Ask Cassandra

An Olympus Inc. Romance

Kate Healey

Contents

Content Note

If you've joined me from the first Olympus Inc. trilogy (welcome!) please do note that this arc is a little darker. We're talking romantic comedies in the Shakespearean sense, in that there's a happy ending and a happy couple by the end, but there's some potentially disturbing material along the way. That's because the original narrative I'm leaning on is that of the cursed House of Atreus, which is a spectacularly messy story of familial strife, even by the grim standards of Greek myth.

This book contains a workplace relationship, where everyone consents and it all turns out fine, but you may well want to shake them. It also includes murder, attempted murder, discussion of suicide, discussion of adultery, discussion of domestic and emotional abuse, mentions of teen pregnancy, and depiction of mental illness.

Unlike the original, it does not include sexual assault, incest, human sacrifice, cannibalism, or sheep-rustling.

Ask Cassandra

Dear Cassandra,

Ten years ago today the love of my life left me for someone else. On our wedding day. It wasn't actually at the altar, but six hours afterwards, at the reception.

It's not an exaggeration to say I was destroyed. In the immediate aftermath, I made some stupid decisions that could have had terrible results (they didn't, but I know I was just lucky).

I know she made the best choice for herself, and I truly don't begrudge her happiness. If she didn't want to be married to me, then leaving was the right choice. But I just don't know how to get over her. She was the kindest person I've ever met, with a fantastic dry sense of humor, and she really understood what it's like to grow up in a family of strong personalities when you're the conflict-avoidant one.

Recently, I've tried to get back out there and date other women and I think it's important to be honest about what happened, so that potential partners know where I'm coming from. But every time I tell my dates about the One Who Left, they stop being interested.

Any advice?

Left Behind.

Dear Left Behind,

First, I hope you had (and maybe continue to get) professional help to manage your feelings about what sounds like a truly traumatic event. My entire insides curdled when I read that "the kindest person" you've ever met left you for someone else six hours after she married you. You're right that if someone wants out of a relationship, they should leave, but the timing on this particular leave-taking was spectacularly cruel. I don't care how conflict-avoidant she is—there were dozens of much kinder ways for her to handle that situation, and she should have chosen one of them!

Second, and I say this with all the sympathy in the world, stop telling other women about her.

The truth is, the One Who Left story is ten years old. It is off the bestseller charts, it is being removed from the library collections, it is no longer accepted for trade at secondhand bookstores, and you do not need to bring it out for review on dates. (I am really hoping not first dates. No, right? Right?)

I don't want to discount the strength and longevity of your feelings—you are clearly someone who loves hard and well. But please put some serious consideration into the idea that this woman is not the *love of your life, but a* love of your life. *As long as you keep telling yourself and other people this story about the woman you don't know how to get over, you are not leaving any space for a different story, the one where you fall in love with someone fabulous who loves you back just as hard.*

This column is firmly in favor of honesty, but that doesn't have to be complete honesty. I don't tell my dates I have a side-gig as an advice columnist. If I ever meet someone I'm serious about, I will of course tell all, but until then, not every twenty-minute coffee or casual movie hang needs to come with a side of my life story.

Don't tell your dates yours. See how that goes. And if you feel up to it, write back to tell us how it works out—I know that the readers are rooting for you just as much as I am.

Yours,

Cassandra.

Chapter One

Cassie Troiades wasn't sure where she was going.

This was unusual. Usually, Cassie made a point of knowing exactly what she was going to do next. But here she was, alone in the countryside upstate, without a map, pulling over again to peer doubtfully at the directions she'd printed before she left the city.

What light remained to the winter evening was making the most out of the scenery; pristine blankets of snow lay over a series of small fields, occasionally bordered by picturesque wooden fences or thick hedges. At intervals, deep rutted dirt roads mysteriously disappeared behind the looping landscape of whitened hills or meandered through the trees of ancient apple orchards, the heavy branches bared for winter, but promising bounty come the next fall through the generosity of their outstretched boughs.

Cassie had lost her taste for Arcadian splendor about three wrong turns ago. Her new boss had warned her that cell reception was spotty in the area. She'd been relying on the printed directions since the maps application on her phone had sputtered itself into confusion. The problem was that while the directions were very clear about when she should turn from the main highway onto Anther Road, no one had bothered to signpost the actual roads. She'd passed a vineyard a few minutes ago, stubby little grape vines spread along long wires—maybe that had belonged to Tantalus Vineyard?

Cassie reminded herself that she wasn't lost, as such. She just wasn't exactly clear on where she was, or how to get to where she was supposed to be.

Her phone pinged, and she dived for it, scrolling rapidly through the list of belated notifications.

Two missed calls from her mom. Her younger sisters had texted. Her younger brother had shared an incomprehensible meme. Iulus was a sweet kid, so it was probably meant to be encouraging, but Cassie squinted at the blurry grid of lines against a starry background and resigned herself to being too old to understand the Youth.

She opened her maps app with more hope than expectation, but was relieved to find a little blue dot pulsing in a helpful reminder that You Are Here. She was on Calypso, which wasn't listed in the printed directions, but if she kept going, she would hit Messina, which was. She could double back to Anther, which was...let's see, two turns down...and then about halfway along that road was the winding driveway that led to the Tantalus Vineyard and her home for the next three months.

There.

She turned the key in the ignition.

Nothing happened.

"Okayyy," Cassie said, and looked out at the encroaching darkness. She tried the key again. There was a grinding noise, which was possibly more alarming than silence. All right. Her gas tank was half full, so it wasn't that. Her internal lights were still on, so the battery was working.

This was the extent of her ability to diagnose motor vehicle malfunction. Fortunately, she had access to an expert.

Her sister picked up on the second ring. "How's wine country?"

"I'm in the middle of a horror movie," Cassie said.

"Uh-huh," Laodice said cautiously. "Can you expand on that?"

"I'm lost in the middle of the countryside, my car won't start, and it's getting dark."

"Stay away from scarecrows with scythes. What's wrong with the car?"

Cassie described the symptoms to the best of her abilities, and followed Laodice's instructions to open the hood and send pictures, shivering in the chill.

"Your spark plugs look okay," Laodice said. "Could be the solenoid, or the Bendix gear."

"Mm," Cassie said, stamping her feet to keep warm. She'd brought snow boots with her, but she didn't want to have to rustle around in the trunk for them. Her bags were heavy. "And assuming I don't know what those are..."

"It wouldn't matter if you did," Laodice told her, sounding both superior and inappropriately enthusiastic. "You'd need a workshop and a mechanic on hand. Call Triple A."

"This is the advice I get from my gearhead sister?" Cassie asked, retreating back into the dubious warmth of the car. "Call Triple A?"

"Hey, if you'd taken that job in the Olympus Archives department, you'd be in the parking building down the street, and I could take a look in person," Laodice said. "But you were the one who wanted to get out of the city to a rural paradise."

"I will be *working*," Cassie said primly, though if pressed, she could admit that the pictures of Tantalus's vine-covered hills and lakeside views had been at least part of the appeal, even if the generous pay and the promise of room and board had been the tipping point in her decision to apply for the job. Her former roommates were pleasant, respectful, and had fallen deeply and desperately into an all-encompassing love on their first week of co-habitation. Cassie was happy for them, but she didn't want to *live* there. When you were a noted cynic, all that stunned bliss threatened to make you outright crotchety.

"Hey, guess what?" Laodice said, with that familiar note of lilting anticipation.

Cassie grimaced, but managed to keep wariness out of her voice. "What?"

"I met someone!" Laodice said triumphantly.

"Oh, cool," Cassie said. "I need to call Triple A, but I look forward to hearing about him later."

Laodice was not cynical. Laodice was a born romantic who fell in love with an ease that was both enviable and deeply alarming, especially because her rose-tinted glasses were so thick that she couldn't pick up red flags when they were waving right in front of her face. And she didn't wait for any hint of reciprocation before she committed herself to the fantasy. A lot of startled men had found themselves in conversations about long-term commitment on the first date.

Laodice was living proof that Cassie could dole out all the accurate predictions and practical advice she liked, but if someone didn't want to hear it, they wouldn't.

"He's so handsome," Laodice said, on a sigh. "And he spelled my name right on the coffee cup, which has to be a sign, don't you think?"

"I have to go," Cassie said, and hung up before she could advise Laodice against imagining her wedding to a handsome barista, no matter how good his spelling was.

Okay. The Triple A card was in her wallet. Even if they couldn't get to her right away, she had her car emergency kit with food and water and a blanket—come to that, she had two suitcases of clothes in the trunk. She wasn't going to freeze, or starve, or be hacked into tiny pieces by a hook-handed ghost revenging himself on sexually active teenagers.

Cassie rummaged through her purse for her wallet, and let out a noise that *absolutely wasn't* a scream when the headlights appeared behind her.

The vehicle was moving fast, and after a startled moment to gather her scattered wits, Cassie hastily turned on her own hazard lights. Getting hit by a car that couldn't see her would not improve her situation, and the driver might be able to help her out.

Assuming they weren't a murderer.

"Stop it," she said out loud, and tried to feel relieved instead of apprehensive when the car pulled to a stop behind her. She did lock her doors, though. That was only sensible.

There was a brief pause while the two people in the other car discussed something—probably her—and then the driver got out. Her rearview lights revealed him to be a pleasant-faced older man. He was wearing casual slacks and a sweater, but tugging on a puffy jacket as he walked towards her, which at least argued for his practicality. She couldn't make out his passenger very well, but something in the profile made her think it was a woman.

Cassie relaxed a little. Her Ask Cassandra inbox was full of evidence that women could be very bad people, but they weren't usually spontaneous murderers. This applied to almost everyone, of course. It was just that when your sister loved statistics and shared them with you constantly, it was hard to avoid the fact that while most men weren't murderers, 98% of murders were committed by men.

"Hello there!" the man approaching her door called, his voice a shade too hearty.

Cassie turned her inside light on, and watched his face lose some tension as he took her in—a round-faced, curly-haired woman in her late twenties, alone in her car, with suitcases and boxes in her back seat. He hadn't known who he was approaching either, she realized, and repaid his courage by rolling down her window.

"It won't start," she said apologetically. "I was about to call Triple A, but—"

"Would you be Cassie Troiades?" he interrupted.

"Oh! Yes!" Cassie said, on rising hope. "Are you Manny Pelopson?"

The man grinned. "His uncle, Theo. We were wondering where you'd got to."

"I'm so sorry. I think I missed a couple of turn-offs."

"Happens all the time," Theo said, waving her apology away. "We have to send the van out for the workers at vintage time, or they wander around for hours trying to find us. You got closer than most."

He gave her an approving nod, as if getting closer than most people was something she should be proud of. Theo had silvery highlights in his thick, sandy hair and his eyes crinkled in a friendly way, and Cassie realized that he was handsome. Also at least thirty years older than her, and her employer's uncle, so definitely off-limits, but there was nothing to stop her appreciating a silver fox when she met one. Especially if he could fix her car.

Theo got her to open the hood and try the ignition again, produced a penlight from his pocket, and stared thoughtfully into the engine for a while, muttering to himself. Cassie's hopes were dashed when he put the hood down and shook his head. "Damned if I can work it out," he said. "I think we'd best just transfer you to the BMW and take you on to Tantalus. I'll get Steph from the garage to take a look in the morning."

"If you and your wife won't mind," Cassie said, although she was already envisioning a hot shower and a mug of something warm.

"My wife?" Theo said, and followed her look to his car. As far as Cassie could tell, his passenger had barely moved, much less bothered to find out what was going on. "Oh, no, that's Aerope, my sister-in-law. Manny's mother. No, she won't mind." He hesitated a moment, as if hearing the words coming out of his mouth made him doubt them, and then added, with more certainty: "It's not as if we can leave you out here to freeze, is it?"

Cassie decided against apologizing for yet another mistake, and instead nodded assent and reached for her purse. Theo hoisted her heaviest suitcase with barely a grunt, and Cassie followed with her laptop bag and smaller case. Theo put everything in the trunk, which had a few grocery bags, but was otherwise unoccupied.

"Do you need those boxes?" he asked.

Cassie was supposed to start work in the morning. She'd need some supplies. "Just the red one," she said, compromising, but when she stepped back towards her car, Theo held his hand out for her keys.

"I'll grab it. You jump in and get warm."

Well, he'd proved himself competent and practical so far. She could probably rely on him to lock up.

Cassie climbed into the back seat grateful for the thrum of the heated air.

"Hello," she said, pitching her voice forward. "I'm Cassie Troiades." When she glanced up at the rearview mirror, she found herself pinned to the smooth leather by a pair of ice-blue eyes.

"Aerope Pelopson," the woman said. Her voice was rich, smooth, and totally devoid of warmth. "You're the archivist."

"That's right," Cassie said. That voice seemed to expect her to add a "ma'am," but she was damned if she'd cower on her first meeting with anyone.

"My late husband had always planned to organize the family archives himself," Aerope said, after a pause that had definitely noted the lack of a "ma'am."

"I'm sorry for your loss," Cassie said politely.

Aerope's gaze didn't flicker. "Are you any good?"

"Yes," Cassie said, and consciously dropped her shoulders. "And I have a lot of experience with private collections."

"Hm," Aerope said, and her eyes flicked away from the mirror, releasing Cassie from their grip. After a moment she added, "You should have brought printed directions."

Cassie held her tongue. When somebody had already made up their mind not to like you, there wasn't a lot you could say to change their mind. Protesting that she *had* printed the directions and it wasn't her fault that local government apparently neglected road signage wouldn't do her any good. She'd rather stay silent than beg for approval.

When it became obvious that she wasn't going to respond, Aerope's eyes flicked back to her, showing a very tiny modicum of interest.

Cassie had met the famed Hera Rheczack, CEO of Olympus Publishing, who had a fearsome reputation as an ice queen. Hera had prevented Cassie from being fired from her advice column side gig, so Cassie could admit she was personally biased, but as far as she'd been able to take in from their one brief encounter, Hera was reserved and a bit chilly, but not actually unfriendly.

Aerope Pelopson made Hera look like a bouncing beam of sunshine.

Fortunately, Theo came back at that point, stamping snow off his shoes and blowing on his hands as he climbed into the driver's seat. It was nearly full evening now, the last bit of daylight disappearing into the gloom.

Cassie thought about being alone in the dark, trying to tell Triple A where she was, and decided to be grateful. Aerope wasn't friendly, but she wasn't kicking Cassie out into the winter either, and Theo kept up a patter of conversation as he drove, genially pointing out things Cassie would be able to see in the morning and assuring her that the guesthouse was snug, fully-contained, and ready for her.

Cassie, relieved that she wouldn't have to share a kitchen or bathroom, did her best to keep up her side of the dialogue. She told Theo a little bit about her family, about her studies, and some suitably anonymized anecdotes about other private archives she'd worked on. The story about the surprise box of preserved lizards was too good to pass up.

"You won't find any lizards in *our* archives," Aerope said, her first contribution to the conversation.

"I don't know, Arry, there could be anything in there," Theo said. "Arthur was a bit of a hoarder," he told Cassie, his voice confiding.

Aerope bristled. "He certainly was not," she said. "He had an eye towards history."

"And now we have an attic full of it," Theo said. He half-turned to Cassie, and she wished he'd keep his eyes on the road. "My vote was that we take everything outside and build a bonfire."

Cassie didn't have to pretend her shock. Torching the historical records of one of the earliest vineyards in the state? Every single one of her professors would have rather gone up in flames themselves. "I'm glad you hired me instead," she said, striving for diplomacy.

"Manny did that, not me," Theo said cheerfully. "No offense intended, but I'd much rather have spent your salary on a new crusher-destemmer."

Aerope had turned her head to glare at her brother-in-law, and if she'd been chilly with Cassie, her voice was positively arctic when she said, "Fortunately, Arthur knew better than to leave the archives to *you*, Theodore."

Cassie caught the glinting edge of Theo's smile. "Yeah, so isn't it good that Cassie's been hired to take care of it instead?"

"I would prefer Manfred to have taken on the task himself," Aerope said.

"Well, that's Manny for you," Theo said amiably. "Still, Cassie, I hope you won't find lizards. Rats, now. Rats are very possible."

And on that encouraging note, they turned down a private driveway, and found themselves passing a house that Cassie could tell, even in the dark, was both historic and *enormous*.

"Drop me off here," Aerope commanded, and Theo obediently pulled the BMW over. Aerope went to the trunk and retrieved two shopping bags with embossed labels. In the golden light streaming from the house, Cassie saw that Aerope was a woman-of-a-certain-age with sharp cheek and collarbones, every blonde hair set in place. She was wearing a wool skirt suit and knee-high boots, which appeared to be her sole concession to the weather.

"It was nice to meet you," she told Cassie through the car window, a social lie she didn't even attempt to disguise.

"You too," Cassie said, lying with a little more effort. "I'll do my best with the archives. No bonfires."

Aerope clearly had her doubts that Cassie's best would be anywhere close to sufficient, but she gave her a wintry smile in appreciation of the attempt at a joke, shot Theo a parting glare, and walked into the big house.

"She took Arthur's death pretty hard," Theo said after a minute.

"It was unexpected?"

"Heart attack. Very sudden. She was away on a weekend trip to the city, and when she came back she found him in their bed. He was already cold. There was nothing she could do, but I think she blames herself for not being there."

"Oh no," Cassie said, feeling a pang of unexpected sympathy for Aerope. Perhaps, having been unable to save her husband, she wanted to save what she saw as his legacy? There was nothing Cassie could do about that, except her job.

Silent for once, Theo drove them away from the main house, down a tidy gravel side-road that went past a small orchard and fetched up outside a—well, not a guest house, exactly. A guest cottage, maybe. Yes, cottage was definitely the word. "Charming" would be another. "Quaint," at a stretch.

Cassie hoped that "good plumbing" and "decent water pressure" were also on the list. The wooden walls looked well-cared for, with no peeling paint, and if the flower boxes on the porch were empty for winter, they also didn't reveal any telltale weedy clumps. The scant snow had been cleared from the path, and as she and Theo walked up the porch steps, suitcases in hand, they were bathed in the light of the glass lantern standing over the cherry-red door. To Cassie's relief, the lantern held a prosaic lightbulb instead of an actual candle, but nevertheless, Cassie could already hear her sister Polyxena insisting she take plenty of pictures of this excellent cottagecore content.

There was light coming from behind the drapes, too, and the shuffle of feet inside.

"Manny must have come over," Theo said. He dropped his keys in his pocket and picked up her suitcase again.

Cassie suppressed an urge to ask how many people had access to the place she was supposed to be living in for the next three months, and turned the handle. Her duffel bag hung uncomfortably off her inner arm as she negotiated herself and it through the door, but the weight disappeared from her awareness as she took in the space.

Polyxena was going to flip out. The cottage screamed "aesthetic," from the adorably wonky bookshelves to the white-painted walls and delicate floral print on the pale blue drapes. The little pot-bellied stove held an already-lit fire, which was cheerily shedding heat over the two cozy, mismatched armchairs facing it. From the door, Cassie could see the small kitchen, with its deep, white stone sink, and the kitchen island topped with a thick wooden butcher's block— pretty and rustic, part of her noted absently, but hard to keep clean.

The floor was stained wooden boards, with rag rugs laid out for warmth. She couldn't see the bathroom and bedroom, tucked away up the stairs, but if there wasn't a claw-footed tub, she would eat one of the innumerable decorations in this place. This room alone might contain more lace doilies than the sum total she'd previously encountered in her entire life.

It also contained a man, busily vacuuming the main rug. He had his back to them, big headphones clamped over his ears, and he was busy shaking one of the finest asses Cassie had ever seen.

Cassie had not previously considered grey sweatpants an attractive piece of clothing, but the firm rump grinding beneath the thin fabric was providing a compelling argument in their favor. Without knowing what he was listening to, it was impossible to judge the man's sense of rhythm, but there was nothing wrong with his moves.

Theo coughed behind her.

Whether it was the noise, or the blast of frigid air that alerted him to their presence, the man, presumably Manny Pelopson, spun around. He was wearing a worn sweatshirt with the logo of Eleusis U's most exclusive fraternity. He had thick, sandy hair, like his uncle, and his beard faultlessly walked the perilous tightrope between hipster parody and full lumberjack. Broad shoulders, a muscular frame, a tempting hint of rounding belly, and—well, those sweatpants really didn't leave much to the imagination, did they? Cassie forced herself to stop ogling her new employer, and yanked her eyes back to his face.

He was staring at her, his entire face beet red. When she made eye contact, he jerked, and dropped his gaze to the floor, then over her shoulder to Theo. He looked humiliated and a little betrayed, and Cassie felt bad for him.

So she gave him her best smile, understanding and a little rueful, and said, "What's the song?"

***

Manny Pelopson had not had the best day.

That morning, the vineyard foreman had said something about pesticides that he was clearly supposed to understand. When Manny had asked for clarification, he'd gotten a bemused look before Jim unbent enough to explain that the organic pesticides Manny wanted to investigate wouldn't work on the most common grape blights in their territory. Manny had pressed for more detail, and the man had promptly buried him in technical jargon and the diplomatically phrased suggestion that Manny should maybe learn a little more about the farming side of the business before he opened his mouth.

When he'd asked Uncle Theo what he thought, Theo had once more suggested that Manny invite Augie upstate for "a few weeks" to "give you more background." Manny was pretty sure that Augie knew even less about grapevine moths and powdery mildew than he did. Augie had been very clear that *he* wasn't going to leave the career he'd spent so much effort building. He'd also shied away from dumping sole care of his four kids on his wife, mostly because Ness would immediately instigate dramatic revenge. So Theo's "suggestion" was less an idea he thought would realistically help, and more yet another indication of his complete lack of faith in Manny's abilities to contribute to Tantalus.

Lunch had been awkward, because his mother was still freezing him out about hiring an Outsider for Family Things. She'd all but ordered him to direct his attention to more serious matters—probate, Tantalus, the refurbishment he had planned for the carriage house—and now she was upset he'd hired an expert to handle the archives. It didn't make a lot of sense. The history of Tantalus was going to be a huge draw to potential clients, but they needed *someone* to bring order to the chaos in the attic before they could realize the full potential of that history. Aerope had made it clear she didn't think Manny should focus on the archives yet. That didn't leave her much ground for objecting to someone else charting that history, but she was objecting anyway.

In the afternoon, Aerope and Theo had gone to Weeping Rock and Manny had wrestled with his father's bookkeeping for hours, missing him and resenting him through every second of it, and then he'd gone for a long twilight run through the quiet vines, trying to shake the tension out. He'd just finished climbing into his softest loungewear after a hot shower when a text message from Theo had told him the archivist was on her way.

At which point he realized he hadn't checked the guest house, nor lit the fire. He was happy to throw money at an expert to have her take at least one task off his horrific to-do list. He'd taken the time to check Ms. Troiades's references, and every single one had said she was capable and efficient. But welcoming her to a cold, dark cottage wouldn't give her any strong impression of his own capabilities, so he'd tossed on his overcoat and hurried over.

The place wasn't dirty, though it was more cluttered than he would have personally liked, and dusting the various knick-knacks and collectibles took a long time. By then the fire had warmed the place up, and he was getting into the groove, so that by the time he pulled the little stick vacuum out of the cupboard under the stairs, he'd relaxed into the beat pounding from his headphones and the satisfaction of restoring a place to good order.

He hadn't *meant* to start dancing. He'd just been happy, for the first time in a long time, and his hips had moved along.

And now he was red-faced and staring at his uncle, who wasn't even bothering to hide his grin.

It was better than looking at his new employee. Cassie Troiades wasn't the skinny, elderly librarian he'd been vaguely picturing, all bones and stern frowns. She was a pretty, lusciously round woman a few years younger than himself with keen eyes and a ripe, red mouth.

She smiled at him, and he saw kindness in her eyes. He didn't want pity, but he'd take kindness over laughing in his face. "What's the song?" she asked, as if she were really interested.

"Um," he said, but he didn't have time to think of a good lie, and he didn't think this woman would believe anything but the truth. "Shake Your Pom Pom."

Theo's laugh was a thunderclap, but Ms. Troiades just nodded. "Missy Elliott," she said, with a note of firm approval. "Classic."

Manny dared to smile back. "Can't mess with Miss Demeanor. I'm Manny Pelopson."

"Cassie Troiades."

Theo was now looking confused and a bit irritated, which was much better than smugly amused. "Take the lady's bags, Manny," he grunted. "Where've your manners gone?"

Manny reached out in automatic obedience, but Cassie said brightly, "Oh, I've got it," and brushed by him. "Bedroom upstairs?" she asked.

"Yep," Manny said, and took the suitcase Theo held out for him instead. He followed his new archivist up the stairs, guiltily noticing the sway of her hips, snugly tucked into jeans. He didn't know if she liked to shake her own pom pom, but if she did, she had an impressive amount to shake. "Bedroom's the door on the left," he called, and heard a murmur of assent.

"Huh," she said a moment later, and he came into to find her staring at the bed. Which was built into the wall, with drawers underneath and cupboards to the side. He'd left the wooden doors open, to air out after he'd put the new sheets on the bed, but if you crawled in there and pulled the doors closed, you were essentially sleeping in a big closet.

"Ah, yeah," Manny said, and put the suitcase down with some gratitude. She didn't pack light. "It's pretty…"

"Cozy?" Cassie asked, still staring.

"I was going to say, comfortable," Manny said. "It's a good mattress." He blinked. "Oh, damn, are you claustrophobic? Because if so, we can work something else out. There's plenty of room in the big house, but I thought you'd want your own space."

"No, no, it's fine," Cassie said, and that full mouth quirked in a smile. "I was just wondering how I was going to get up there."

Manny stepped forward and pulled the handle directly beneath the bed. A set of steps slid out.

"Ah!" she said, and climbed up to bounce experimentally on the edge of the bed. "Oh, it *is* a good mattress," she said, and beamed at him. "Not a lot of headroom, though."

Manny, still disconcerted by the bouncing, tried very hard not to think about the activities that might require *headroom*. "There's a light," he said. "And a bookshelf, if you like reading in bed."

"Love it," she said promptly. "One of my favorite things to do in bed."

A moment later, she appeared to replay what she'd just said, and her cheeks flushed pink, but her smile stayed determinedly on as she climbed down. "So, I should probably unpack if I'm starting work tomorrow."

"Yes," Manny said. "You're welcome to join us for dinner, but I put some groceries in the pantry and fridge, too. If there are items not to your taste, you can just bring them over to the big house tomorrow."

"Thank you," she said, sounding surprised. "This is... I mean, not to be accidentally insulting, but I really wasn't expecting you to set me up this well. I really appreciate it."

"I used to be in hospitality," Manny said, and pretended not to see her interested look. She couldn't actually want to know about his previous career, and he didn't really want to tell her. And he didn't have to. Ask Cassandra's advice was over a year old now, and as challenging as he'd found it to keep his mouth shut about Helen, he couldn't deny the effects. The moment he'd stopped telling women his entire backstory, the easier it had been to go on second, and even third dates.

He'd even thought about taking things further with one of those third dates, a lovely speech therapist named Rose, who'd hinted at wanting to explore commitment. *That* would have been the time to talk about Helen, and how the happiest day of his life had become the worst in the few minutes it had taken him to read her scribbled note. But six months ago, on the morning of their scheduled fourth date, his mother had called, sobbing incoherently, only managing to force out the words, "Manfred, *come home.*"

And after that, he'd had a new worst day.

His new employee was looking at him uncertainly, because his face, his stupid honest face, was obviously revealing the knot of obligation and resentment and helpless love that pulled tight around his heart every time he thought about that moment.

"I might just settle in here tonight, and get a good start tomorrow," she said.

Manny nodded. "Then I'll come over tomorrow morning and take you over, show you around," he said. "Is nine o'clock okay?"

"Perfect."

"The archive is a mess," he warned her. "I'm not sure what you're used to, but it's not really organized at all."

"That's why you hired a professional," she said. She wasn't bragging, just confident in her experience and skill, and Manny felt both relieved and incredibly envious. He'd *been* that confident, before. When he'd been where he belonged.

Cassie looked around the room, obviously figuring out where to begin putting her stuff, and he backed towards the door. Something niggled at the back of his brain. "Is Cassie short for Cassandra?" he asked.

"That's what it says on my birth certificate," she said, her tone distracted. "But I don't use it. Just Cassie is fine."

"Cool," he said. "Well, there's a folder on the kitchen table that has some details about the cottage, including the Wi-Fi password."

"Wi-Fi! Great."

Manny grinned at her. "It's a guest cottage, not a yoga retreat."

Cassie looked pointedly at the bed nook, then raised her eyebrows at him.

"Rustic vibes, not actually rustic," he assured her. "Plumbing, heating, and all the necessary comforts."

"Does the bathtub have claw feet?" she asked intently.

"Of course."

She looked skeptical. "Will it fit me?"

"Definitely," Manny said. "It's sized for two." His brain helpfully presented an image of a naked Cassie in the tub, smiling at him in amused anticipation. The image was necessarily fuzzy—all he could see of her right now was her face and hands—but he was aware of an inconvenient desire to fill in the details.

"My phone number's also in the folder," he said hastily. "Text me if you need anything. Good night, Cassie."

"Good night," she said, and he went down to cadge a ride off Theo back to the house. The price for the ride was a series of questions about Manny's goals and priorities, all of his answers clearly unsatisfactory, but for once Manny didn't really mind. He was thinking of Cassie Troiades, kind and confident, bouncing on that ridiculous bed.

Chapter Two

Cassie woke up disoriented, and reached for her glasses.

They weren't on her nightstand. The nightstand didn't seem to be there either.

It took a confused moment before the dimensions of the space translated from her expectations into reality, and then she sat up and groped around in the shelf set into the head of the bed, until her fingers hit her glasses case.

Right. *Right.* She wasn't in her apartment with Ilione and Lyz. She'd sublet her room and come upstate, to where they didn't believe in road signs, but passionately adored patchwork.

And her boss was coming to pick her up soon, so she had a precious hour to get dressed, fed, and work on her *other* job, the one she didn't put on her resume or mention in interviews, other than to say she did some freelance writing.

This was true. She could even point to a few articles with her byline. Laodice was really good at letting her know when Olympus editors were looking for pitches, and had the inside track on what kind of work might best appeal.

But her *real* freelance writing was answering questions for Ask Cassandra.

The name was an unfortunate coincidence. *Agora* had first been published in the 70s, one of the new women's lib magazines following *Ms.* magazine's spectacular debut, and Ask Cassandra had been a staple feature from day one. The original advice columnist, Cassandra Donovan, had been a firebrand who'd told her letter writers how to demand better from their communities, dump their abusive boyfriends, walk away from their heinous families, and fight for their rights to bodily autonomy, gender equality, and basic human respect. Cassandra had been lauded and reviled, viewed as a hero and a demon, and she'd received so much hate mail during her decade-long tenure that the next Ask Cassandra columnist had taken "Cassandra" as a pen name and remained anonymous.

Daphne Trần had only revealed her role years later, on a *Gaia* TV special focusing on the women's magazine movement. When Gaia had asked why she'd decided anonymity was the way to go, Daphne, now a Pulitzer Prize winning novelist, had been blunt: "It was all the death threats," she'd said. "If they were going to threaten that middle-class white woman with murder, I thought they might actually murder me."

After Daphne had come more Cassandras. Some of them had chosen to reveal their own names alongside the pen name, but most of them had sheltered behind the tradition.

Like the original Cassandra, Cassie was a middle-class white woman, but she'd never considered using her own name. She lived in the era of doxxing and cyber terrorism, and she was telling people how to demand better from their communities, dump their abusive partners, walk away from their heinous families, and fight for their rights to bodily autonomy, equity, and basic human respect, because fifty years after Cassandra Donovan, that was still work that needed to be done.

And the best way she could think of to maintain the energy and will to keep going was to make sure that nobody knew she, Cassie Troiades, was the one doing it.

Five people knew the truth: Cassie's sisters, her editor at *Agora*, the payroll supervisor who handled her checks, and Hera, the CEO of Olympus. The filters designed by the Olympus IT department screened out most of the hate mail that came in for "Cassandra," and her editor handled the rest. Cassie got the *real* letters, from people who wanted her help, with problems large and small. Occasionally she got mail from someone who was very much in the wrong, but telling those people to get lost was also fun (and was great clickbait, according to her editor).

She ventured downstairs, shivering in her bathrobe, and found the space heater hidden in the cupboard under the stairs, right where the folder of useful info had said it would be. She didn't know why Manny Pelopson wasn't in hospitality any more, but it clearly wasn't because he was bad at it.

She fixed a bowl of cereal while the living room heated up, sat down in a comfortable armchair, and opened her laptop.

Dear Cassandra,

Last month I (18f) was at the beach with some friends, and someone dared me to climb up some rocks. Long story short, I did, and I got stuck there when the tide came in. It was really stupid, and I totally know that now.

My friends didn't even notice, they kind of all took off and left me there (we're not really friends any more) and I was freaking out, because I can't swim very well, and the tide was getting higher.

Then a guy on a surfboard (let's call him Percy, 22m) paddled over to me and got me to climb on his board and he swam me back to shore. He kept saying all this stuff about how I was so beautiful and he was so honored to be the one to rescue me, and honestly, I don't know what I said back, I was mostly just crying, but I guess I must have said something to encourage him.

Percy said he'd take me home, so I gave him my address, and he did, but that turned out to be really dumb too. Now he knows where I live and he follows all my socials and he keeps asking me out. So far I've been like, oh, I made plans with my friends, or, sorry, I've got a big test and I need to study. He asks me at least twice a week. There's nothing wrong with him, but I just don't want to go out with him, and I think if I say yes I might be leading him on, but I don't want to say no because that feels mean. I wish he'd get the hint.

I don't want to be mean to this guy, because he for real probably saved my life. I don't know what I would have done if he hadn't turned up, and people have drowned on that beach before. My dad says that I should at least go on one date, just to be polite. Is he right? Is there something else I should be saying so that Percy gets the message, but doesn't feel rejected?

Yours,

Galaxy Brain

(My real name is Andromeda but please don't use that, I really don't want to hurt Percy's feelings and idk if he reads your column.)

Cassandra cracked her knuckles.

Dear Galaxy Brain,

First, your dad is wrong. You should not ever feel obliged to go out with someone, or feel that it is rude to decline.

Second, Percy (possibly) saved your life; that is unequivocally a good thing. You can be grateful that he was there and thankful for his efforts on your behalf.

Third, asking you out is an entirely separate issue, and frankly, he's being a dink about it. He should be getting the hint.

I don't think you need to worry about not hurting Percy's feelings. His feelings are his business. He's asked you a question, and he has the answer, even if he's unable to acknowledge it. Honestly, he's scored a real own goal here. If he'd just left things at "I rescued another human from a scary situation" he would get to be the hero of the story. But "and then I persistently asked her out over her consistent evasions" is not a good addendum, and I have to think that it's spoiling all your gratitude and relief.

Consciously or unconsciously, Percy is using that lack of a firm no as an excuse to keep asking. It's time to remove that excuse and say that you don't want to go out with him. Don't say "maybe later," don't say "when I'm less busy with school." I'm going to advise that you don't even say "thanks for saving me but—" because I think that Percy is the kind of guy who will leverage your gratitude for a pity date if he can.

(Aside to readers in the comment section: A reminder that "why didn't you just say no in the first place?" is not a helpful comment. If Galaxy Brain felt comfortable and safe saying an immediate flat no, she would have already done so. What is she supposed to do, build a time machine to meet your expectations?)

But before you say no, there are two things that concern me here: he knows where you live, and he's been asking you out "at least twice a week". I want you to go and read the safety resources for leaving an abusive relationship linked in the sidebar. Not all of these apply to your situation, but—

Cassie scowled at the screen. She didn't want to coach yet another young woman through the terrifying prospect of her first no. She *did* want to reach through time and space and give "Percy" a good smack, and then she wanted to lay waste to the patriarchy, possibly burning down late-stage capitalism on her way out.

So, a normal work day on her side gig.

Her phone rang and she picked up without looking.

"Hey, Mom," she said, still glaring at the screen. Nobody but Hecuba Troiades called her this early.

Her mother's voice was warm and breathy. "Honey, are you checking your breasts regularly?"

"Every month, Mom."

"Oh good, because I just saw this terrible story on the morning show. Are your sisters checking their breasts?"

"It hasn't come up in conversation lately."

"I'd better call them," Hecuba decided. "I'd *hope* that Polly is checking her breasts, she's showing so much of them on her little videos. I'm sure those flashy sports bras can't be very supportive."

"She's a fitness influencer, Mom. Her sponsors send her clothes."

"Well, all right," Hecuba said. "At least she's making a living."

Polyxena was a millionaire, and had been before her twenty-second birthday, but Cassie knew better than to start that discussion again.

"So I'll call Dicey next, and then Polly. Have you started your new job?"

Someone knocked at the door. Cassie startled. "Mom, I've got to go," she said, getting hastily out of the chair.

"Are there any good prospects there?" Hecuba said, talking faster. "Because the story on the morning show said it's best if someone else checks your breasts, that's what happened to the woman on the show, her husband found the lump, although it was very sad in the end, because—"

"I love you, Mom, talk to you later, bye," Cassie said, and hung up as she opened the door, letting in a blast of frigid air.

"Sorry," Manny said. "I know I'm early, but—" His gaze snagged on the front of her bathrobe, and he cleared his throat. "I can come back in ten minutes?"

"No, come in, it's freezing," Cassie said. "It's my fault, my mom called and I lost track of time." She went up the stairs to change into jeans and a thick sweater, grateful that she'd checked the weather forecast for the region and packed appropriately. In the bathroom, she brushed her teeth, splashed water on her face, and finger-combed her hair into place, wondering if her mother would consider Manny a "good prospect."

Probably. He was a business owner with a property portfolio. And Cassie thought that he wouldn't mind checking her breasts for lumps.

She thought she wouldn't mind either.

But he was her employer, and she was the sensible sister, too sensible for workplace romance, and she could palpate her own boobs, damn it. She packed her stray thoughts away with her pajamas, pushed under the pillow, and went downstairs fresh-faced and ready to go.

Manny was standing in the middle of the room, frowning at his phone, but he slid it into his pocket as she reappeared. "My brother," he said, by way of explanation.

"Family, huh?" Cassie said. "Can't live with them, can't stuff them in a sack and throw them into the river without answering some awkward questions."

Manny huffed a laugh, and she wondered belatedly if that was a diplomatic thing to say to a man who did live with family. She covered the awkwardness by slinging her laptop bag over her shoulder and picking up the red box that held her archival kit. "Shall we? I'm dying to see this fabled attic."

***

Cassie Troiades looked just as good in the morning as she had last night, her eyes bright and cheeks pink with the cold as they walked over to the main house.

"I think this is what they call brisk," she observed.

"I should have driven," Manny said. "Sorry."

"No, it's fine," she said, sounding slightly surprised at her own demurral. She took a deep breath, which made her sweater move interestingly. It was a dark orange that picked out the russet highlights in her dark curls. "The air really does smell fresher out here."

"You don't spend much time in the great outdoors, I take it."

"Only when I'm on a run. And even then, it's the suburbs."

"You run?" Manny said. "Me too. I can tell you about a few good routes around here, if you like."

"That'd be great," Cassie said, but she was looking at the big house as it loomed above them. "Wow. I didn't quite realize how impressive this was last night."

Manny knew what she was seeing. The big house was technically Pelopson Manor, but no one ever called it that except on address labels. It stood at the top of a small rise. The slope was barely noticeable, but the effect was of the house looming over you like a disappointed elder. The building was three stories tall, and clad in grey masonry blocks. The arched windows on the lower two floors looked over the precise squares and rectangles of the French-style garden. The narrower windows of the third floor, designed as servant's quarters, were a neat row on top, and the pointed, gabled roof, dusted with snow, gave the impression of eyebrows arched in disapproval.

Or maybe that was just him. Probably Cassie only saw the elegant lines and obvious wealth that had gone into the house. Inside, she'd probably appreciate the polished floors and massive rafters, the lead window detailing and the wooden panels on the interior walls.

What Manny saw was the massive heating bill and the antique wiring, the plumbing refit his mother was still paying for and the roof replacement that his father had been putting off for five years. The gardens were beautiful, but they'd been designed in the time when the servant's quarters had been occupied by actual servants. They were meant to have a groundskeeper, not his mother doing what she could on top of her other job.

"Home sweet home," he said, more grimly than he'd intended. He tried to recover, adding, "Most of this dates from the 1920s rebuild. The architect's blueprints should be in the archives somewhere."

"Oh, excellent," Cassie said, sounding genuinely enthusiastic. "Architects are generally very good with records."

He led them past the tennis court to the back, where a porch had been added in the 70s and they went carefully up the ice-slick steps. They stamped the snow off their boots in the mudroom. The kitchen was warm and bright, and there was half a pot of coffee left. Aerope was sitting at the kitchen table, fully dressed in a tweed skirt set, sipping from a cup while she did the crossword.

"Good morning," she said, her face neutral.

Manny stooped to kiss her cheek, wondering if she'd truly repented of her opposition to bringing in a professional, or if she were biding her time. His private bet was on the latter. "Morning, Mother."

"Hello, Mrs. Pelopson," Cassie said, and Aerope nodded at her.

Or, rather, at the red box in her gloved hands.

"You might need more than one of those," she said, with glacial good humor.

"This is just my essentials kit," Cassie said. "Gloves, mask, Post-it notes—a bunch of stuff, really. But you're right." She turned to Manny. "What do I need to do about my car? The rest of my kit is in there, and I don't want it getting snowed in." She smiled. "Though I guess I don't have to worry about it being stolen."

"I wouldn't say that," Manny said. "We've got a group of kids round here who think it's funny to steal anything that isn't nailed down, and some of the things that are. They mostly leave it somewhere after they get bored, but no guarantees."

Cassie's eyes narrowed. "Do they steal road signs?"

"Good guess."

"Theodore already left to notify the mechanic," Aerope said, taking another sip of coffee. "You could wait to start until you know what's happening, if you like."

"No, thank you," Cassie said politely. She smiled at Manny. "Which way to the attic?"

"Right this way," Manny said, and shot his mother a warning glance behind Cassie's back. Aerope ignored him.

The house had three main floors, with the attic on top of that, and there was no elevator installed. Manny's job listing had specified that the candidate had to be physically capable, and indeed, Cassie climbed the first two flights of stairs without slowing down. She did pause when Manny opened the hidden door at the end of the third-floor hallway, revealing the narrow, steep set of stairs that led to the attic. It wasn't *quite* a ladder.

"Do you want me to carry that?" he asked, nodding at her box.

"I'm fine," Cassie said. It had the cadence of an automatic response, but Manny nodded and went up the steps first, hand groping above his head for the string that dangled from the antique light bulb. He caught it on the third swing and tugged.

The attic lights flickered into feeble life, and he cleared the steps so that Cassie could come up too.

She stopped dead at the top of the stairs, her lips parting in wonder.

The first manifestation of the Pelopson house had been built in 1863. Successive generations had taken turns to tear down and rebuild the space as the family size and fashions changed. Most of the structure now dated from the 1920s rebuild, and the fittings were much newer, but Pelopsons didn't throw away things that were still perfectly good, if a little old-fashioned.

They stored them instead.

Dust sheets shrouded the furniture, most of it wooden, some of it elaborately carved. One wall held a perilous stack of dismantled platform beds. Manny hadn't known what a box spring was until college. From previous explorations, he knew there were sideboards and bookshelves, washstands and wardrobes, dining chairs, arm chairs, reclining couches, innumerable footstools and side tables, and one huge antique desk that had apparently been dismantled before it went up the stairs and reassembled afterwards, for reasons that entirely escaped him, because nothing had ever been put in its many drawers.

Then there were the boxes. Some were plastic storage tubs, some were cardboard, some were wooden harvest crates salvaged from the vineyard. All of them were crammed with toys, clothes, books, kitchenware, dining sets and mementoes, and all of them had been put up there by Pelopsons who probably sincerely meant to clean up the attic once they had the time.

"Believe it or not, it used to be worse," Manny told Cassie.

"I bet those help," she said, and pointed at the shelves. They were utilitarian stainless steel, obviously modern.

"That was me and my brother, about ten years ago." He thought. "Wait. Oh man, it has to be fifteen years now. It was the summer I turned sixteen."

Manny and Augie had spent a substantial amount of the summer installing the shelving units and packing them with boxes. Their dad had made them keep all the paper records separate, placing them in the little room he'd built in the far corner.

"One day, I'll turn this into a proper archive," he'd said.

Manny remembered the sting of barked knuckles, the irritation of sweat getting into his eyes, the tang of the cold beers Augie had snuck upstairs for them. And the pride on his father's face as he put his hands on his hips and rocked back, surveying the shelves with the Tantalus archives. "Nearly two hundred years, boys," he'd said. "That's what we're looking at here. Seven generations of good work."

Manny coughed to clear the lump in his throat.

"This is incredible," Cassie said, rotating slowly. "I'm not archiving the entire attic, am I? Because your ad said a three-month contract and this is...much more than that."

"Oh no. Most of it's just ordinary attic junk. Old toys, clothes, sporting equipment. The archives are this way." He led the way, skirting the elderly steamer trunks too large to go on shelves with the rest of the luggage. Cassie followed, making gratifying noises of interest and curiosity.

They came to the small enclosed room at the far end of the space, and he opened the door, leaving the key in the lock. "Here it is," he said, and watched Cassie's face as she took in the space.

Three rows of aluminum shelves had been crammed so closely into the narrow space that getting the boxes in had required some careful maneuvering. Some of the more heavily laden shelves were actually dipping slightly under the weight of massive photos albums, record books, and whatever other ephemera had been deemed worth keeping by the Pelopsons. There was a strange, not entirely unpleasant odor, of musty paper and worn leather. He felt as if the archives were surveying them too, cynical of any changes, but not entirely closed off to hope.

Cassie's mobile face went from intrigued to intimidated to determined. "Ah," she said, and put her red box down. "Okay. I can see I've got my work cut out for me. Okay if I move furniture around to set up a workspace here?"

"No problem. There's a bathroom on the third floor, and my office is there too if you need anything," Manny said. "I'll be around most of the day, I think, but feel free to text any questions if you can't find me or don't want to climb down." If she were a new employee at Delphi he'd be letting her know about break times, but that seemed inappropriate. Cassie was clearly a competent person capable of managing her own time, and it wasn't as if the archives had a concierge desk that needed manning. "Help yourself to anything in the kitchen for lunch and snacks, or head back to the guesthouse, whichever you prefer. I'll let you know when I hear about your car. Do you have any questions?"

"Just one," Cassie said. She lowered her voice, and Manny instinctively leaned closer to her. There was a faint scent of something herbal coming from her hair, and it mingled pleasantly with the dusty aroma of the attic. "I don't want to get in the way of any family conflict or pry into stuff that isn't my business but can you tell me anything about why your mom doesn't want me here? I'd rather not accidentally poke any sore spots."

Manny stiffened. The knee-jerk reaction to protect his family was something he'd been working on, but it still took him by surprise sometimes. "My dad died six months ago," he said. "He'd been talking about going through the archives for years, but he'd actually started poking around up here. He told Mom he was going to cut back on his hours running the winery and write a book about the family history. And then he died, very suddenly."

"I'm so sorry."

"Yeah. And it's funny—Mom isn't the Pelopson, you know? She married in. But she cares about the history, maybe even more than he did, and now she wants me to do the organizing and research and Augie—that's my brother—to write the book. But only when we have time, which we really don't right now."

"So I'm treading on hallowed ground."

"Yeah." Manny rubbed the back of his neck. "I'd like to say she'll come around, but I don't know if she will. And I know that might make the job uncomfortable from time to time. But let me know if she says or does anything out of line. You're working for me, not her, and it's my job to look out for you."

"Family conflict actually comes up a lot in this job," Cassie said. "People have different ideas about what to do with their private archives, where they should be stored, whether they should call in a professional—all that stuff. You're not alone."

"Huh," Manny said, feeling a bit better. "I hadn't thought of that, but yeah, that makes sense."

She gave him a professionally sympathetic smile. "I'll do my best not to hit your mom where she's hurting. Thanks for letting me know the background." She rolled her shoulders and stepped back, and only then did Manny realize how close she'd been. Close enough to confide in. Close enough to kiss.

"Okay," he said hastily. "I'll let you get to work."

***

It took very little effort to find a table Cassie could use. The real difficulty was resisting further exploration. This attic was a wonderland, a gorgeous chaos that tugged at every instinct she had to investigate and make orderly.

But she had a job to do, so once she dragged the table over, she set up her laptop and kit just outside the archive room. There wasn't really room for her to do much in there; she was going to have to go in, pull boxes out and go through them, one-by-one.

Crammed and cramped as it was, the little room in the attic was very far from the worst storage facility Cassie had ever seen. That dubious honor still went to the basement in Florida, which was not even a place she'd thought you could put a basement. This space was dry, and unless the roof leaked there wasn't likely to be much in the way of water damage.

Dust, though. Dust was definitely going to be a problem. Cassie hunted through her kit for a mask and gloves, and briefly contemplated the plastic hazmat overalls. Normally she wouldn't bother unless there was a recognized danger, but she also didn't want to get mouse droppings or dirt all over her new sweater. Well, wear the overalls for the initial assessment, then, and she could take them off after that.

Aerope Pelopson was also going to be a problem. She'd been friendly enough in the kitchen, but Cassie could recognize a woman plotting a strategic shift when she saw one.

She'd encountered a lot of strong-willed, family-focused women in her job, because those were often the people who held the family history and decided that the records needed to be cleaned up. The matriarch of the Florida estate had been a tiny, wizened great-grandmother with a razor-sharp mind and a tongue to match.

But Nana Sue had also been Cassie's staunchest defender, as numerous branches and sub-branches of the family argued about what she uncovered and what they ought to do about it. Cassie had left Nana Sue planning to leverage her vast network of family connections to get the archives admitted to one of the local universities, and she was pretty sure Sue was going to manage it somehow.

Nana Sue had also been adamant that Cassie should date one of her single grandsons, marry into the family, and move to St. Augustine. Wayne was a nice man with an even nicer body, but he was also not the sharpest tool in the shed, so Cassie had declined, with regrets, and driven north with the feeling that she'd just escaped a very friendly trap.

Cassie zipped the hazmat suit up, grimacing at the sound of plastic rustling. She got her gloves on, adjusted her glasses and stepped inside the little room.

The Pelopson family history surrounded her.

Cassie did not normally think of herself as fanciful. But every time she first walked into an archive, full of primary records and first-hand accounts, photographs, bank statements, diaries, receipts, and countless bits and pieces that had once been considered essential enough to keep, she felt history pulse around her. At the moment, it was a vast and formless chaos of experience and impression. Her job was to bring order to the chaos. Just by being here, by noticing things and sorting them into categories, she was changing the way those things could be recognized and accessed. She was exerting, however lightly, her own narrative control over someone else's story, and she never took that responsibility lightly.

It was also the kind of deeply addictive buzz that meant she'd never even considered applying for that archivist position at Olympus Inc, no matter how much Laodice would have loved to work in the same building. Magazine archives, however well-organized and funded, could never provide the same wild thrill.

She picked up the first box on the top shelf, closest to the door, and carried it back to her table. One by one, she lifted out the items within, and identified what they were, entering them into her spreadsheet. Close examination was a job for another day. The initial survey was all about categorization.

And if this box was any indication, the initial survey was going to take at least a week or two. It wasn't just the shelves that were crammed. The Pelopsons obviously believed in making use of any available space.

As far as she could tell, there was no real established order, either chronological or categorical. This box had contained a sheaf of handwritten recipes on yellowing paper, the vineyard's tax records for 1973, 1987 and 2004, a bunch of fading receipts with no annotation stuffed into envelopes, a macaroni-decorated art project that had suspiciously rodent-like nibbles, and three family photo albums.

Photo albums were *great*, and also time-consuming, especially if people weren't in the habit of identifying who was who and when and where the photos were taken. Cassie could already tell she'd be spending a lot of time trying to track down who was pictured in each photo, but that was a job for another day. She stuck the Post-it listing the contents on the side of the box, carried it back to the shelf, and picked up the next one.

Three hours later, she finished the fifth box, rolled her shoulders, and resolutely ignored the desire to go through just one more. Her stomach was protesting, and she wanted to find out what was happening with her car.

As she hit the third-floor hallway, she saw Manny coming towards her, carrying two plates. "I was making myself a sandwich, and wondered if you might want one," he explained.

Cassie took one of the plates. It looked like an egg and cheese sandwich, cooked in the best bodega tradition. He'd even added a pickle spear and a side of chips.

"Are you trying to win some sort of best boss ever award?" she asked. "Because you're making a really good play for my vote."

Manny smiled. "Who's my competition?"

"A little old lady named Nana Sue. She'd serve you a slice of key lime pie in one breath and cut you off at the knees in the next."

"In that case, I happily concede my inevitable defeat."

"It's the only smart choice," Cassie agreed. She hesitated, not sure of whether he meant her to go and eat in the attic, or head down to the kitchen, or...

Manny opened a door. "My office is in here, if you don't mind company."

"Sure," Cassie said, and followed him in.

The archives were practically tidy in comparison. Here, dusty bookshelves were crammed with texts and ledgers, and knickknacks and antiques were cluttered on every flat surface. Computer equipment was piled in one corner. She spotted at least two monitors, and a huge processor tower that looked decades older than current tech. Under the windows was a massive oak desk with sturdy carved legs, an ancient computer, and folders and printouts and reference texts, all piled haphazardly on top of each other.

Cassie's archivist instincts itched.

"Uh, yeah," Manny said. "Sorry about the mess." He moved a few cushions, a pile of origami animals, and a tennis racket (how? why?) from an armchair and gestured her into it, taking the rickety wheeled office chair himself.

Behind him, Cassie spotted the slimline laptop taking up the single cleared and dusted corner of the desk, mouse and mousepad neatly aligned beside it. The one piece of order in the chaos.

She bit into the sandwich. Melted cheese oozed into her mouth. "This is really good," she said.

"Thanks."

"But what were you going to do if I were vegan? Or lactose-intolerant?"

Manny shrugged. "Eat two sandwiches."

Cassie could see his point. She wouldn't mind eating two of these. They ate off their laps in companionable silence. At about the point she was starting to miss her water bottle, still upstairs, Manny said, "Oh, right," and opened a mini-fridge holding an array of sodas. "Would you like something to drink?"

"Okay, you've got to tell me what 'I was in hospitality' means," Cassie said, selecting a root beer. "Because this is starting to look like magic."

Manny laughed. He had a nice laugh, kind of a happy rumble. "I managed a boutique hotel in the city. Delphi."

"Oh, I've heard of that! The fancy one downtown?"

"That's the one."

"And now you're managing Tantalus?"

"It seems so," Manny said, and smoothly shifted gears before she could ask more about that. "How're things going upstairs?"

Cassie took the hint. "Pretty good, so far. I should have an initial survey done by the end of the week. That's mostly just saying what's in each box at first glance. I keep a spreadsheet that catalogs the items. After that I go through everything piece by piece and start tentative categories. That's where the real fun happens."

"You actually mean that," Manny said, sounding faintly surprised.

Cassie shrugged. "I like things organized. Classic eldest daughter. But there's always the part where you might turn up something interesting."

"Interesting? Like, scandalous?"

"I can't reveal client information," Cassie said primly. "But I *can* say that a few families have skeletons in their closets."

"Literally?"

"No! Well, unless it's rats, and even then, they tend to mummify." Manny shuddered.

Someone banged on the door, and then opened it without waiting for Manny to reply. It was Theo.

"Manny, what stupid fucking nonsense have you been telling the boys at the winery," he said, storming in, and then halted in his tracks as he registered Cassie's presence.

It would almost have been funny, how quickly the rage was swallowed by cheerful good humor, if it hadn't also been deeply alarming. "Well, aren't you two cozy?" he said, eyes glinting.

"Just taking my lunch break," Cassie said, standing up and brushing crumbs off. She collected Manny's plate as well as her own. "I'd better get back to it. But I'll take these down."

"Thank you," Manny said quietly.

Cassie looked him straight in the eye. "Thank *you*. Lunch was delicious."

"Steph from the garage said she'll give you a call later this afternoon," Theo told her. "She's got a few jobs this morning."

"Right, thank you," Cassie said. She didn't want to be in this room, where the air had turned sour with the threat of recrimination. She almost wished she could take Manny out with her.

But he was a grown man and could presumably take care of himself. Indeed, as she let herself out, she heard him say, patient, but firm, "Theo, I've explained why investigating organic makes sense."

"Liberal hippie bullshit," Theo snorted, and then she was far enough away that she couldn't hear them.

***

"We can't afford to go organic," Theo said, his face like a thundercloud, and Manny wanted to leave him and chase Cassie instead, offer to take her anywhere, as long as he could escape and she could be with him. He'd felt calmer in her presence than he had in literally months.

But he had duties and responsibilities, and he wouldn't ignore them for the illusion of freedom.

"We can't afford to go organic right now," he said. "But when we refurbish the carriage house and open for visitors this summer, we could put aside some of the projected profits for crop overhaul. Organic is a way for us to stand out in a crowded market dominated by the Californian wineries. We can't compete with them in quality, quantity, or price point, so we have to find other points of differentiation and target a tighter demographic."

"There's nothing wrong with our wine's quality. The cellar door does great."

"It really does," Manny said. "I was surprised by how much it brings in."

The Tantalus cellar door was Theo's pride and joy, an add-on profit stream he'd proposed, created, and managed for nearly twenty years. It was essentially a small tasting room with shelves of wine for purchase, cash only, and a stool behind the counter that Theo occupied whenever he felt like it.

Manny had visited a couple of times since he'd been back, and he could see some distinct areas for improvement. The room's décor was outdated, and not the cute vintage kind of outdated that attracted antique hunters or day-trippers. The sign by the highway was small and unenticing, the hours were variable, and the whole place could have done with a vigorous deep-cleaning. But Theo must have been doing something right, because the direct sales from the cellar door turned a decent profit.

Theo grunted, unappeased by this praise for the project he'd originated. "You'd know the wine was good if you *drank* it."

Manny shrugged. Most wine tasted like sour grape juice to him. He'd drunk half a glass of champagne on his wedding day, and vaguely recalled it being pretty good, but the subsequent disaster had forever tainted that experience.

He was forced to rely on other data to judge Tantalus's products. And the dwindling sales and smaller profit margins told their own story. Theo could point to stellar reviews from the wine appreciation titles of the 80s all he wanted, or protest the success of his cellar door sideline, but modern cuisine magazines concentrated on the big guns or exciting newcomers, not family vineyards with mid-shelf reds. Their sales to wholesalers were drying up. If Tantalus was going to survive, they needed to position themselves as a boutique vineyard, and switching to organic was one way to do that.

Manny didn't know how to make wine. But he knew hospitality. He knew the kind of person who'd love to stay in the carriage house of a historic vineyard, go on a guided walk through the vines, visit the cellars and maybe even have an expensive high tea at the big house. That last was a thought he hadn't dared to suggest to his mother yet. But she and Augie had approved his plans to refurbish and rent out the carriage house.

Manny's grandfather had left the house and grounds to Arthur, but the business to his sons, so while Theo couldn't stop Manny from renting out the carriage house, he could veto any major changes to the winery. Most of what Manny was doing at the moment was gathering information and trying to show Theo how change might benefit them all.

"Have you had a chance to consider refurbishing the cellar door?" he asked. "Modern cellar doors have the store, but also make it more of an experience—a bar with tasting flights and platters, or even a full restaurant."

"The cellar door is fine the way it is," Theo said, immediately and predictably. "Why don't you reach out to your work friends and get more of our wine in hotel bars, hm? *That*'s a way you could help this family."

"That's a good idea," Manny said, and Theo paused, looking suspicious.

"No, I mean it, it's a really good idea. We could set up a tasting experience for beverage managers at hotels and restaurants. Some of those people oversee contracts worth millions. If we invite them to stay in the carriage house, then take them on a tour, get them to see a new cellar door experience—"

"Oh, here it is," Theo said, snorting. "Manny, I've been looking after the business for thirty years. You'd be better off learning how it works now than trying to change it."

"I have an MBA with specializations in Marketing and Analysis," Manny said. "I'm not a viticulturalist, but I do know how to run a business."

Theo looked disgusted. "But you've never owned one. You ran that little hotel for rich people—"

"We're rich people, Theo," Manny said wearily, and rubbed his temples. "But yes. I ran the top-rated private hotel on the Eastern Seaboard for an excellent salary. I didn't own it myself. And that's actually good for you, because when you and Mom wanted me to quit and move here,

I could do that, instead of trying to find a buyer. Why did you even want me to come, if you weren't going to listen to me?"

Perhaps some of the regrets he had about that choice were showing, because when Theo next spoke, his voice was more tentative. "I thought I'd teach you how it worked. Not that you'd start poking your fingers into every damn pie."

"I'm learning as fast as I can," Manny said. "But I think we need to make changes before I've learned everything. The books are messy. I've done the best I can, but I wish you and Dad had hired an accountant years ago. If we get audited, I can't guarantee we'll be found compliant."

Theo shrugged. "Arthur told me he had a system. We don't owe much, do we? Or are there problems with Arthur's accounts? I've got some savings, if you need a loan."

Manny felt a burst of warmth at the offer, which was given as carelessly as Theo offered critique, and with about as much forethought. Whatever anyone said about Theo, no one could accuse him of being ungenerous.

"No, it's okay. The vineyard doesn't owe anything at the moment, and there's enough in Mom and Dad's account to pay off the rest of what we owe on the house electrical refit."

"Then don't worry about it," Theo told him. "If it's not a problem, it's not a problem."

"I'm not actually worried about debt," Manny said. He hated it when finance guys said things like "you've got to spend money to make money," usually right before they tried to get you to invest in something shady, but he'd run the projections. The way the vineyard was going, they'd be in the red within five years. Right now, Tantalus could get a loan without much trouble. But if they didn't make an effort to turn things around now, while they were still making a profit, it would be too late to ask. At that point, investors would consider a loan throwing good money after bad.

At that point, they wouldn't be able to correct the slide.

Tantalus Vineyard really did need to spend money to make money, and they needed to spend it soon.

"We don't need to make any changes right now," Theo said dismissively. "It's only six months since your father died—aren't you supposed to hold off on changes for a while anyway? That's what the grief brochure said."

Well, he wasn't wrong about that. Manny's therapist had said something similar. Unfortunately, the numbers didn't lie, and they didn't care about his feelings. "Uncle Theo, I just want us to think about the possibilities."

"Waste of time. Come out and help me with the mulcher today. You need to get your hands dirty, and you'll feel better if you get outside for a bit."

Manny looked out the window. "Let me get my coat," he said, and when Theo beamed at him, he found himself regretting the sharp tone he'd adopted earlier. Everyone was grieving Arthur Pelopson in their own way. Aerope was wound tighter than a spring, Theo was picky and critical, and Manny was...urgently trying to address everything at once, as if acting on a time limit would give him back the time he'd missed with his dad.

He hadn't called Augie for a few days. He should do that tonight, ask him to put the kids on the phone. Remind himself that under all the frustrations and quirks of family life, they loved each other.

And that he should make the most of what he had, every day, because he never knew when tragedy might strike.

By late afternoon, Cassie had sore eyes, a runny nose, and a scraped elbow. The space between the shelves was much too tight for easy movement. Even thin people would have had some trouble. At her size she had to practically hold her breath and suck it in to get the boxes out. How had Manny gotten those boxes in there in the first place? He had less breadth in the stomach than she did, but more in the shoulders. Maybe his brother was smaller.

She entertained herself for a moment, picturing the contortions Manny Pelopson might make in order to prevent his juicy ass from knocking anything over. Then she took off her glasses and rubbed the bridge of her nose. The lights up here were giving her a headache, and she'd need a double dose of her antihistamine to deal with the dust. But she'd made good progress; the top shelf of boxes had been cataloged, and this last box had been half-empty, which had definitely sped up the process.

She picked it up, ready to return it, and set it back down when something fluttered to the ground.

It was a photograph of a dozen or so kids in swimsuits, clustered on a dock jutting into a lake, with an adult couple in the middle. The photo had been caught under the cardboard flaps, as if someone had tucked it in at the last moment. Cassie hadn't spotted it on her first survey, a sure sign that she'd reached her capacity for the day. There was no notation on the back for time, place, or people, but the clothes and condition of the photo provided some clues. She dutifully logged "Loose photograph, c. 70s?" on her spreadsheet and returned the picture to the box.

The door to Manny's office was ajar, but he wasn't there. She quelled a momentary disappointment, and went down the stairs, which made enthusiastic noises as she went, retracing her way to the kitchen and the back door. She would have loved a chance to look around the house, but it would have been unforgivably nosy to take herself on a tour. Maybe she'd ask Manny for one tomorrow.

On this hopeful note, she opened the back door, and jumped back when she saw Aerope Pelopson standing right outside it, her hand reaching for the handle.

"Oh!" she said, and then, feeling like a fool. "Sorry, Mrs. Pelopson, I didn't know you were there."

The other woman looked equally startled, but recovered swiftly. No bulky puffer jacket for her; she wore a navy wool coat, belted at the waist, and a pristine white scarf wrapped around her throat. Cassie was willing to bet the scarf was cashmere. "Ah, Miss Troiades," she said. "I was planning to fetch you, as it happens. Stephanie Marshall at the garage came into the library and said she'd just finished work on your vehicle. She's closed the shop for the day, but you'd be welcome to come pick it up in the next hour."

"Oh," Cassie said. "Uh, thank you. Manny said he'd take me into town to get it, but I don't think he's around."

Aerope hesitated a moment, then nodded. "I'll take you," she said. "If now is good?"

Cassie hesitated in turn. "I appreciate the offer, but didn't you just drive out from town?"

"It's no distance, and you need your vehicle," Aerope said, and turned on the heel of her practical, yet stylish snow boot. Cassie followed, very aware of the sweat that had gathered under her breasts and the dust that was no doubt clinging to her curls.

She felt slightly better when they rounded the corner to the parking spaces, and discovered Theo and Manny getting out of Theo's BMW. Both of them were red-faced and grimier than she was. Manny had a swipe of dirt on his cheekbone, just above the line of his beard, and a dried leaf actually stuck in there.

"What on earth have you two been doing?" Aerope asked.

Theo thumped Manny on the back. "Teaching this one how to use the mulcher! We'll be ready for spring, once the first thaw comes. Where are you girls off to?"

"To fetch Cassie's car," Aerope said.

"I can take you," Manny said immediately. "Uh, if you give me ten minutes to shower and change."

Cassie grinned at him. "You do have a little something there," she said, and gestured just below her chin.

Manny swiped uselessly at his beard a couple of times and she shook her head. "May I?" She stepped closer when he nodded, and plucked the scrap from his beard. When she glanced up and met his eyes, she was suddenly aware that they were very close. Touching distance, in fact. It would be nice to touch him again.

From the spark in his eyes, she didn't think he'd object.

"Um, so, yeah, I can wait ten minutes," she said, and stepped back again.

"Don't be silly," Aerope said, her eyes very sharp. "I'm ready now. And we shouldn't keep Stephanie waiting." She smiled. "Besides, it'll give us a chance to get to know each other. Just us girls."

Damn. Clearly Cassie wasn't the only one who'd noticed that flare of mutual attraction. But there was no graceful way out of it. She climbed into the SUV with Aerope, and waved at Manny as they departed.

According to Cassie's research, though there were smaller villages and hamlets scattered all over the region, the town of Weeping Rock was the only real urban space in the Lake Lydia municipality, and it was what everybody seemed to refer to when they said "in town."

"It's lucky for me that you were in the library at the same time as the mechanic," Cassie said.

Aerope sounded surprised. "Of course I was in the library. I work there."

"Oh," Cassie said. She had immense respect for librarians—more than half of her graduating class had gone into library work—but she'd thought the stereotype of the stern librarian had dropped out of real life years ago. "In administration, or...?"

"I'm the head of the Children and Youth department. Stephanie brought her daughter in for my story time this afternoon."

Cassie pictured Aerope reading to children. Probably a sprightly tale about a very naughty archivist who invaded the ice palace of a beautiful blonde queen, and had to be severely punished until she learned the error of her ways. "That's good," she said inanely, and watched the countryside darken around them as the afternoon slipped into evening. It was about the same time she'd been stuck on the side of the road yesterday.

Only yesterday? It felt like it had been longer than that.

"So!" Aerope said brightly. "Is there anyone special in your life? Manny has been seeing a nice psychologist in the city."

Oh, very subtle. "Not at the moment. I'm dating, but there's nobody serious."

"Very wise. No need to narrow the field at your age." Her tone turned inviting. "You must miss the city, though. Not many dating prospects here."

"Actually, I have a date scheduled with someone local tomorrow night," Cassie said. She might be a romantic cynic, but she firmly believed in the appeal of a casual hook-up. There hadn't been *many* possibilities in the area, it was true, but the dating apps had supplied one guy who had good photos and a fine line in flirty texts.

"With whom?" Aerope asked, grammatically correct and frigid as an ice floe.

Cassie seriously considered telling her it was none of her business, but that might spark more conflict than she wanted to deal with, and besides, Aerope was a local. She probably had more information than Cassie could get in a quick session with a search engine.

"Isaac Corey."

"One of the Idlewild Coreys?" Aerope said instantly. "The one who went to medical school or the banker?"

"The banker, I think," Cassie said. Their texts had included some references to finance.

"The banker divorced recently, I remember that. His ex-wife taught at Weeping Rock elementary school and had an affair with a student's father. Terrible business."

"Ah," Cassie said. Well, it wasn't necessarily a red flag that Isaac hadn't mentioned that. She'd frequently advised people looking for casual dates not to tell potential hookups their entire life story. "Thank you for letting me know."

"Not that you should let that put you off," Aerope added, apparently remembering that she was trying to keep Cassie away from her son.

"Everybody has some baggage, as you young people say. Besides, you won't be here long."

"Three months," Cassie agreed.

Aerope took them over a bridge, and onto a road that looked more well-traveled. There were other cars on it, at least. "Maybe less time than that," she said.

Cassie contemplated leaving it alone. But they were sweeping past the sign that read *Welcome to Weeping Rock*, and she'd be out of the car in a minute or two. If there was going to be a confrontation, now was a good time. "What do you mean by that?" she asked, her voice as neutral as she could make it.

"Just that you might find some reason to leave early," Aerope said. She pulled the car to a stop outside a shop with a bright pink sign reading "Marshall Auto." She leaned across the car seat towards Cassie. "You might find a better opportunity somewhere else. I wouldn't blame you, if you did. I'd be happy to pay the rest of your fee if you left sooner than expected."

Holy shit. Cassie had been telling Manny the truth when she'd said that archivists often uncovered family conflict, but she'd never had anyone try to bribe her before.

"That's very generous of you," she said, in lieu of anything else.

Aerope smiled, or at least bared her teeth. "I can be very generous, when merited." She left unspoken how she might behave towards people who didn't merit generosity.

"Well, see you later," Cassie said, and got out of the car. Did she need to tell Manny about this? It seemed like someone attempting to bribe you away from your job was something you should tell your boss, but what if that someone was your boss's *mother*? And what if she was grieving her husband and his father, and living in the same house with your boss, and maybe part of his business structure?

What would Cassandra say, if someone wrote in with this problem?

"Hey! Are you Cassie?"

Cassie jerked out of her daze, and smiled at the woman walking out of the garage, wiping her hands off on a rag. "That's me."

"I'm Steph Marshall." The woman rocked back on her heels and looked Cassie over. Cassie returned the favor. Steph Marshall was only a couple of inches taller than her, but just as broad, filling out her blue overalls with sturdy muscle. Her hair was cropped short and dyed bright pink, the same flamingo shade as the sign above her head. "Nice to meet you. I'd shake your hand, but I'm covered in grease."

"I'm covered in dust," Cassie offered. "I've been in the Pelopson attic all day."

Steph whistled through her teeth. "I bet that's an interesting place."

"It really is," Cassie said, more enthusiastically than she'd meant to.

"You cleaning up there?"

"No, I'm an archivist. I mean, there'll be some cleaning, but I'm mostly there to catalog and organize their documents. I'll do some preservation too, if I have time left over."

"Damn, that sounds amazing."

Cassie nodded. "I've only just started, but the archives have already offered some fascinating glimpses into local history."

"Do you know what the family plan to do with them? Donate to the library or something?"

"I don't actually know," Cassie said. She wouldn't say if she did, of course—that wouldn't be ethical—but she found herself pleased she didn't have to obfuscate anything to this woman.

Steph looked enthusiastic anyway. "You know, I bet Mrs. Pelopson could get a display at the library."

"Oh, yes," Cassie said. "She's... A children's librarian?" She couldn't help the questioning inflection that crept in at the end.

"Yep. Best librarian in the state. She's so great with those kids. I used to wish she was my mom."

"Really?" Cassie said.

Steph caught the doubt that time and blinked at her. "You bet. My mom wanted a girl who'd dress up and date quarterbacks. I wanted to wear jeans and date cheerleaders. She thought it was a phase I'd grow out of, and we argued a lot, so I spent plenty of time in the library. Mrs. Pelopson's warm and kind, but she's a fighter, too. She used to get queer books in for me, and every June she puts on this massive display for Pride Month." Steph snorted. "One of the local ministers tried to challenge that once. Just once."

Cassie tried to reconcile the idea of Aerope as *warm and kind* with the woman she'd met, but her brain flatly refused to do it. *Fighter*, now, that made sense. "I'm glad you had someone to fight for you," she said, in lieu of *are we talking about the same Aerope Pelopson?*

Steph grinned at her, and Cassie realized she'd just passed a test she hadn't known she was taking. "But I'm yammering on and you'll want your car," Steph said easily, and gestured Cassie into the garage. Cassie's car had pride of place in the center of the workshop. "Nice little vehicle. You look after her yourself?"

"My sister does. She likes cars."

Steph nodded approvingly. "She knows what she's doing." She went on to describe what the problem had been and how she'd fixed it, but Cassie didn't have a good memory for mechanics at the best of times, and was too busy eying the trunk and backseat for anything missing. Manny's talk about the local teen thieves had alarmed her, but everything seemed to be there. Teens probably weren't all that interested in her stationery supplies anyway, not when there were road signs for the taking.

"How's Manny getting on with being back?" Steph asked.

"I don't know him that well yet," Cassie said, and her brain added, all unbidden, *but I'd like to*. "Fine, I think? He's really made me feel at home."

"I used to stare at the back of his head in AP English and wish he were a girl," Steph confided. "He's such a good guy. His brother's an asshole, though. He was a senior when we were freshmen, and you've never seen a dude so high on his own ego. Don't ever ask Augie a question unless you want a ten-minute monologue."

"Got it. I'm not sure if I'll meet him."

"Best to avoid it, if you can."

Cassie nodded. "So, what do I owe you?"

Steph eyed her up and down, then looked at the car again. "Ninety dollars, plus tax," she decided.

Cassie raised an eyebrow. "Are you cutting me a deal?"

"I'm charging you what I'd charge a local," Steph said, unruffled.

"I'm not local."

"But you're a guest, not a tourist." Steph nodded firmly to herself. "If you feel bad about it, you can buy me a drink sometime." She caught Cassie's hesitation. "Friendly drink. You're interesting, and you have an interesting job. And you're staying with the Pelopsons, who have been good to me. And I like your vibe. I'd be happy to show you around some, introduce you to a few people."

"I like your vibe too," Cassie said, with complete honesty. "I'll be in touch about that drink." She paid her bill, exchanged numbers with Steph, and reclaimed her car, feeling the warmth of making a new friend. She wasn't as social as her sisters, but she liked people and her job sometimes isolated her from them. Especially in small communities, which didn't always warm up to strangers.

It would be nice to get to know some people.

Chapter Three

[Cassie] Got my car back!

[Laodice] What was the problem?

[Cassie] *shrug emoji*

[Cassie] Honestly, the mechanic did tell me, but all I heard her say was "not a big deal, ninety dollars please."

[Laodice] *crying emoji*

[Cassie] Next time I'll take notes for you.

[Laodice] Ys pls. How was your first day?

[Cassie] My boss's mother hates me, and his uncle is an Old White Dude Who Knows Better Than You

[Laodice] boooooooo. How's the boss?

[Cassie] He's good.

She hesitated, but...

[Cassie] Kind of hot, actually. Though obviously not going there. And his mom says he's seeing someone.

[Laodice] 60% of adults have a workplace romance!

[Cassie] It can't possibly be that many. What were the criteria for "romance?"

[Xena] do me and Zac count as workplace romance?

[Cassie] No, you're both self-employed in the same field. You just guest on each other's content a lot.

[Xena] hm

[Xena] not much from this manny guy on socials. Just linkedin and old facebook.

[Cassie] It doesn't matter, because I'm not going there. Go stalk my date for tomorrow, Isaac Corey from Idlewild. Banker.

[Xena] hmmmmmmmmmm

[Xena] even less.

[Xena] honestly, could be scrubbed

[Xena] red flag

[Cassie] Not everybody is online fourteen hours a day, Zee

[Laodice] Some of us are even detoxing from social media because it's better to be in the now.

[Xena] did your barista say that when you asked for his insta?

[Laodice] He said he prefers face to face interactions

[Xena] yeah, at his job, where he works

Three dots appeared by Laodice's name, then disappeared, then appeared again

[Cassie] Okay, time out. Do you want some advice?

[Xena] no

[Laodice] sure

[Cassie] L, stop flirting. Ask him out, *once*, and if it's anything other than an enthusiastic yes, it's a no. And prepare for no, btw, this is what happens when you crush on people whose job it is to literally serve you.

[Laodice] uggggggggh ok

[Cassie] Zee, as requested, no comment.

[Xena] yeah but I can feel you thinking it. FINE i'll stop being a bitch. Sorry L.

[Laodice] <3 everything okay?

[Xena] the comments were a lot today.

[Xena] DO NOT READ OR RESPOND

[Xena] CASSIE THIS MEANS YOU

[Cassie] You tell off the people being mean to your little sister ONE time...

[Xena] fr tho don't!!

[Cassie] No, I won't. I'm sorry.

[Laodice] Did Mom tell you guys to check your breasts?

[Xena] yeah

[Xena] think I might use it for content

[Xena] you guys want in? Family bonding over boobs?

[Laodice] No thanks

[Cassie] Absolutely not

[Xena] weenies

***

Around noon the next day, Manny wondered if Cassie might want a break. He'd seen the lights of her car drive in last night, and heard her footsteps along the third floor while he was on the phone with a wholesaler, but he hadn't seen the actual woman all morning.

He'd thought about her, though, once or twice or half a dozen times. The way she'd thanked him for lunch and admired his hospitality. The way she'd plucked that leaf from his beard and grinned up at him with her soft, lush mouth.

He went up to the attic, to see if she wanted lunch, but Cassie wasn't there. Her work was. He must have missed a couple of journeys to the attic, because she'd brought up more equipment. More archive boxes, flattened. Scissors, several different kinds of tape and glue, a roll of white paper, so thin it was almost translucent. Her laptop was closed, but he spent a minute admiring the stickers collaged on the lid. There was a great one of a deranged raccoon eating potato chips, and another that declared "Archivists do it in the metadata", but his favorite was a Maenad College alumna sticker showing a snake-haired woman holding a man's decapitated head.

When he went looking for Cassie downstairs, he found her trapped at the kitchen table with two empty plates and his mother.

"—don't really mind the cold that much, Mrs. Pelopson," Cassie was saying. She sent him a single panicked glance as he walked in. She was too well-mannered to mouth *help me*, but Manny got the message.

"But surely you find it gloomy, with all the—oh, hello, Manfred."

"Hello, Mother," he said, and sat on Aerope's other side, so that she was forced to turn away from Cassie to talk to him. "Weren't you working today?"

"Berenice swapped shifts with me so she can get a mammogram next week." She swiveled back to Cassie. "I thought Cassie might want something for lunch."

"I don't think I've ever had a better quiche," Cassie said. "You're an amazing cook, Mrs. Pelopson."

"Yours is keeping warm in the oven, Manfred."

"Thank you."

"It's a shame I can't serve it cold. I prefer cold quiche, personally, but it's just too chilly for it. Did you say your last job was in the South, Cassie? You must be finding it difficult to adjust."

"It's nice and warm in the house, even in the attic," Cassie said. "I've been meaning to ask, Manny, can I actually light that fire in the guest cottage?"

"You bet. I had the chimney checked when I refurbished. There's a wood pile out the back."

"That sounds *amazing*," Cassie said, and he got a little dizzy with the idea of her sprawled in front of that fire, heat glowing in her cheeks.

He coughed. "We're supposed to have good weather this afternoon and evening, so I planned a run. If you didn't have plans, I could show you one of the routes I use, maybe get the fire started for you?"

"Cassie has a date tonight," Aerope cut in. "With Isaac Corey."

"Oh," Manny said. "Oh, cool. Did you guys meet yesterday or…?"

Cassie gave him a look he couldn't quite interpret. "We chatted a little bit before I started the job," she said. "Maybe you and I could go for that run tomorrow?" She stood up. "Thank you for lunch, Mrs. Pelopson. I'd better get back to it."

"I imagine you want to leave early," Aerope said. "To get ready for your date." She gave Cassie a smile.

"That's very kind, but I'm happy to keep going. I've got good momentum."

The smile disappeared. Manny spotted the signs of his mother readying another sortie and stepped hurriedly into the breach. "What's that really thin paper called?"

"Glassine," Cassie said. "It preserves and protects photographs."

"But we have albums," Aerope said, momentarily diverted.

"Photos fall out," Cassie said diplomatically. "I found a loose one yesterday." She nodded at both of them and left, probably before Aerope could find a reason to be offended at that.

"Thanks for lunch, Mother," Manny said, and pulled his quiche out of the oven warmer. "I thought I'd walk through the carriage house after lunch, start making some lists of what we'll need for the renovation."

"That sounds nice, dear," Aerope said, but she was frowning at the door Cassie had just walked through. "That young woman has an answer for everything."

"Yes, because she's good at her job," Manny said. "Please let her do it."

Aerope transferred her frown to him. "Don't think I don't see what you're thinking."

"This quiche smells great," Manny said, and tucked in.

***

Cassie had come to the conclusion that, since bribery hadn't worked, Aerope Pelopson was trying to drive her from the job through sheer irritation. After that agonizing lunch, Aerope had come into the attic three more times, offering coffee, fresh-baked scones (admittedly delicious), and reiterating her offer for Cassie to leave early to get to her big date.

That last time, she'd stuck around the archives, watching Cassie work, claiming to find it fascinating, and asking questions about her previous jobs.

Cassie couldn't concentrate on the work, she couldn't tell her to go away without being rude, and she couldn't walk away herself because that would be letting Aerope *win*. Her pace slowed to a crawl, and she'd caught herself accidentally entering data in the wrong cells twice, which meant she'd probably done it more often than that. She was going to have to doublecheck the spreadsheet tomorrow.

And that was only if she could get any more concentration time tomorrow. Aerope had brightly informed her that while she had the morning shift at the library, she'd be home all afternoon. Cassie reminded herself that Steph Marshall liked the woman, so there must be something to like, gritted her teeth, and kept doing the best she could.

She made it to 5pm, barely, and returned the half-completed box to the archives before she locked the door.

"Do you lock it every time?" Aerope asked, for once sounding genuinely interested instead of ice cold or syrupy sweet.

"It's protocol for any archival space that can lock," Cassie said. "Our instructors were very firm about securing archives. It's one of the best ways to guarantee provenance."

She was half-expecting Aerope to object or frostily point out that only the Pelopsons had access to the house, and it was *their* archive, but the woman just nodded and followed Cassie down the stairs, wishing her well on her date.

The back door shutting behind her sounded like defeat, and Cassie walked back to the guest house, thinking hard. If Aerope pulled something like that again, she was going to have to speak to Manny about the hostile working environment. The problem was that there wasn't an HR department here, and her line of report was one person. And she didn't know where Aerope fitted in.

The archives belonged to Manny; that much she'd gathered from the car conversation between Aerope and Theo on her first arrival. Manny should therefore be legally allowed to employ anyone he wanted to do things with them. But *legal* wasn't always the same as *possible*.

For example, was Tantalus a company that employed Manny, or had Aerope inherited an owner's share from her husband? And if so, was that where Cassie's fee was ultimately coming from? Would telling Manny about the bribe and asking him to keep Aerope out of the attic result in an ultimatum from his mother-boss?

If she were giving advice in Ask Cassandra, she'd tell the letter writer to put everything in writing, where it could be referred to later in case of a legal dispute. But she thought Manny was on the level. And he'd told her to tell him if Aerope were getting out of line. Actually, he'd said *"it's my job to take care of you"* and he'd sounded like he'd meant it. Which was just an employer's obligation, of course, no need to get quivery over it.

She ran a bath, still thinking, and sank into the hot water with a sigh. Probably everyone who thought their boss was a good guy would be reluctant to tattle on his mom in writing. But "he has an excellent butt" and "he fed me a sandwich" and "I'm pretty sure he wants to make out with me, and that's flattering" were not a good basis for business decisions. She wrapped herself in the plush, oversized robe Xena had given her for her birthday, and tapped out a quick email.

She left it in the drafts folder. Sending it could wait until after this date.

***

Cassie's first impression of Isaac Corey was favorable. He was big and handsome, a hefty guy who'd obviously shaved and showered for the occasion. That was a point for him, and so was the fact that, allowing for some minor filtering and different lighting, he looked like his pictures.

He was sitting at a table near the wall, and he looked up hopefully as she approached. She'd considered wearing the one dress she'd brought with her, but she could bring that out for a second date, if there was to be one. Instead, she was wearing black pants and a sparkling, galaxy print top that she knew for a fact made her breasts look fantastic.

Isaac's eyes snagged on her cleavage for a moment, and then went to her face, which was another point in his favor.

"Isaac?" she said. "I'm Cassie."

"Hey!" he said, and stood up, going for a hug.

Cassie thrust her hand out instead. He hesitated, and shook it. "Nice to see you in person."

"Ditto," Cassie said. "This place is neat."

Isaac looked around as if he were seeing the bar for the first time. The low ceilings and exposed rafters were probably compulsory, but whoever had decorated had veered away from the traditional colonial vibe. The tables were topped with grey and white tiles set into timber frames. Isaac had taken a table in the middle of the room, but against the walls were booths with high-backed, red-cushioned benches. Above each table was one of those complicated folded lightshades, which looked to be made out of comic book pages, although closer inspection revealed it to be some kind of plastic—hopefully heat-resistant. Stylized vector art of cult films lined the walls, and a funky plastic stegosaurus sat on their own table, a hand-lettered RESERVED sign sticking out of a slot cut in his back.

"I guess," he said. "It didn't used to look like this."

Cassie sat down. The lamp on their table was a glass alien skull with a tealight burning merrily inside. "What did it used to look like?"

Isaac looked around the bar again. "I don't know. More adult."

"Most of those are films for adults," Cassie said, pointing at a cheerful rendition of *The Exorcist*. "I think there's a lot of room for fun in adult lives."

Isaac grinned at her, eyes glinting. "Yeah? When was the last time you had some adult fun?"

Cassie smiled. "Oh, I don't think we know each other well enough to compare schedules."

"Me, two months ago."

So she'd signaled a boundary, and he'd ignored it. Awesome. Well, she had a guaranteed subject-changer. "Two months ago I was down south, finding pressed lizards in a Florida basement."

"Huh," Isaac said. "That's weird." He waved at the bartender, a pretty woman with long dark hair, and after a moment she came over. "What do you want to drink?"

"Do you have any Tantalus wines?" Cassie asked the bartender.

"Sure do. Their merlot's pretty good."

"One of those, thanks."

"Whiskey on the rocks," Isaac said. He winked at the bartender. "But just one, this time, Laura."

Laura made an expression that wasn't quite a smile and turned back to the bar. Cassie looked at Isaac. "Just one?" she asked mildly.

"Oh, three months ago I was ordering two at a time," he said, and gave her a sidelong look. "Not now. But things were pretty rough after my wife left. Did I mention that?"

"I don't think so," Cassie said, opting not to tell him that Aerope had.

"Well, she did. She was cheating on me, not the other way around, if you were worried."

"I'm really sorry," Cassie said. She meant it. The betrayal had clearly left a mark.

"But I'm over that now," Isaac said, and spent the next twenty minutes telling her what a massive bitch his ex-wife was. Cassie's sympathy drained rapidly. She limited her responses to nodding, vaguely affirmative noises, and "that sounds hard." Isaac seemed to be veering between getting his resentment out or making a play for her sympathy, neither of which were pleasant as an audience. He also didn't ask her a single question about herself.

Sadly, Cassie had had worse dates. He wasn't getting sloppy drunk, or making negative comments about her body designed to lower her self-esteem. But he was rude and boring, and she didn't like some of the phrases he used about his ex, so this was definitely a one-and-done first meeting.

She thought about staging a retreat via the bathroom and the back door, but she wasn't sure he'd done anything bad enough to warrant a ghosting. Instead she waited for a brief pause, and put her glass down. "Well, that's my drink done," she said.

"Did you want another?" Isaac said. "Do you want to get dinner? Or we could get out of here. My place isn't far."

For the love of all that was holy. If he thought she was going home with him, he hadn't paid any attention whatsoever.

"No, that's all right," Cassie said, standing up. "I think I'll call it a night."

Isaac stared at her. "What? Why?"

"Well," Cassie said, rapidly discarding possible answers, "It was good to meet you, but I'm going to get going now."

"You only just got here! It's been like ten minutes."

It had, in fact, been half an hour of her life that she was never getting back, but Cassie didn't want to be drawn into an argument that would waste even more time on this man. "Okay," she said. "Good night." She should probably offer to pay for her drink, but the way he was squinting at her was setting off alarm bells.

Sure enough, the next thing out of his mouth was, "That's pretty fucking rude."

Okay, then. He was definitely on the hook for her drink. "I guess so," Cassie said, and walked towards the coat rack. She'd hoped to get away smoothly, but she heard the scrape of his chair on the wooden floor.

"Hey! I said, you're being really rude!"

"I heard."

"What the hell is wrong with you?"

Cassie zipped up her jacket and surveyed the bar for possible assistance. The bartender was coming towards them, her pretty face determined. Some of the locals were pretending not to notice, which wasn't useful, but some were definitely paying attention, which...could go either way, really.

"I'm leaving," she told Isaac again, and took a step backwards. She didn't want him right behind her, and she wanted to know he wasn't going to follow her into the parking lot.

He grabbed the sleeve of her jacket and tugged. Cassie wasn't normally very tuggable, but Isaac was a big man, and she rocked forward a couple of steps.

Right. The line was well and truly crossed.

"Let me go, asshole," she said, loud and clear. A few more locals were definitely paying attention.

"Look," he said, forcing a smile. "Look, just give me a chance. You haven't really given me a chance—"

"The lady's leaving, Isaac, and you ought to stay put while she does," the pretty bartender said, and Isaac glared at her.

"Stay out of this," he said.

She shook her head. "Stay out of you making trouble in my bar?"

"I've been drinking in this bar from before you were born, Laura May."

Laura rolled her eyes. "You're only six years older than me, Isaac Corey. If you were drinking in this bar back then, it was soda."

Cassie took advantage of the distraction to tug her arm free, and felt the door open at her back.

"What the hell is going on here?" someone demanded, and Cassie risked a glance over her shoulder. Steph Marshall had just come in. With her candy-pink hair and a white puffer jacket, she looked like an adorable cartoon mascot, but the scowl she was directing at Isaac ruined the effect a little.

"I'm leaving," Cassie told her. "Isaac wanted me to stay, but I think he gets that's not going to happen now."

"I'll walk you to your car," Steph said instantly, and Cassie could have hugged her. She was too angry to be actually scared, but she absolutely did not want to be alone in that parking lot.

"Now, Isaac, you come with me and I'll get you another gin and tonic," Laura was saying, her tone conciliatory, and Cassie knew exactly what she was doing. She slipped out while Isaac was distracted, and Steph fell in beside her as they crunched through the parking lot grit.

"I'm sorry," Steph said. "What a welcome we've given you. Broken down car, terrible date, and there'll probably be a storm within a week or so."

Cassie looked up instinctively, and Steph laughed. "Not right away! We're clear for the next few days, at least."

"I sort of hoped the snow would melt soon," Cassie confessed.

"Well, the first thaw won't be too far away. But we'll likely still get some snow through to April, and I've known storms in late May. Not recently, though, given climate change and all." She stopped by Cassie's car. "There you go."

"Is this going to make any trouble for you?" Cassie asked as she climbed in.

"Me? No. Trouble for Isaac, maybe. He's been pushing his luck as it is." She rapped her knuckles on the hood. "Text me when you get home? Safe driving."

***

Manny tipped another armful of trash into the dumpster and took a moment to stretch and breathe. It was just after noon, and one of those bright winter days that you learned to cherish out here. Light gleamed on the bare tree limbs in the apple orchard, and made even the churned snow and mud in the yard more appealing. He was eager to get the carriage house cleared before the weather turned, but his body was humming with the warm satisfaction of physical exertion, and in this brief pause, he drank in the peace and the cold air.

Then he turned back to the carriage house, and felt worry grip him again.

The guest house had been built in the 1930s, reputedly to house the irascible father-in-law of Theophilius Pelopson. They'd kept it as a guest house ever since, renovating as fashion and changing building standards demanded. Privately, Manny thought his cottagecore redesign was the best of the lot. Sure, Cassie seemed to find it hilarious, but she'd still praised the comfort.

The carriage house was a different story. It was a big building, built in the late 1890s, designed as part-stables, part carriage and tack storage space. The introduction of the automobile soon after had eliminated the need for the Pelopsons to keep horses, and the space had been used for a garage for a while. Eventually, it had suffered the fate of many garages and become a repository for stuff to be thrown away "later."

The Pelopsons had put the things someone thought were worth keeping in the attic. Everything else had come out here. Leftover tiles and bricks, lumber off-cuts, half-full paint cans, obsolete machinery and other trash, all of it just stacked against walls or piled up on the concrete floor. The building itself had been well-maintained—no derelict hulks allowed on Pelopson property—and the brick facade and exposed beams would appeal to exactly the demographic he was hoping to lure. The architect at Appleton Construction had agreed when she'd come out to do the initial planning survey, enthusiastically maneuvering around the obstacles to measure and plot out the possibilities. But all those obstacles had to be moved before the real work could begin.

And his projections for clearing it out himself had been...optimistic.

"You're making excellent progress, dear," Aerope said behind him, and Manny straightened.

"Are you developing psychic abilities, Mother?" he asked.

She smiled fondly at him. "I've always had them, Manfred. How else would I have survived bringing up you and your brother? Come into the house for a bite." She linked her arm in his and drew him towards the big house. "Here's a thought. Since you're paying Cassandra to sort and organize things, why don't you ask her to help you clear out the carriage house?"

"That's not the job I hired her for."

"Very similar, though," Aerope said brightly. "Lots of family history in there. You should at least show her around. She might spot something that might be better off preserved."

"I suppose," Manny conceded. Would Cassie like the carriage house? He wouldn't ask her to cart trash out, but there was enough antique machinery in there that it might have some historical interest, at that.

"You should call her down for lunch, then take her out to see it."

That was his mother's planning voice. She was definitely planning something. Manny squinted at her suspiciously. He could have sworn that yesterday, she'd wanted to keep Cassie away from him, but now she seemed eager to toss them together. Or was it just that she wanted to keep Cassie out of the archives, and thought the carriage house presented an appealing alternative?

Nevertheless, he washed his hands and headed up to the attic, where Cassie was just locking up the archives for her lunch break. "Oh, hey," she said, and smiled at him.

Manny's spirits instantly lifted. *Down, boy,* he thought, but the problem was that she was just so damn appealing, all wrapped up in those chunky wool layers he wanted to peel off her.

"I wondered if you'd like to see the carriage house," he said. "I can't claim there's much in the way of written records, but you might find it interesting."

"Is that the big building next door? How many carriages did your family have?"

"I'm going to assume too many," Manny said dryly. "It was the Gilded Age, and they weren't really going for discreet. It stabled all the horses for the manor house and the vineyard, too, and it had bedrooms for the grooms, although they probably got less space than the horses."

"I thought it was a really fancy warehouse."

"Well, essentially that's all it is now. But we're refurbishing it into a boutique hotel."

"Oh, cool! Sure, I'd love to have a look sometime."

"It was Mom's idea," Manny said, giving credit where it was due.

A complicated expression passed across Cassie's face. "That was nice of her," she said, and Manny winced.

"Is she giving you a hard time?" he asked. "Please tell me if she's interfering in your work."

"I wrote an email draft," Cassie said, half-turning towards her laptop, and then she swiveled back to him. "Okay, yes. She spent most of yesterday afternoon up here, and it really impacted my work flow. I didn't directly ask her to leave because I wasn't sure if that would be appropriate. I'm not a hundred percent certain on the chain of command and I don't know what the business situation is."

Manny nodded. "Okay. Dad left the archives to me, and I'm paying for you to deal with them, out of my own pocket. It's not a Tantalus business expense, and you're not responsible to my mother."

Cassie exhaled. "Okay."

"On the other hand, I can understand why you wouldn't like to outright tell her to leave, especially when this is her home. I'm happy to run interference, and to tell her to leave you alone during your work hours. Hopefully, that will be enough. But if necessary, I'll escalate."

"*Thank* you," Cassie said. "Man. I bet your employees loved you."

Manny's face heated. In fact, they had. His performance reviews had always been good, and he'd enjoyed managing people. At least, when he was managing people in his area of expertise. The guys at the winery weren't that interested in being told what to do.

Was that why he was so focused on the carriage house refurbishment, he wondered uncomfortably. Was he so eager to get back to hospitality management that he was pushing his family business in a direction it didn't need to go?

He refocused on the problem at hand. "How about this. You still want to go for that run?"

"Yes, absolutely."

"Then let's say your work day finishes now. We can grab lunch, I'll talk to Mom while you get ready, and then we can run after."

"Avoiding potential backlash and giving everyone a chance to chill out," Cassie said admiringly. "Very smooth."

So over soup and sandwiches, Manny mentioned that the weather was nice if Cassie wanted to go for a run, and she agreed that yes, it would be lovely to take advantage of the afternoon sunshine. Aerope's enthusiastic encouragement was another tick in the "anything to keep her away from the archives" column.

And when Cassie left to change into her workout gear, Manny turned to his mother and firmed his resolve. "Please don't go up to the attic while Cassie's working," he said.

Aerope looked as if she was trying to decide between denial or outrage, and settled for mildly peeved. "Well, really, I was just being friendly."

"Mom. I'm serious. I hired her for a job, and I need her to be able to concentrate on it."

"It's a job we don't need her to do!"

"We're not having this conversation again," Manny said. His voice was calm, but his heart was pounding. "I know you disagree with how I'm choosing to handle the archives, but it was my decision, and I've made it. It all ties into the changes you've already approved. People love a story, and telling the story of Tantalus can only improve our chances to hit our niche."

"There's no big rush. Why don't you take a few months and think about—"

"Are you going to continue to harass my employee?" Manny cut in. "Who has done *nothing wrong* and doesn't deserve it?"

Aerope opened her mouth. Then she closed it again, her jaw tightening. "I'll stay away from the attic," she said.

Manny stifled a sigh of relief. "Thank you."

"And you should do the same," Aerope added. "Just because she had the sense to tell Isaac Corey to get lost doesn't mean she's good enough." She stalked away from the dining table before Manny could ask what she meant by that.

On second thought, he was pretty sure he knew. He headed upstairs to find his own running clothes, shaking his head.

Cassie was waiting for him outside the guest house, doing some stretches. Manny's mouth dried out as he watched her lunge. Cassie in jeans was fun to look at, but Cassie in tight leggings...

"I spoke to my mother," he said. He sounded businesslike. Professional. Damn, Cassie's ass was amazing. "She's undertaken to stay away from the attic while you work. Let me know if there are any more problems."

"Thank you," Cassie said, on a relieved exhale, and Manny knew he shouldn't feel like a hero just for doing his job, but when she smiled at him like that it was hard *not* to feel good. He started stretching his own hamstrings.

"What kind of run are you looking for?" he asked.

"I like something around a 5k. A bit of slope is okay, but no mountain climbing. And I'm pretty slow."

"I'm happy to go at your pace," Manny said. "Or if you're faster than me, I promise I won't mind if you take off ahead."

Cassie laughed. "I won't be faster. I drive my sister crazy. She's a fitness influencer, and she's always like, you could go faster than that, you can work on your speed, you should do interval training!" She shrugged. "But I don't want to. I just like to run."

They set off, jogging slowly down the driveway as their muscles warmed and loosened. Manny turned left at the gate, and they went down the road for a little bit before he turned left again, into the Tantalus vineyards. He was choosing a route he'd run many times before, over ground that was hard, but not snowy. He didn't want to be the guy responsible for making Cassie run through a snowbank and break her ankle. True to his word, he let her set the pace. She did go slower than he'd normally prefer, but he was perfectly content to keep step beside her, watching the effort pinken her cheeks and the focus sharpen her gaze.

"You don't wear your glasses for running?"

"Not since the second time I broke them," she said. Her breath was elevated, but even. "I mostly need them for close up work, anyway." She gestured at the vines. "Those are a bit fuzzy, but it's not a problem."

They kept going, the pallid sun illuminating their path. "Okay with that hill?" Manny asked.

Cassie looked at the slope. "Sure," she said gamely, and they both put their heads down and dug in for the climb. Cassie's breath was coming faster, and Manny was panting a bit himself when they hit the crest and Cassie slowed to a fast walk.

"Whoa," she said. "I can see your house from here."

Manny grinned at her. Lake Lydia stretched below them, placid and smooth, with fields and orchards and home estates edging onto it. He pointed. "If you look behind the big house, you can see the path down to the lake. And there's our dock."

"You have your own private dock," Cassie said. "Of course you do." She shaded her eyes. "Oh, actually, I think I've seen the dock in photos. There was a loose one with a lot of kids in the 70s."

"My grandfather used to bring out disadvantaged kids from the city in the summer. I think it was some kind of back door philanthropy thing. Dad and Theo used to talk about it."

"Did they do the same thing?"

Manny shook his head. "Though Augie and I used to bring friends out, when we got old enough. We had some good times at that lake." He'd proposed to Helen on that dock, that bright summer after they'd both graduated from college.

He'd known Helen for a while. Her sister Ness had been going out with Augie on and off since their freshman year. And Helen was beautiful, of course, easily the most beautiful woman at Eleusis. Just knowing her had given Manny a social boost, though he'd quickly stopped introducing his frat brothers to her when it became clear she was too shy to enjoy meeting boisterous strangers. He and Helen were the quiet ones, happy to cover for each other or slip away for private conversation when the family struggles got too loud.

Ness and Augie, against the advice of nearly everyone who knew them, had gotten married three years after college. He and Helen had spent more time together during the build up to that spring wedding. She'd seemed a little sad and distant, and he'd done his best to cheer her up and make her feel welcome.

He'd discovered that she had shy, but decided opinions on music and art, she had a sense of humor that only came out when she trusted people, she was kind and sweet, and very easy to fall in love with. Hanging out had led to making out had led to a slow-blooming romance. For all that, he could sense a reserve that went miles deep, and felt that there were parts of herself that Helen had always kept back. He'd never imagined that she'd actually agree when he asked her to marry him.

But, after a pause he later told himself he'd imagined, she'd said yes. He'd never been happier.

"Do you need a minute?" Cassie asked, and he realized he'd stopped moving altogether.

"No, sorry. I was just thinking about someone I used to know." He started jogging again, leading them along the crest of the hill, and down the gentle slope that would let them loop back around the first vineyard and back out to the road—if he was remembering correctly, that would be just a shade under 5k.

By silent, mutual consent, they slowed down again as they went back up the main house driveway.

"You haven't asked me about my date," Cassie said suddenly. "Nor did your mom. Does that mean you already know how it went?"

"It could mean I thought it was none of my business," Manny suggested hopefully, but he caught her look and sighed. "No, you're right. If it's any consolation, Steph only texted me to make sure you got home all right."

Cassie looked skeptical. "And did you?"

"I can see the guest house from my window," Manny said, and pointed it out as they walked past the manor. He didn't *need* to walk her back to the guest house, she was perfectly capable of that, but it would be rude to just cut off the conversation. "I saw your car drive in." No need to mention the wave of unexpected relief that had rolled over him at the sight.

"Mm," Cassie said. "I realize that in small towns, people talk, but I don't necessarily want to know what they're saying about me."

"Okay," Manny said.

After a moment, Cassie looked at him. "Maybe I want to know a *little* bit more about what they're saying about me."

"Nothing bad," Manny said promptly. "Steph said she only saw the tail end, but it looked like he didn't want to let you leave, and that she was glad you'd told him where to shove it."

"I wasn't quite that rude." Cassie's mouth quirked. "I mean, I kind of wish I had told him to fuck off, because he was seriously out of line. He actually grabbed my jacket to stop me leaving."

Manny stopped still. "He *grabbed* you?"

Cassie met his eyes. "Just my jacket. But I wasn't very happy about it."

Manny had never been the violent type, but he had a sudden desire to pummel Isaac Corey.

"I got the feeling he'd been going through a rough patch," Cassie said, and led them up the porch to her door. Manny followed without thinking about it, hesitating only at the threshold when she paused to take off her shoes.

"I'll get you some water," Cassie said.

"Sure, thanks," Manny said, and waited in the doorway. This wasn't crowding her. He wasn't in her space. Just…at the threshold of it. "Um, you know that no matter how rough a patch he's going through, that wasn't okay, right?"

"I do know that, yes," Cassie said, sounding faintly exasperated as she walked into the kitchen. "I'm not letting him off the hook. People are responsible for their choices, even when they're heartbroken."

Manny nodded. "Someone broke my heart, once. And in the immediate aftermath I reacted badly. But my reaction was my fault, not hers." He didn't wake up with the nightmares any more, but he could remember it, he and Augie and the boys, crammed into Jax's truck and driving all over Ithaca, following Odysseus Turner's directions. He'd been hollowed out, nothing inside him but that gaping wound where joy had been. He'd been desperate just to talk to Helen, to make sure that she meant it, that she was really leaving him for real.

It wasn't until later that he'd realized what a bunch of drunken, angry idiots trying to hunt down the woman he loved could have turned into. It wasn't until later that he was sane enough to break out in a cold sweat, and thank whatever gods there were that they'd never caught Helen and Paris that night.

Cassie handed him a glass of water, and he drank half of it in a single gulp, reviving at the cold, clear taste.

"I'd hate to think that gossip might turn the community against me," she said tentatively, and he realized she was trying to find out if people would be on Isaac's side.

"I wouldn't worry about that," he said immediately. "Isaac had a lot of goodwill in this town when his wife left, but he's burned through most of it. People have started saying that if he was this sulky and selfish in the marriage, no wonder Janine looked elsewhere."

"Do you think he was?"

Manny shrugged. "I wasn't around when it all went down."

"I keep forgetting you only came back recently. You seem as if you belong here."

Manny thought about Theo's resistance to change, his mother's inexplicable opposition to organizing the archives, the effort it took to lay any claim on this place. "You might be the only one who thinks that," he said quietly. "Thanks for the water."

"Thanks for the company," Cassie said. "Let's do it again. But right now I have to get out of this sports bra."

Manny felt the blood rush to his cheeks at the same time the vision flooded his brain. He could so clearly picture Cassie's groan of relief as she released the catch, the abundant spill of flesh as her breasts were freed, how he could take the weight with his hands instead, and soothe the tender skin with his lips. He met her eyes, and knew that she had some idea of what he was thinking. She might have even reciprocated. Her own cheeks were flushed, and the tip of her tongue darted out to wet her lower lip.

They both stepped back at the same time.

"Okay, so, see you tomorrow," he said.

"Yep!" Cassie said. "I'll work extra hard to make up the hours."

"Awesome. Great. See you then. Tomorrow, I mean." He jumped off the porch without bothering with the stairs. "Yep. Bye!"

"Bye!" Cassie said, and if laughter was bubbling up in her voice, Manny couldn't blame her. He was acting exactly like an idiot with a crush on a pretty girl.

Because that was what he was. And he wasn't sure what to do about it.

Chapter Four

For the next two weeks, Cassie tried very hard not to act on her attraction to Manny Pelopson, no matter how good some action sounded.

There were a couple of problems. The first problem was that Manny was kind and interesting and a good listener and obviously laboring under the massive burden of revitalizing the family business without, as far as Cassie could tell, a single complaint.

Another problem was that he was grieving. Everyone in that house was grieving. The absence of Arthur Pelopson was a gap in every conversation. Theo didn't officially live in the big house, but he stomped in and out, berating Manny whenever he thought he'd overstepped his bounds. Cassie didn't know if he was always that irascible, or if the loss of his brother was rubbing his nerves raw.

Aerope had gone from icy observation to being overly solicitous to ignoring Cassie completely. Cassie honestly preferred the last, but she couldn't see any sign of the fierce, loving defender that Steph so admired. Steph had known Aerope for years, and was clearly a good judge of character, but any glimpse of that woman was buried under bereavement.

"And the third problem is that he's my boss," she concluded.

It was her second weekend in Weeping Rock, and Cassie had elected to spend the Saturday exploring the area with Steph and her daughter. They'd hiked one of the easier Lake Lydia trails, eaten enormous burgers at a local bistro, and visited the agriculture museum, at Keyshia's request. Keyshia was a serious little kid, but Cassie hadn't known what to make of a three-year-old who was into agriculture museums. It turned out the actual appeal was the playground, which was full of kid-sized farm equipment. Keyshia had climbed into the tractor cab and had had to be bribed with jelly beans before she'd leave.

Hanging out with Steph and Keyshia hadn't been her only option this weekend. Manny had asked if she wanted to go for another run, or maybe a drive around some local spots. Unfortunately, if she spent more time alone with him in an enclosed space, she was going to do something stupid like tell him to pull over and take his clothes off.

Steph grinned at her. "The boss thing isn't that big a deal. I read somewhere that 60 percent of Americans have had a workplace romance."

"My sister says that too."

"The hot sister who's into girls?"

"No, not the hot sister who's into girls *and* boys and is currently filming in Toronto with her boyfriend of two years," Cassie said pointedly. "This is Laodice, the *other* hot sister, who's exclusively into boys."

"Laodice is the one that's into cars, right?" Steph tapped her fingers against her mug of hot chocolate. "How exclusive is exclusively, if you know what I'm saying?"

"Just boys. But so many boys. They only have to give her a soulful look or say her hair looks nice and she starts writing their names together in her journal." She glanced at Keyshia, who was sitting on the kitchen floor with Play-Doh, utterly uninterested in the complications of adult love lives. "I'm exaggerating for comic effect, by the way. Don't tell Laodice I said that."

"I'd need to meet her for that." Steph waggled her eyebrows until Cassie laughed. "Seriously, though, you're only here for three months. Ten weeks, now. Make out with Manny a little. Do it for me. Do it for the kid I was in AP English."

"Make what with Manny?" Keyshia asked.

"A cake," Steph said, without missing a beat.

"Do we have cake?"

"Not today, hon."

"Okay," Keyshia said, and solemnly held up her Play-Doh sculpture. It was a squashed orange ball with four spindly tentacles hanging off it, and a second, slightly smaller ball on top. "This is you, Cassie."

"Oh," Cassie said, unsure of the etiquette. "Thank you?"

Keyshia nodded. "I'm going to make a cake next," she announced, and squished the Play-Doh into a disc.

"Your mama's coming to pick you up soon," Steph told her. "Do you want to check your bag and make sure you have everything you need for the week?"

Cassie hadn't met Steph's ex-girlfriend yet, but it didn't seem the time to linger in the doorway. She stayed at the kitchen table instead and caught only a glimpse of a brown-skinned woman in a heavy overcoat as she carried Keyshia out to the car, calling friendly enough farewells over her shoulder.

Steph came back in and sat down, her cheer dimmed.

"Everything okay?"

"Sure. Yeah, I'm fine. Just, you know, we were great together until we weren't, and sometimes I remember. Idunnu's so good with Key, and it's not like the feelings ever went away. We just couldn't live together. Sometimes I think, oh maybe we could try again, do it right this time." She sighed. "But I shouldn't lay this all on you. I should write to Ask Cassandra or something."

Cassie's heart jolted. "The advice columnist?" she said, making it come out as a tone of vague interest.

"Yeah! Have you read her stuff? I think she's a genius. She wrote this amazing response to a woman who'd gotten pregnant and engaged, and her rich fiancé was a one-man parade of red flags."

"I think I've read some of that column," Cassie said. Which was true, after all. She hadn't gone through *all* of the archived letters and responses. "Isn't it like Dear Prudence, though? Like, lots of different authors who are just called Cassandra?"

"Oh man, I love Prudie too. And Captain Awkward is incredible, and I'll scroll through the Am I The Asshole subreddit posts occasionally. Although I'd never be brave enough to crowd-source advice. I sometimes think there are more assholes in the comments than the letters."

"Have you ever written in to any of them?"

"Once to Cassandra, when things were going sideways with Idunnu. But she didn't write back." She shrugged. "She must get so many emails, though. And I read some of her other replies to couples with kids breaking up, which were actually pretty handy. Step one, staying together for the kids does both you and the kids a disservice. Step two, no matter how amicable the break-up, get a lawyer."

Cassie smiled. "What do you think she'd say if I wrote in asking about Manny?"

"Don't sleep with your boss," Steph said, without hesitation.

Cassie forced a laugh. "Probably."

"Definitely," Steph said, and topped up Cassie's hot chocolate. "But in this case, she'd be wrong. You're adults, you like each other, and this isn't a long-term working relationship."

"There's still a power imbalance, at least in theory."

"Now *you* sound like Cassandra," Steph said. "Theoretically, if you sleep together and Manny fired you right after, not that I think he ever would, what would you do?"

"Demand he pay the rest of my fee and leave him off my reference list," Cassie said. "And be very disappointed in myself for my bad judgment."

"And if *you* wanted to leave early, what would you do?"

Cassie pursed her lips. "I guess...the same thing I'd do if I had to leave a job for any other reason. I'd refund his deposit, minus the work I've already done, and offer to put him in touch with some of my colleagues."

Steph grinned at her. "Sounds like you've got it all sorted out."

Cassie's laugh was more sincere. "Theory is one thing. It's practice that's messy."

"Messy can be good," Steph told her. "You want a shot of something in that hot chocolate? Ward off the chill?"

"I'd better be driving back," Cassie said reluctantly. She would have liked to stay and dish with Steph some more, but her inbox was getting crowded, and her backlog of answered letters was running out. "I have some work to do tomorrow."

"I thought you had the day off?"

"I do, but I've got some freelance writing gigs too. Gotta hustle and grind, you know how it is."

"You write? Like, for newspapers?"

Cassie was used to obfuscation. Still, she couldn't help feeling a little bit guilty. And proud too, that Steph liked her work and it had apparently helped. "Sort of," she said. "My sister throws me some stuff from her bridal magazine. It's nothing very important."

"Oh yeah, because love's super easy," Steph said. "I bet it's way more important than you think."

Ask Cassandra

D ear Cassandra,

I've been with my partner O (he/him) for nearly ten years. We met at our performing arts high school, and we had an instant connection. It was thrilling to meet someone who loved music as much as I did, and we fell for each other deeply and immediately.

There was no question about what we would do after high school—we were staying together. We went to the same conservatory, and joined the same orchestra. Then he went solo.

He thrived as a solo artist. I won't share any specifics but we're talking big events, big money, the kind of opportunities you don't walk away from.

He didn't want to travel the world without me (he said he wouldn't go if I wasn't there, and he wasn't joking) and I wasn't getting many big breaks of my own, so I kind of shelved my career to support his. I quit the orchestra, and followed him around the world.

And gradually I became aware of how much world there was, and how much I'd constricted myself to a world that was made up of just this man and me. My life sounds like a dream to most people. I've traveled all over the world, eaten at the best restaurants, visited all the sights, and seen him perform at the most exclusive venues. He showers me with affection and buys me anything I want. In every new city he puts money in my hands and tells me to go shopping.

I do love him and we've shared so much, but the terrible thing is that I don't think I can be what he needs anymore. I want to stop touring, start applying to orchestra openings, and spend more time on my own work.

Just bringing this up makes O panic. He calls me his muse and says he doesn't know how he could live without me. He's committed to performances two years in advance, but he says he would give up anything and follow me everywhere to be with me. He swears that even if I never work another day in my life he'll always take care of me and give me everything I need.

He's always said this stuff, but it used to sound so romantic. Every love song I've ever heard is about how incredible it is to find someone willing to give you everything. But the truth is, I no longer want to take it. Not from him, not from anyone.

Does that make me a cynic? I don't want to be.

But I also don't want to be supported and adored. I don't want to be a muse. I don't want to inspire someone else. I want to find my own inspiration, figure out what makes me thrive, what makes me alive and creative and joyful.

I once brought up the idea of a break, so that we could see what life could be like if we were independent of each other, and he went into a depression that lasted for weeks. He missed performances, stopped eating, and I was seriously scared he'd hurt himself. In a panic, I promised I'd stay with him forever, and he's reminded me of that constantly ever since.

Sometimes I fantasize about running away, but I know he'd follow. Lately, I've caught myself thinking that it might be better if I died—I don't want to actually hurt myself, but if I were dead, he couldn't argue me into *staying any longer, could he? Those thoughts have scared me enough that I'm writing to you.*

What do I do? If I leave, how? If I stay, how? Will I ever be free?

Yours,

E.

Dear E,

First, I want to congratulate you on maintaining your sense of self and a desire for your own fulfillment despite every encouragement you've received—from your partner, from our world, from those stupid love songs—to subsume yourself entirely in his work and wellbeing.

Second, if you haven't already, I want you to go see a mental health professional as soon as possible. I believe you when you say you don't actually want to hurt yourself, and that these thoughts scare you, and I think that's a great sign. But I am not a doctor, and even if I were, I'm not your doctor. Please see your doctor. If your peripatetic life doesn't allow for a regular doctor, call one of the mental health hotlines listed in the sidebar.

Third, yes, you should leave. You should definitely leave. You can leave always, for any reason, but "being with him makes me want to die" is pretty much the best reason there is to get yourself gone.

Normally I'd be telling you to gather up your friends and family to support you while you made a plan to go, but, honestly, I don't want to assume that's a possibility this time. Your letter makes you sound so isolated, and I do wonder how much of that is deliberate. He's taken you away from everything familiar, and engineered a life so unstable that you could never build new friendships or make connections with anyone but him? How very convenient for the man who wants you to be each other's only person.

Let me be very clear, if I haven't been: O is emotionally abusing you. He may not see it that way (I guarantee he doesn't) but "you are the only person

I need and I need you always" is not romantic. It is deeply controlling. It places an unconscionable burden upon the other person, especially if, like you, they are generous and loving and feel the pressure to reciprocate. Especially when the merest hint that you might like to be an independent person prompts "a depression that lasted for weeks"! I won't suggest that he was faking it; I believe that his sadness and panic were genuine emotions. But he definitely took advantage of that state, and of your reaction to it because, and this is the kicker: he reminds you of that promise. The promise you made under duress, when you feared for his health, is one that he should have explicitly released you from as soon as he was less distressed. That he didn't is very telling.

He could be genuinely upset and still recognize your right to make decisions for your life. He could be depressed, and still understand that you have autonomy and agency. He could choose to feel his feelings and make dealing with them his responsibility, not yours.

He didn't make that choice. He chose to extract a promise that you would never leave, and now he waves that over your head as if it were a blood pact you can't break.

It's not.

People leave people they have promised not to leave every day. That's what a divorce is. That's what the majority of long-term relationship break ups are. We promise to stay when things are good (or in your case, when they are very bad) and later, when circumstances change, or they do, or we do, we break that promise. This is sad, but it's absolutely normal. We cannot predict what's coming next.

But, that said, let me predict some things for you.

He will not get better. He will not loosen your leash. There will always be a reason why you shouldn't pursue a job or stay in one place for long enough to put down roots. He reacts very poorly to any hint that you might leave, and that means that he could become dangerous. You don't mention physical abuse, so this might seem overly dramatic, but people can do terrible things when they're panicking, and this guy has stalker written all over him. When you say "I fantasize about running away, but I know he'd follow," I **believe** *you.*

This is why I want you to be very careful and very secretive about your next steps. If you're not doing this already, put aside some of the money he gives you. Ideally, put it into a bank account in your own name, that he cannot access. Money is one route to freedom.

Information is another route—check out the links in the sidebar on the right, especially the ones for leaving an abusive relationship. Don't hint at your plans. Do all of the information safety things recommended in those links: get a burner phone, change the passwords on your devices and accounts, clear your browser history often.

I'm so sorry. This is scary and lonely work, and I wish so much that you didn't have to do it. There are people and groups ready and willing to help you, and I hope you reach out to them as soon as you feel safe to do so.

I have another prediction for you. I predict that there's a day when this man and this life are behind you. There's a day when you wake up and feel inspired instead of trapped. There's a day when you are your own muse.

On that day, you will be free.

Love,

Cassandra.

Chapter Five

Manny hadn't seen Cassie all weekend, and was a little alarmed by how much he'd noticed that. It wasn't as if he hadn't been busy. He'd spent the daylight hours hauling more trash out of the carriage house. Theo actually helped him with that on Sunday afternoon. There was a certain joy to be had from dropping stuff into the dumpster and hearing it smash, and Manny thought Theo felt it too.

Certainly, his uncle had relaxed enough to reminisce about earlier times.

"—and our dad said that if your father wanted to go to college, he'd better find better uses for his head than cracking it," Theo concluded, chortling.

Manny shoved at the heavy wooden filing cabinet they were trying to muscle across the floor. It was too heavy to lift with just the two of them, and it would have been easier if they could have taken the drawers out, but the damn thing was locked, and the key had probably been lost decades earlier. "You dared Dad to jump off the roof?"

"Only the roof of the carriage house, and into a leaf pile," Theo said. "I'd already done it, and only got a couple of scratches. But damn, your grandfather was mad." Something passed across his face. "Guess we'll never know if Arthur would have done it. Myself, I always thought he'd chicken out at the last second, but he kept saying he would have, if Dad hadn't caught us in time. But if his college had been threatened…" He shoved at the cabinet again and grunted. "He really wanted to go."

"And you?"

"Not so much," Theo said. "Dad said he'd only be paying Eleusis fees for one of us, so I could take out loans or get a scholarship. I got some track and field scholarships to other schools, but in the end I decided to stay here and get my hands dirty." He grinned at Manny. "Just as well for you, eh?"

"You definitely know the business better than anyone else," Manny said. He could recognize Theo's expertise. It was just expertise that was more useful for a different market, in a different branding environment. "Doesn't seem fair that he'd only pay for Dad, though. Couldn't he have split it? Hang on, I'm going to put my shoulder into this instead."

"Well, Arthur was the oldest, and the smart one," Theo said. He leaned into the cabinet beside Manny, and they got a few more inches. "Not that I was a dummy, but…" He shrugged. "Arthur didn't think it was fair either. He offered to pay my way later."

"I didn't know that."

"You weren't even born. But Augie was, and I figured Arthur would need the money for his own kid. And I was too old for college then. Wasn't like I could pledge Arthur's fraternity, was it? Hold on, there's a piece of lumber in the way." He reached down and yanked it free, and the sudden motion tipped the cabinet forward. Manny grabbed at it, but too late to stop it toppling. The cabinet spun and smashed into the concrete floor, and both men jumped back.

Manny stared at his uncle, who stared back. He wasn't sure who'd started laughing first, only that they were both suddenly howling, leaning on each other and gasping for air.

"You can't do this stuff by hand," Theo said after a minute, wiping water from his eyes. "Definitely not by yourself, or even with two of us. What's with the rush, anyway? It's going to take a little more time to finalize the plans and get the loan approved, right?"

"I want them to be able to start construction without waiting on me," Manny said.

Theo rubbed his chin. "How about this. Call your brother, and see if he can come up for a weekend. I'll bring the hand-truck and the pickup from the vineyard, and all three of us can work on it." He looked around, a little dubious. "Maybe I'll bring the forklift, at that."

Now there was an idea. He couldn't take Augie from his family for a few weeks, but he could probably borrow him for a weekend. Or hell, Augie could bring the whole family up here. Manny hadn't seen the kids for months, and he missed them. He even missed Ness, a little bit. His sharp-tongued sister-in-law looked a little too much like his ex for him to ever be completely comfortable around her, but her acerbic wit could be very entertaining, when it wasn't aimed at him.

"Good idea," Manny said, and twisted to one side, trying to ease a tight spot. "I'm not sure I'm built for manual labor."

"You're doing okay," Theo said, which felt like the most positive thing he'd said to Manny in months. He rotated his shoulder a couple of times, looking away. "It meant something, you know. That your dad offered to send me to college. He always wanted things to be fair."

Manny swallowed past the lump in his throat. "He was a good man."

"Yes, he was," Theo said. He was shading his eyes, squinting into the fading light. "I'm going to get going."

"Stay for dinner," Manny said. For once, he meant it.

"Nah, that's okay. Feels like I've been hanging around like a bad smell lately. How are things going with that Cassie girl?"

"I think we could safely call her a woman," Manny said. "And really well. On Friday she told me that she'll finish the initial survey sometime this week. Then she'll figure out a category system and start sorting things into it, and documenting everything in more detail. She's making incredible progress."

Theo's voice was amused. "I wasn't asking about her work ethic."

"Oh," Manny said. "Okay, well, I'd better get back to it. Bye."

Theo laughed and walked away, and Manny straightened, absentmindedly poking a bruise on his hip. After nearly two weeks of concentrated effort and three filled dumpsters, the carriage house was beginning to look better. Not great, exactly, but they'd gotten rid of most of the stuff that was easy to move, and the cleared space made it easier to see the bones of the building.

He'd mentally reserved some of the antique machinery and tools for refurbishment. He could use them as décor, or put them on display, or hell, sell them online to collectors to help fund the renovations. Most of the interior partitions had been removed years ago, and what remained were the load-bearing walls, which he intended to work around rather than remove. There wasn't any rot or insect damage, and the concrete floor could either be polished or covered, depending on how the design worked out. He could easily get six small suites on this floor, but perhaps he'd go for four small, and one luxury apartment, with a full kitchen.

It was ambitious, it was all ambitious, but it was also very doable. He knew contractors, he knew designers, he knew how to navigate codes and regulations. He knew the many intricate moving pieces that could and would get out of alignment, and would need someone to notice and shift them back into place. He could find and train good staff. He could make this work.

"I can make this work," he said out loud, and pictured himself in the carriage house on its opening day, welcoming people in to look at the rooms, each with a slightly different theme, but working harmoniously together. He was going to do eras, with textiles and decorations appropriate to each. Not cheesy, corny fake history, but something real or at least respectfully replicated. A 20s suite, a 50s suite, a 70s suite... It would work.

In his head, he turned to the person beside him, smiling.

It was Cassie.

Manny's eyes sprang open, releasing the vision.

In his secret fantasies of the past, it was always Helen who'd come back to witness his imagined triumphs, Helen who'd repented and left Paris, or maybe Paris had left her, or even died (of something swift and non-painful, he wasn't a total monster) and Helen had returned, now delighted to accept the support and love he'd been so willing to give.

But ever since Ask Cassandra had told him to stop telling himself that story, he'd rejected that fantasy, forcing it out of his head every time it tried to wiggle in. He'd gone back to therapy, with a new therapist who'd guided him towards healthier ideations. "Visualize yourself succeeding, by all means," he'd said. "But don't make that success dependent on someone else's approval—not your parents, not your brother, and certainly not your ex-wife. See yourself accomplishing your goals and focus on how good that will feel for *you*, because you did it."

And he had. He did. He'd felt the joy himself, and he'd turned to Cassie, not so that she could approve, but so that she could *share* it.

"What the hell?" he muttered. Cassie wasn't going to be here when the carriage house opened for visitors. She was leaving in ten weeks.

He was attracted to her, of course. Who wouldn't be? She was pretty and smart, and she smelled great, and she wore tight jeans and warm chunky sweaters he wanted to just snuggle into. And they clicked. Lunch had become something he looked forward to. He'd shown her the vineyard on their runs and talked a little bit about his plans, and she'd been encouraging and interested. She'd told him more about what she'd been finding in the attic, and that had been interesting too. Not just the history of his family, but the enthusiasm with which she approached the task. She'd been utterly delighted when she'd discovered a treasure trove of love letters from the early 20th century, and it had been all he could do not to kiss her right then.

But it didn't mean anything. He shouldn't be placing her in his daydreams.

He'd stopped moving, and it was getting colder with the dimming light. Manny fetched his discarded jacket and shrugged it on over his thick plaid before bending to inspect the fallen cabinet.

It had landed on a corner before thumping flat onto one side, and the impact had cracked and twisted the burnished oak, huge, raw splinters jutting out. The frame was askew, and Manny squinted, playing his phone light into the gaps. There was something in the bottom drawer.

He went to the put-aside tools section, and after a few minutes of rummaging, came back with a crowbar. The craftsmanship was solid, but he was able to wedge the bar in a crack and lever it back and forth until something gave way and cracked. When he yanked at the drawer handle this time, it reluctantly shifted under his hand, and he could retrieve the object—a notebook covered in fuzzy green suede, stamped with the word RECORDS.

He flipped through it, but it was handwritten in fading pen, and seemed to be mostly numbers, with a few initials here and there. Probably more bookkeeping.

Cassie would like it. He'd show it to her tomorrow and ask where it might fit into the archives.

He tucked the notebook into his jacket and left, half his mind on being able to give Cassie something and the rest on what he might be able to scrounge up for dinner.

He spared only a brief thought on wondering why the ledger had been there in the first place, when the rest of the cabinet was empty and all the other documents were in the attic. Thinking about Cassie was much more fun.

***

Cassie slept well on Sunday night in her snug bed cave, and emerged to find new snow on the ground. It was just a light dusting, but she wrapped a scarf around her head before she traipsed to the big house. She probably wouldn't get a run this afternoon

On the other hand, she could use a night at home to get more work done. She'd only managed to write one Ask Cassandra response the day before, and that wasn't going to do much for her backlog. She'd thought too hard about it, that was the problem. She'd been trying to find the perfect words to persuade "E" that her worthless musician boyfriend's devotion was more suffocation than support. He'd tried to make one person his sole support system, and she'd inevitably buckled under the weight. It was selfish at best and cruel at worst.

She'd spent far too much time worrying that "E" wouldn't be able to see that.

Cassie took a deep breath, and regretted it as soon as the frigid air seared her throat. The reality of her job was that she couldn't make anyone do anything. She could only tell the truth as she saw it, as clearly as she could. What they chose to do with that advice was up to them.

So tonight, she'd give more people more advice.

And maybe do some laundry. She was definitely running out of clothes.

With that in mind, she walked through the back door. She was hoping she'd find Manny in the kitchen, where she could ask about whether she could use the family laundry, or if she should find a laundromat in Weeping Rock. The kitchen was empty, and so was the stairwell, but she heard a muffled sound from the living room, and poked her head in.

Manny wasn't there.

Aerope was. She was sitting cross-legged on the plush rug in the middle of the floor, surrounded by piles of neatly folded clothes that she'd obviously ferried down from a bedroom. More clothes, still on their hangers, were laid over the backs of chairs and sofas.

They were all men's clothes. Blazers, button-ups, a lifetime's supply of t-shirts and socks and underwear.

Aerope had an empty cardboard box in front of her, and a black plastic trash bag to one side. There was a pair of worn corduroy pants in her lap, and she was gripping them in both hands. Her face, when she met Cassie's eyes, was absolutely blank.

Cassie froze. She desperately wished she'd never even thought the word laundry. "I was looking for Manny," she said.

"He's in Weeping Rock this morning," Aerope said, without changing expression. "He'll be back later this afternoon."

"Right. Sorry. For intruding, I mean. And also... I'm so sorry."

"I thought I'd get this out of the way before he came back, but I can't seem to get started," Aerope said, her voice conversational. "It made sense, because the dumpster is right there, by the carriage house. I could box up the clothes good enough to donate and throw everything else in the trash. They're no use to anyone. They just take up space in the wardrobe. I can't give them to the boys because they're both so much bigger than Arthur. So, donation or garbage. That makes sense, doesn't it?"

Cassie nodded. Her throat was tight with sympathy.

"I watched a show last week, with a very nice woman who said the best way to let go of things you loved was to thank them. I imagine she's right. She helped a lot of people on the show. But I can't thank these clothes. I'm not grateful."

"I— can I help, Mrs. Pelopson? Is there something I can do to help?"

"You can leave," Aerope said. She relaxed her grip on the pants and smoothed them with her palms. "I am aware that you don't deserve to be chased away from this job. I know I have no authority. I understand that I must appear totally irrational to you. But if you want to help me, you'll destroy your spreadsheets and notes and you'll leave. I'll make it right with Manny. I'll pay your fee." She looked straight at Cassie. "I'll double it, if only you'll go."

"I can't," Cassie said. "It wouldn't be right."

The fierce light in Aerope's eyes dimmed. "What would you know about right?" she said bitterly, and Cassie slipped away.

She went up the stairs quickly, a hard lump in her chest. What would she say if Aerope wrote in to Ask Cassandra? Seek professional help, definitely. Some gesture towards time making grief easier, something glib about there being a day in the future when she'd no longer be in this much pain? It was true, mostly, but it didn't do much for people who were hurting right now.

And besides, Aerope *hadn't* written to Ask Cassandra. She hadn't asked Cassie for advice or welcomed her sympathy. She'd told her what she wanted, and it was something Cassie couldn't—wouldn't—do. So they were at an impasse.

At least the work was going well. The initial survey was nearly done, and she was delighted at what even that very cursory overview had turned up. She hadn't been able to sit down and read any of the journals, commonplace books, or ledgers yet, but there were so *many* of them. The Pelopson hoarding habit had turned nearly two centuries of history into tangible artifacts, each one a piece of a long and complex story. It could all be very dull—the harvest went well, here's what I paid for the new wagon—but even that could be of assistance to, say, economic historians or climate researchers.

Or, her personal favorite, the artifacts could be interesting in their own right. The Paston Letters of Norfolk had recorded five generations in the lives of that English family as they navigated the stormy waters of the Wars of the Roses. They were an invaluable resource for anyone studying daily life in medieval England, and also incredibly useful for anyone looking at the way language had changed in that period. The Pastons themselves weren't always particularly admirable, but they were shrewd political strategists. They'd survived the war and dragged themselves up the social ladder in a time that had ruined many family fortunes.

The Pelopsons reminded her of them, in more than one way. Continuous sources for post-colonial American history weren't as rare as they were for medieval England, but Cassie had the thrilling suspicion that the Pelopson archives could turn out to be a real find. She wouldn't know for sure until she started the deeper examination.

After that, the big concern would be preservation. This airless attic wasn't the best place for documents, and the storage in the tiny room left much to be desired. She could recommend digitization, which would take a long time and cost a lot if Manny hired someone privately, or she could recommend turning the collection over to an institution. Most big libraries and universities were wary of taking on new archival collections, but if this collection was even half as valuable as she thought it might be, they'd be jumping at the chance.

"Don't get ahead of yourself," she muttered, and went to work on the next box. They contained green suede-bound record books from the 60s and 70s, tracking profits and losses. It looked as though those had been good years for the winery, but she firmly resisted the urge to examine them more closely and added "Financial record books, handwritten entries, good condition, 1960-1977" to her increasingly lengthy spreadsheet, before adding a few more details on each one.

The work soothed her, as it always did. The past was messy and often terrible, but it was also done. It was past pain, not the present grief that was tormenting Aerope, or the issues that had Cassandra's readers writing in, desperate for the advice of a stranger.

A stranger who was increasingly uncertain of her ability to give good advice, particularly when her own romantic life was a mess. She hadn't had a real relationship for two years. Most of her dates weren't as disastrous as the Isaac Corey incident, but they never really went anywhere past reasonable sex and some fun hangouts. She could have perfectly good sex with herself, and hang out with her friends and sisters, without all the extra effort that went into finding dates and screening strangers. Maybe she should stop trying, at least for a while.

Maybe she should look a little closer to home, at somebody she already thought was fun and sexy…

Cassie shook her head hard, and went back to work.

***

Manny was driving back from Weeping Rock when he saw the pickup truck on the corner, parked suspiciously close to one of the road signs the town had just re-erected.

Sure enough, when he slowed down to take a closer look, two local teenagers were standing in the ditch, trying to look innocent. Manny parked and walked back to them.

"Car trouble?" he asked genially.

The two teens looked at each other, then at him.

Manny knew Hercules Stormson on sight. He showed up on the high school digital billboard, usually holding a wrestling trophy and grinning, but occasionally holding a football (and grinning). The girl beside him was someone he didn't recognize. She wore a long, pleated skirt in dark purple, a grey oversized woolen sweater with a cowl-neck, and black fingerless gloves that wouldn't do anything to keep her hands warm.

"We're fine," Hercules said, flashing a charming smile. "But thanks for stopping, sir."

Ow. He was being called *sir* by a teenager.

"Herc Stormson, isn't it?"

Herc winced. "Uh, yes, sir."

"No school today?"

"It's a half day for seniors," Herc said quickly.

"That must be nice. I hear you pulled off a great win against the Nemean Lions last week."

"Oh, yeah! I mean, thanks, sir."

Manny nodded. "And your dad told me you'd got some great scholarship offers. It would be a shame if something happened to sully your record. Like, for example, vandalism of public property and road sign theft. Especially when your dad's the Weeping Rock chief of police."

Herc's eyes darted down the road as if Tyron Stormson might be hurtling towards them in his blue-and-white.

"Um, are you, like, accusing us of something?" the girl asked. She wasn't smiling. She was staring right at him, as if she could bore a hole in his skull with her gaze. "Because that's pretty creepy, just stopping by the road to harass teenagers."

Herc muttered something that sounded like, "shut up, Trace," but the girl ignored him. Her eyes were outlined with heavy black eyeliner, and her burgundy and black hair was in two long, limp braids. She looked like an updated version of the Goth kids Manny had met at college.

"You don't know anything about us," she continued passionately. "I don't want your stupid road sign."

"Great," Manny said, feeling decidedly off-center. "Glad to hear it. Have a nice afternoon."

He walked away, hearing the hushed whispers start behind him. Herc's voice rumbled something in a warning tone, and he heard Trace's voice break high and clear over it: "—*he* didn't know that!"

Aha. So he hadn't actually been wrong. Trace, whoever she was, clearly valued a strong offense as the best defense, but Herc had had the look of a kid rapidly deciding whether looking cool to his peers outweighed wrestling scholarships. That particular road sign was probably safe for now.

He and Augie had never gone for sign theft, though they'd done their fair share of dumb pranks. He'd snuck booze into school formals, helped prank call Augie's Algebra II teacher, and assisted in the senior skip day prank, which had been led by the shop kids that year. They'd constructed various metal panels, all of which fit together during a sweaty early morning hour to convert the statue of the town founder into a lopsided T-Rex.

His own senior prank had involved something with the drama kids and an impromptu musical on the main quad. It was somehow less memorable.

Well, that had been how it went, when he was a kid. Augie was strong and confident, the big man on campus—any campus. And Manny had been right beside him. Or, often, behind him. He'd never resented his brother for getting so many accolades. He admired him too much, was too delighted by every scrap of careless attention. He'd patterned so much of his early life after Augie. He'd gone to the same college, pledged to the same frat. If he hadn't been gently guided away from Communications and towards Business Management by his advisor, he might have tried to follow Augie's footsteps into journalism, a career he would have hated, and also been terrible at.

Hell, he'd even tried to marry Augie's wife's sister.

Something had changed, in the years since Helen. Manny respected and loved his brother but he didn't have that same unthinking admiration any more. He didn't like the way Ness and Augie interacted, no matter how much Augie swore that it worked for them. He didn't want to cheat and fight and make up all the time. He wanted an equal partner and true friend. Not someone endlessly accommodating, the way Helen had tried to be, but someone willing to stand up for herself, someone who could call him on his shit and make him laugh. He wanted someone he could look after when she needed it, and someone who could look after him when he needed that.

He wanted...

He wanted what his parents had had. Before Arthur had died, and left Aerope devastated with loss.

Manny pulled up outside the house and braced his hands on the sides of the wheel. After a few minutes, he blew his nose and wiped his eyes.

When he went into the kitchen, his mother was sitting at the table, her hands wrapped around a mug, staring into nothing.

"Mother?"

"Hm? Oh, hello, Manfred. How did things go with the accountant?"

"Federal estate tax return signed, sealed, and delivered," Manny reported.

"That's good," Aerope said, a little more life coming into her face. "Thank you for doing this. I still remember what a nightmare probate was for my mother."

Manny smiled. "I don't mind. It was... I don't know, it felt like a weird vote of confidence that Dad made me the executor of his will. I mean, I know it was probably because Augie's busy..."

"It's because he knew he could count on you," Aerope said, and patted his hand. "Also, we decided we'd only make one of you do it for each of us, so we flipped a coin to decide. Augie gets me."

"That's nice?" Manny said. "Speaking of Augie, would you mind if he and the family came up for a weekend?"

Aerope's face softened, as it always did at the mention of her grandchildren. "Goodness, no. We've plenty of room."

"You might not see so much of Augie," he warned. "I'm planning to exploit him for his labor to help clear the carriage house."

"Exploit away," Aerope said, her own tone slightly waspish. "He shouldn't be leaving all of this to you anyway." She pulled out the chair beside her and patted the seat. "Sit down, Manny. I need to talk to you about Ms. Troiades."

Manny's alarm bells started faintly ringing. "Really? And that's a sit-down conversation?"

"She was terribly rude to me today," Aerope said. "Pushy, intrusive, called me names..."

"What names?"

Aerope's eyes darted around the kitchen. "I couldn't possibly repeat them."

"Okay," Manny said slowly. "So I guess I should fire her."

Aerope's shoulders relaxed. "Maybe that would be for the best."

"Actually, you know what? She called my mother names? I'm going to call her out online."

"Oh, that's not really necessary."

Manny pushed back his chair with some force and stood up. "No, it really is. Don't worry, Mom. I have a lot of contacts in social media."

"There's no need to drag her name through the mud."

"Sure there is. By the time I'm through with her, Cassie Troiades will never get another job." He stared at his mother. "She'll have to completely rebrand, maybe spend thousands on training in a new career, leave the country, change her name..."

His mother's eyes, which had widened with alarm, narrowed. "Very funny."

"I'm not laughing, Mom. Butt out. I don't understand where this hostility is coming from, and I've got to say I'm starting not to care."

"But—"

"But *nothing*. Cassie is a good person and great at her job." He pointed at her. "And by the way, you expecting me to fire someone because you say so doesn't say much of how you think of *me*, either. You know you raised me better than that."

"Manny," Aerope said, her eyes closing. "I'm sorry I lied to you. It was stupid. But I don't know what to do. She has to go, and you won't listen to me..."

"Nope," Manny said, and stomped out of the kitchen.

Halfway up the stairs, he realized he'd better talk to Cassie about this. He couldn't think of a conversation he'd enjoy less, but at least he had something to sweeten the deal—the record book he'd yanked out of the broken filing cabinet.

Cassie was sitting at her customary table, looking intently at a photo album. She hadn't heard him yet, so Manny stopped for a moment to look at her.

She was so pretty, with her round, pink cheeks and her bouncy curls. The light coming in the skylight above her desk turned the dusty attic air into a column of sparkling light, gilding her hair and reflecting off her glasses. A perfect picture of the modern scholar at work.

She lifted her head. "Hey."

"Hello," Manny said, smiling despite himself. "I brought you a present."

He realized it was potentially misleading as soon as he'd said it, but Cassie lit up over the notebook as much as Helen had lit up over concert tickets.

"Where did you find this?" she asked, gazing at it with greedy eyes.

"In the carriage house, while I was cleaning it out. Locked inside a heavy filing cabinet, if you can believe it. It broke, and I saw that in the wreckage. Some kind of finances ledger. But there's no name or date on it and I don't know who wrote it when."

"Were the other records in the location?" she asked. "What period was the filing cabinet? Were there any provenance details?"

"Should I have taken pictures?" Manny asked.

"Yes," she said absently, and then blinked at him. "Oh, I'm sorry, that was rude. You didn't know."

"It's still on the carriage house floor," Manny said, amused. "I didn't see any other records, but we can go look at it later, if you like."

"Yes, please," Cassie said. "Actually, I think I might know where this guy belongs. Wait here a second." She walked into the archive room and came back a moment later with a box. The post-it on the front read "Assorted Record Books/60s-70s" in loopy, round letters. "This green suede is pretty distinctive," she said, taking off the lid and carefully pulling out a couple of other notebooks. "Yes, I thought so—the same style of notebook. And even though your one isn't dated, if we look at the handwriting... See those narrow H's and slanted T crosses?"

Manny stepped closer behind her. He wasn't above inhaling the scent of her hair as he looked over her shoulder. "It looks the same."

Cassie nodded. "People can have similar handwriting styles, of course, especially if they're writing in the same time period. I can't really tell your great-great grandmother's writing from her mother's. But it's easier the closer we move to the modern day, and less prescribed handwriting styles." Her hands, nimble in their latex gloves, carefully flipped pages. "And if we could find some phrases or even words the same in both, we could make an even firmer identification. Look. There. 'School fees,' the same in both books."

Manny squinted. "You're right."

Cassie tilted her head and beamed at him.

She'd smiled at him before, but he'd never been this close, inches from her lips. It was like staring directly into the sun, beautiful and blinding.

"I think I can safely say that this book was used by your grandfather," she said. "Dating could be trickier. It looks like he ordered a bunch of these green notebooks in 1959. He must have liked them, because he kept using them, right up to 1977, where he started using some brown ones. In the early 80s, the vineyard switches to typed ledgers, and after the mid-90s, all of the financial records are printed." Her eyes crinkled. "We lose the clues of handwriting and idiosyncratic materials when that happens, but we gain a lot in clarity."

"You're amazing," Manny said, with sincerity. She hadn't consulted her spreadsheet for a single one of those dates; it was all just sitting in her memory. "Wait a second, though. School fees aren't a vineyard expense."

"Oh, people with a family-owned business aren't always great at separating personal finances from the business ones," Cassie said. "Or they keep the records for both in the same ledger, which I think is what your grandfather did with this one." She checked the notebook she'd pulled from the box. "Yes, vineyard expenses at the front, family expenses at the back."

"My accounting professor would have a heart attack," Manny said, and then heard the words that had come out of his mouth.

Cassie picked up the change in mood immediately. She didn't pull away, but her expression shifted from one of avid interest to compassion.

"Well, that's a turn of phrase that has a new meaning," Manny said ruefully. "Too soon for jokes?"

"It's never too soon for jokes," Cassie assured him. "Humor is a very human reaction to grief."

The phrase pinged something in the back of Manny's brain, but before he could chase the thought down, Cassie turned away from him to put the notebooks back in their box, adding the one he'd brought her. "Speaking of grief," she said carefully. "I think I need to tell you about an encounter I had with Aerope this morning."

"Right," Manny said, and took a step back, so he wasn't looming over her in her space. "She um, she tried to tell me some story about how you'd been intrusive, and rude."

Cassie winced.

"And called her names," Manny added. "I pushed back a little, and she admitted she'd exaggerated." Actually, Aerope had admitted she'd lied outright, but he discovered that he didn't want to say that to Cassie. "I thought I should come up and ask you about it."

"I didn't call her names," Cassie said, her eyes steady. "I think I did intrude on her in what she thought would be a private moment."

Manny blinked. "Oh?"

Cassie looked down. "She was sorting your dad's clothes, for donations or to throw away. It looked like she was finding it really difficult."

"Oh," Manny said. "Okay, yes, that explains some of it. We're WASPs. We don't like to emote in public." He rubbed his forehead. "But she's got to stop trying to get you fired."

"I think she just wants me to leave, whatever it takes," Cassie said. "I didn't tell you this before, because you were already addressing the problem, but when she took me into Weeping Rock a couple of weeks ago, she offered to pay me the rest of my fee if I left early."

"She *what*? Like a bribe?"

"That was the impression I got," Cassie said. "I figured maybe she'd thought better of it, but she brought it up again today. She seemed very...determined."

"I will talk to her again," Manny said grimly.

"Today, she offered to double the money," Cassie said, and met his startled gaze. "And she wanted me to delete my spreadsheet and toss all my notes. It's maybe not my place to say anything, and I really don't want to interfere with your family. It wouldn't matter if she just disliked me. I don't expect everyone to like me. But from what Steph Marshall has said, your mom normally doesn't act anything like this. I think there's maybe something else going on."

Manny tried to keep his voice steady. "You think she might be unwell? Mentally?"

"That's also a very human reaction to grief," Cassie said steadily. "Look, if you wanted to release me from the contract so you can look after your mom, I'd understand. I could look at my schedule and maybe see if I could come back later in the year. You'd want to do some work on preserving the archives in the meantime, that little room isn't the best place for them, but I *get* it."

Manny blew out a breath. "That's an incredibly kind offer."

"If it were my mom…" Cassie said, and trailed off, shaking her head. "I absolutely would want the rest of my fee, of course," she added, grinning impishly at him. "I'm not *that* altruistic. But you wouldn't need to double it."

Manny thought about it. His automatic response was that he didn't want Cassie to leave, but she was bringing up some valid concerns. "Room and board is also part of your contract," he said. "Would you be able to return to your previous living situation?"

"I've sublet my room," Cassie admitted. "But I could ask my sister if she'd be willing to let me sleep on her couch for a while. Or I could move back in with my parents."

"From your expression, I'm guessing that's not the ideal solution?"

"Oh, don't get me wrong. I love my parents. But they live in the suburbs and they…man, there's just no non-crude way to put this. They fuck like bunnies. I've got three younger siblings, and if it weren't for birth control, there'd probably be fifty of us."

Manny began to laugh.

"Don't mock me," Cassie said ominously. "The number of times I've walked into a room to find them making out, it's got to be some form of psychological torture."

"I'm so sorry," Manny said, wiping his eyes. "If it helps any, my dad just could not keep his hands off my mom's ass."

Cassie's eyes widened with horror. "Why would that help?"

"Shared pain is halved pain?" Manny offered. "Okay, look, I really appreciate your offer, but I hope we can work something else out. If nothing else, I'm on a tight schedule for the carriage house refit, and using the archives will add a lot of appeal to potential guests."

Cassie nodded. He'd spoken to her about his plans for the carriage house. "If it helps, I think I can already point to some things you might want to put on display or document in a brochure," she said. "But honestly, there's so much here. It deserves detailed attention."

Manny nodded. "I want you to stay," he said, perhaps with a touch too much honesty. "Do *you* want to leave?"

"No," Cassie said. "I really don't. This is maybe the most promising archive I've ever worked with. I wake up every morning excited to see more of it."

"Of course," Manny said, feeling a little deflated.

But Cassie wasn't finished. She looked undecided for a moment, then her jaw firmed, and she took a step closer. "And that's not the only thing that excites me."

"Oh?"

"The job's good. And the company's better." She glanced up at him, her tongue darting out to wet that tempting lower lip, and Manny saw her pupils flare.

He was very aware of their breathing, their closeness, the pounding of his heart. "You appreciate the company, huh?" His voice dipped lower, and this was unprofessional, this was dangerous, he had a million other things he should be thinking about, and he didn't care.

Cassie's scent was driving everything else out of his head. He dipped to meet her, and she rose to meet him, and then they were kissing, sweet and hot and good.

This was right. Whatever else was happening, this worked.

121

Chapter Six

"This is a bad idea," Cassie said after several breathless minutes, and Manny got out of her space immediately.

"Do you want to stop?" he said.

"Nope," Cassie said. Heavy, liquid warmth was spreading through her body, desire like honey in her veins. "Wait, what about your psychologist? Did your mom make that up too?"

"Mom told you about my therapist? What about him?"

"No, your mom said you were seeing a nice psychologist in the city."

"Oh," Manny said. "No. I *was* seeing a nice speech therapist in the city. But that was months ago, and things ended with Rose pretty quickly after my dad died." He grinned at her. "She was warning you away from me."

"Well, she's got a point," Cassie said. "This isn't very smart of us."

"So dumb," Manny agreed, his eyes on her lips.

Cassie kissed him, a light, teasing touch, and pulled back. "I've been wanting to do this since I met you."

"Me too."

"But it's definitely inappropriate."

"We're risking a solid working relationship," Manny said, and slid his hands gently down her arms. Cassie shivered.

"Right," she said. "So I just thought we should acknowledge that this is a fundamentally bad idea, and then do it anyway."

Manny's grin was slow and seductive. "You're right. I definitely shouldn't get my hands on your breasts, but I'm going to enjoy it."

The words zinged through her, desire sparking in their wake. Cassie's voice was shaky. "I absolutely shouldn't grope the ass I've wanted to touch for weeks"

"I shouldn't bury my face between your thighs."

"I shouldn't explore your cock with my tongue."

They were pressed against each other now, eyes locked. Her nipples were hardening at the contact, and she could feel an impressive erection pressed against her belly.

"I shouldn't slide inside you," Manny said, and Cassie's core went molten at the thought.

"I shouldn't ride you till you break," she whispered, and Manny shuddered.

"Right, since we're agreed," he said, and his mouth descended on hers.

This wasn't tender. It was a devouring kiss, lips and tongue and teeth *eating* at her, and Cassie gave as good as she got, pushing against him until he groaned into her mouth. She grabbed his ass—*finally*—and felt the tight muscle flex under her hands as she pulled his pelvis flush against hers, grinding shamelessly against him.

"Okay," Manny said, tearing his mouth away. "On this desk, or...?"

"On the *archives*?" Cassie said, sounding scandalized even to herself.

"Right, don't know what I was thinking," Manny said. He grabbed her hand, and Cassie reluctantly gave up her handful of excellent ass so that he could tug her further into the attic proper. The place was full of furniture. There were even a few deconstructed beds, though the thought of rodent nests in the old mattresses was a disturbing possibility...

Cassie was just about to suggest they go downstairs when Manny said, "Great, here it is," and swung her around, using the momentum to half-lift her onto a sturdy old desk.

Cassie didn't think of herself as particularly liftable, but Manny was evidently stronger than he looked. Or granted desperate strength by lust, because the second her butt hit the surface he was on her, hands sliding up under her sweater.

"Oh," Cassie said, as his hands gently lifted the weight of her breasts and then "*oh,*" as his thumbs stroked over her nipples.

Manny was watching her, his eyes flicking from her face to the movement of his hands under the cloth. "Yes?"

"Fuck, yes," Cassie said, and grabbed her sweater hem.

Getting the sweater off was slightly awkward, partly because Manny didn't seem to want to let go of her boobs long enough to help, and partly because she just had to kiss him several times along the way.

"Is the beard okay?" he mumbled.

"It's working for me," Cassie said honestly. She'd kissed bearded men before, and the experience differed a lot depending on the man, his technique, and his general beard care practice. Kissing Manny was easily at the top of the list. She licked the seam of his lips and he opened for her again. She plunged in, enjoying the heat and the dizzy sensation of his hands as much as the soft tickle of his beard against her skin.

He pulled back, gasping, his eyes narrowed with intent, and suddenly she was lifting her arms and he was peeling her sweater off.

"Holy shit," she heard him say while her face was still muffled in fabric, and when she got it all the way off, he was staring at her breasts, resplendent in red silk.

Cassie found time to thank the fates that she'd run out of laundry and put on her good underwear that morning. Then his mouth closed on her right breast and she momentarily lost the ability to think at all. Manny sucked her nipple through the fabric, his tongue toying with the hardening point, as his hand stroked the other breast, silk sliding against the tender skin. His free arm was around her back, helping support her weight and keeping her within ready range of his mouth and hands.

He switched to the other breast, and she arched her back in encouragement, bracing herself with her hands. Her legs were still dangling off the edge of the desk, parted so that he could stand between them, and she looped her calves around his back and tugged him closer.

Manny made an urgent sound, and his free hand leaped from her breast to the top button of her jeans. "Can I taste?" he said, his eyes glazed. "Please, Cassie, let me eat you out. I've been thinking about it for so long."

"Well, since you asked nicely," Cassie said, and when his fumbling wasn't fast enough for her, she popped her own buttons and shoved her jeans and underwear down her hips. Manny peeled them off her legs, and she was suddenly naked from the waist down, splayed out in front of him.

This was the moment she'd never been able to talk herself out of, the moment where she wasn't sure how a new partner would react to the silver stretch marks on her full stomach, or the dimpled, pale flesh of her rounded thighs. One glance at Manny's face showed her that regardless of her own momentary uncertainty about her body, he definitely appreciated it.

In fact, he looked downright ravenous as he went to his knees. He ran his hands along the back of her knees, grinning as she jumped at the pressure, and then hooked her legs over his shoulders, his hands pressing her thighs wide so that he could lick a slow, lavish path up her cunt.

"Oh, fuck," Cassie panted, and abandoned herself to being worshiped.

Manny took his time at first, learning what worked for her. Once he'd figured out the pressure she liked, he sped up. Cassie's muscles tightened, her breath coming in tiny, gasping pants. This was great, this was fine, she could definitely come like this, but...

"I want you *in* me," she said, on the edge of delirium.

Manny lifted his head and grinned at her. His mouth and beard were glistening. "If you think I'm heading downstairs to find condoms right now..."

Cassie's mouth nearly said, "fuck that, and fuck me," but her brain smacked her before she could voice it. Sex with the boss was already a mistake; unprotected sex with the boss was an undeniable step into outright stupidity. She whined in the back of her throat instead, and Manny slid two fingers into his own mouth, sucking deeply. He ducked down again, and she pushed herself up on her elbows so that she could see the golden head buried between her thighs.

Then he slid his fingers inside her and she thumped flat onto her back. His tongue was doing something incredible, circling around her clit, then pressing flat against it, while those magic fingers stretched her open.

"More, more, more," she said, the words babbling out of her, and he withdrew his hand, then thrust in again, three fingers this time. No careful stretch now, he knew she could take it, and he gave it to her, over and over and over while his tongue kept the rhythm on her clit, and the pleasure built and built, until she hovered right on the cliff's edge.

He pressed his tongue flat on her clit again, and *kept it there.*

Cassie flung her arms over her face and bit down on her wrist as she came, waves of pleasure rolling over her as her muscles shook and her toes curled.

Manny was suddenly leaning over her, looking smug. Well, he had every right to.

"Holy shit," she said, when she got her breath back. "That is some *serious* hospitality."

He laughed, but his eyes were still hungry, and she could feel his cock through his pants, jutting eagerly at the crease of her hip. She lifted her hips to give him a little more friction, and he groaned.

"Come here," she said, and sat up again. She reached between them and unzipped his pants, eeling her hand between fabric and flesh until she had his erection in a firm grip, squeezing the base. "Hello, there," she said, and Manny groaned again, tossing his head back.

"Are you trying to kill me?" he said through clenched teeth.

"Given the available options, how do you want to come?" Cassie said sweetly, and his eyes flew open, staring at her.

No, at her breasts, enclosed in red silk, still with the telltale wet patches where he'd done devastating things to her nipples. They peaked again at the thought of his clever mouth, and she squeezed her upper arms together, plumping her breasts so that they strained at the lace.

"Oh, fuck," Manny said, his eyes locked on her cleavage.

"You want to come on my tits, baby?" Cassie said, and felt his cock jump in her grip. That was answer enough. She laughed and pushed him back far enough that she could slide down the front of the table to kneel at his feet while he made fast work of his pants. Her sweater was probably a lost cause, so she folded it under herself for a pad and sat back on her haunches.

Manny was staring at her, his breath coming in shallow pants. He was holding his cock in a tight grip, running his thumb over the head. Oh yeah, she wanted to taste that.

Next time, she thought, and then tried not to consider the part where she'd already assumed there was a next time. "Keep my bra on?" she asked.

"Off," Manny said. "I want to see." He stroked the mound of her breast with his free hand, and she felt her pussy clench again at the contact. She made short work of the clasp at the back and let the bra tip down and off her arms, tossing it to one side without breaking eye contact. Manny made a noise low in his throat and stepped closer, hand working roughly at his cock.

"You're so beautiful," he said, so low it was nearly a growl. "I've been thinking about you, Cassie. I've been thinking about what I want to do to you, what we could do together, and it's wrong, it's so wrong, but I can't stop."

"Tell me. Tell me all of it."

"I want to bend you over this desk and pound into you from behind. I want you to ride me until you scream. I want you to come on my cock, again and again."

Cassie licked her lips, slow and deliberate.

"I want your hands on me," he said, his own hand working faster. "I want your mouth on me, fuck, Cassie, your mouth is a dream, your breasts are a miracle, you're so soft, so gorgeous, so—" His eyes rolled into the back of his head, and his face froze in an expression that looked on the edge of pain. He grunted as if someone had hit him, and then he was coming in thick, hot spurts across her breasts. It wasn't Cassie's favorite sensation, but it was worth it to see his jaw drop, his eyes shining with something that looked very close to worship.

He braced himself on the edge of the desk, panting. Cassie thought his knees might be wobbly. She was feeling shaky herself.

Also, now that the fevered rush of sex was dying down, a little chilly. And sticky. There were wet-wipes in her archive kit. She got up to fetch them, and Manny's eyes widened.

"I'm not running away," she said. "Just cleaning up."

Manny nodded and scooped up his pants and underwear. He'd somehow managed to keep his top layer on, which now that she was thinking about it, wasn't completely fair. Cassie wiped herself clean and climbed back into her clothes.

Manny sat down on the attic floor beside her and wrapped his arm around her shoulders, and she leaned into the heat.

"Regrets?" he said quietly.

"Nope," Cassie said. "Although I wish we'd got as far as a bed."

"Next time," Manny promised, and then winced. "I mean, assuming you want a next time."

"I was making the same assumption," Cassie told him, and he relaxed against her. "We should talk about this, though. For now, can we say no complications and no expectations?"

"Meaning?"

"I don't sleep with people who are sleeping with someone else. That would be a complication for me."

"Not an issue," Manny said, a note of something dark in his voice. "I don't do that either."

"And as for expectations… You're planning to stay here and open your new business, and I'm planning to go back to the city. Any expectation of commitment past that would be a bad idea."

"Right. That makes sense." He didn't say it with any great enthusiasm, but he didn't sound upset, either.

"What about you?" Cassie said. She was remembering every time she'd written advice to people telling them to *use their words* and *be open and honest* with partners. Definitely one of those things that it was easier to preach than practice. "What would be a complication for you?"

Manny was quiet for a moment. "Don't sleep with someone else kind of covers it for me," he said. "And don't… Don't try to keep things from me because you're afraid it'll hurt my feelings or whatever. Just tell me if I'm doing something you don't like, or if you want to end it."

Ouch. There was obviously a backstory there, but now wasn't the time to pry. He'd tell her more if he wanted to.

"I tend to be upfront," Cassie said.

"I noticed that," Manny said, and shook his head at her, grinning faintly. "I can't believe you just straight up asked if I wanted to come on your tits."

"Didn't seem much point in being shy, considering where your mouth had been."

"My mouth would be happy to return to that location any time." He stretched. "So, in summary, we're currently exclusively having sex with each other, but we're not planning for anything beyond that?"

"And we're going to be honest and not keep things from each other."

"Great. Then I can honestly say that I want to see you tonight." He stroked a line down the center of her chest, and she shivered. "Hopefully, with condoms."

"I'd like that."

"Your place or mine?" Manny asked, and Cassie pictured sneaking out of his room and being caught by Aerope.

"Mine," she said firmly. "And this time, you're getting naked first."

He laughed, and kissed her again. No heat this time, just a friendly smooch that was somehow very touching. "I know it was a bad idea," he said, nuzzling at her neck. "But I don't have any regrets either."

***

"I need a bath," Cassie said.

Manny shook himself out of the light trance he'd fallen into, lulled by the warmth of her body against his. "Does that mean I have to move?"

"Ideally," Cassie said, and gave him a gentle nudge. "I also need to do some laundry. Can I use the house facilities, or should I go find a laundromat?"

"Let me have an awkward conversation with my mother and get back to you," Manny said. He shoved himself upright and held out his hand. "How serious is the laundry situation?"

Cassie grabbed his hand and levered herself up. "I'm wearing my fancy undies because I've run out of the normal ones."

"And may I say that I appreciate that?"

Cassie kissed him. "You may. But I've got one pair left, and I intend to use them tonight." She grinned at him. "You'll appreciate those too."

"Copy that," Manny said, with feeling, and reluctantly left while Cassie locked up. He was hazily imagining it would probably look better if they didn't leave together. Not that he intended to keep his expanded relationship with Cassie a secret, but the way his mother was acting right now inclined him towards discretion.

With that in mind, he stopped by his bedroom ensuite to quickly clean up, and then headed back to his office.

His mother was standing in the middle of the room, her hands clenched.

"I wanted to fetch something from the attic," Aerope said, her eyes blazing. "And I heard *noises*."

Manny controlled his automatic flinch. "Please tell me you didn't keep going upstairs."

"Certainly not," Aerope said. "I cannot *believe* you slept with that woman. Now she can sue you for harassment when you fire her."

Manny couldn't remember ever raising his voice to his mother, but the temptation had never been stronger. He stalked to his desk and sat down. "I'm not firing her, Mother," he said flatly. "And you're not bribing her to leave, either."

Aerope flinched.

"Yes, she told me," Manny said. "Of course she did. Because she *is* being harassed in her workplace. By *you*."

"You don't understand," Aerope said, her lips white with strain. "She has to leave."

"Why, Mom? We might be able to work something out if you tell me why."

The tendons in Aerope's neck were rigid. "Because we don't need outsiders in the archives."

"That's not a good enough reason, Mom. I don't think that's even *your* real reason." He gestured to the armchair he'd cleared for Cassie's lunch breaks. "Come on, sit down. Tell me about it. I know you're hurting. We're all hurting. If you need some extra space, we can discuss it, but these ultimatums have to stop."

Aerope didn't move. "This is my house, not yours," she said unsteadily. "Your father left it to me for the rest of my lifetime. If I say she's not welcome here, she has to go."

Manny rubbed his temples. "He left the archives to me. If you bar Cassie from the house, then I'll move the archives out." Actually, that might be the best solution. Then Cassie could keep her contract, his mother couldn't interfere, and Aerope would maybe get some respite to work on whatever the underlying cause was. "She said the documents need better storage anyway. Okay, this works. Tomorrow I'll look into office space downtown."

"*No*," Aerope said. "You can't take the archives!"

"Mom, legally, they're mine."

"I'll contest the will," Aerope said.

Manny froze. Dragging the family through the court system, exposing them to the speculation of the community... Whatever this was, it wasn't just Aerope's usual certainty that she knew the best course of action. If she was willing to contest the will to get her own way, she must be truly desperate.

"Mother," Manny said. "Mom. Please, tell me what's going on."

Her chin lifted proudly, but he could see her wavering. "Can you not just trust that I know more about this than you do?"

"I can see that you do. But I need to know too, because Dad did leave the archives to me. I'm not willing to default on that responsibility."

Aerope snorted, and Manny held up his hand. "Calling in a professional *was* responsible," he said. "You'd agree to that if it wasn't for... Whatever this is. I'm genuinely worried about you."

"I'm not *crazy*," Aerope said.

"You're not really presenting the best case for sanity," Manny said. "That was a damn stupid lie you told me this afternoon. Next thing you'll be drawing lines of salt across the doorways to keep Cassie out."

"Well, that wouldn't work," Aerope said practically. "She's not a demon. I'm sure she's a very nice woman."

Manny wouldn't have called Cassie *nice*. Kind, yes. Perceptive, absolutely. Gorgeous, oh fuck yes.

He tore his mind away from an inconvenient vision of Cassie on her knees, grinning up at him, evidence of their recent activities painted across her spectacular breasts, and refocused on his mother, who had lost the moment of levity.

"You really want to know?" she said.

"I think I need to."

Aerope sat down as if her knees had been cut out from under her. The bleakness in her face warned him even before she opened her mouth.

"Your father didn't die of a heart attack," she said. "He killed himself."

Manny felt it like a punch to the face. "No."

Aerope's eyes were glossy with tears that didn't fall. "I didn't want to believe it either. But he did. He waited until I went on that trip, and he washed down some sleeping pills with whiskey. He didn't leave a note, he didn't...not a single hint. After the autopsy, Doctor Olsen said that maybe it was accidental. Maybe Arthur had taken a pill to get to sleep, and gotten confused. Maybe he'd forgotten he'd taken it, so he took another and another. But I think he was just trying to be kind."

"Did Dad even use sleeping pills?"

"No," Aerope said, and her face crumpled in on itself. "They were mine."

"Mom. Mom, it's okay." Manny went to her and wrapped his arms around her while she sobbed.

"He left us," she said after a few minutes, her voice raw. "He left us, and he let me find him like that."

He wouldn't, Manny thought, feeling cold to the core. But everyone must think that, when they first heard about an unexpected suicide. He couldn't argue with an autopsy.

"Does anyone else know?" he asked.

"Only our doctor, and the coroner." Aerope said. "And Theo. I didn't want to tell you boys. I didn't want to hurt you."

"So you've been carrying this alone?" Manny said.

"I'm tougher than I look," Aerope said, with dignity, and then she sighed, her face settling into lines that somehow seemed deeper, now he knew. "I'm sorry, Manfred. I know I've been just awful. But I never wanted you to know."

"Mom, it's okay. I'm glad you told me." He hesitated. "I just don't understand what it has to do with the archives."

Aerope nodded. "He started researching last summer, after everyone came out for Midsummer. He said he was finally going to write that book."

"But he seemed so happy about that."

"At first. Then he stopped talking about it. He kept going up to the attic, but he didn't share his new discoveries with me or show me old recipes he thought I'd like. I thought that maybe he was just finding it more work than he'd expected. You know how your father was, every month a new enthusiasm." She gestured at the clutter in the office, the half-built model airplanes and redundant computer equipment, the stack of dusty origami paper on the bookshelf.

"I thought he'd move on to something else soon." A spasm of pain crossed her face. "I didn't recognize his reluctance to talk as a symptom that he might be unwell. I didn't notice anything at the time. It was only afterwards, when Theo asked if Arthur had said anything about the archives that I realized."

"Did he say something to Theo?"

"No, he clammed up on him as well." She took a deep breath. "Theo thinks he might have found something terrible up there, something that might have... Well. Prompted his choice."

Manny didn't know what to say. He wasn't a health professional, but it didn't seem likely to him that a man who had no history of poor mental health could be driven to suicide by a historical scandal. "Had Dad been depressed before?" he asked gently.

"I don't think so," Aerope said doubtfully. "I mean, he had the occasional down day, but he was usually so optimistic."

"Was the vineyard in trouble? The accounting's kind of messy, but as far as I can tell we're still in the black."

"That was my impression, too." Aerope sighed. "There was one sign, perhaps. He increased his life insurance coverage. At the time, I thought getting older was making him more cautious. And perhaps it was—that was months before he even started researching. But it's the only other thing I can think of."

"It just doesn't make sense. What on earth do you think he could have found?"

"I don't know. It's such a mess up there. It could be anything—embezzlement, tax fraud, shady land deals."

"Almost everything around here is built on stolen land, Mom."

"Well, yes. But I meant more recently stolen." She patted him again. "At least now you know why you need to fire Cassie."

"Absolutely not," Manny said, before he could think about it.

Aerope drew herself up. "Is this because you slept with her?"

"No!" he said then reconsidered. "Well, maybe a little. You're right that she'd absolutely have a wrongful dismissal case against me and I wouldn't blame her for pursuing it. But more importantly, Mom, we need her *help*. Whatever's up there, we need to find it. That's her job, and we need her to keep doing it."

Aerope's lip quivered. "But what if it kills you too?" she said, her voice wavering.

"Mom, I love you," Manny said. "So please hear me when I say that's not going to happen."

"I know," Aerope admitted. "I know I sound crazy. I think I *am* a little crazy right now. I miss him every single day. I know that I'm probably blowing it all out of proportion, but I keep thinking that maybe Theo was right. If the archives hold something that could hurt *your father*, when he was so strong... Maybe we should have just burned it all."

Manny shook his head. "I don't think there's any secret that bad. I mean, I'm sure there are some skeletons in our closet. Every family has those, and we're wealthy WASPs descended from colonists. I could name three or four awful possibilities off hand. But... We don't even know that it was the archives. You and Theo were just guessing."

Aerope stared at her hands. "If it's not the archives, then neither of us noticed anything at all," she said. "And that might be worse."

"Mom," Manny said. His voice came out thick, and he had to cough to clear his throat. "Mom, he waited until you'd left. He didn't want you to know anything was wrong. He chose to shut you out. It's not your fault."

Aerope didn't say anything for a moment. "Do you trust Cassie?" she asked.

"Yes," Manny said promptly.

"You trusted Helen, too," Aerope said, and Manny reared back.

To her credit, Aerope looked like she wished she could grab the words out of the air and stuff them back into her mouth. "I'm sorry," she said immediately. "But it's true."

"As far as I'm aware, Helen never betrayed a confidence," Manny said, trying to keep his voice steady.

"Just you."

"It wasn't—Mom, it's been nearly twelve years."

"So?" Aerope said. "I will never forgive her."

Manny sighed. "What was she supposed to do? Stay with me when she didn't want me, didn't love me? That would have been a worse betrayal."

"She should have been brave enough to tell you," Aerope said, unbending.

Manny had come to agree with that, but he knew he wasn't entirely blame free either. "I knew something was wrong. I should have been brave enough to ask. But, look, this is a different situation altogether. I'm not trusting Cassie with my heart or my future. But I do trust her to do her job, and she'll do it better if she knows that she's looking for something."

"All right, tell her," Aerope said, with sudden decision. "Make her sign an NDA."

"I can't ask Cassie to cover up a crime, Mom." Manny thought about it. "I don't think *I* want to cover up a crime, especially a historical one."

"It might not be anything criminal. And if it is, you can ask her to show you the evidence first. If it involves the family, it would look better if we go to the police instead of her."

All right. Aerope was clearly more concerned about the optics than any notion of justice, but he couldn't say she was wrong. If his family had done something terrible in the past, it *would* look better for the current members to present the evidence themselves.

"Fine," he said. "I'll ask her to show me first, on the condition that you go and talk to Doctor Olsen about how you feel."

"I was thinking I should probably do that anyway," Aerope conceded. She smiled tremulously at him. "Although telling you *has* made me feel a little better. Even though I know that it's made things worse for you. Does that make me a terrible mother?"

"You're a great mother," Manny said. "Recent aberrations aside."

Aerope gave him a stern look.

"And you need to treat Cassie better, okay? You don't have to be her best friend, but basic politeness would be a decent start."

His mother pursed her lips. "Well. At least she has good taste in men."

Chapter Seven

"Hm," Cassie said, and plumped her breasts experimentally. The plum-colored straps clenched around her flesh, and she grinned.

Her red silk set was sexy, but still everyday wearable. This particular lingerie set offered no support for vigorous movement, and if she tried to wear pants over the flimsy panties, they would quickly work their way down her hips and belly to end in an uncomfortable wedge of material between her thighs.

But what the set lacked in practicality, it made up for in seduction. Her nipples were barely covered by the low, lacy cup, and silky straps curved over her upper breast, rising to join a ring in the center of her sternum, before fanning out again to hit her shoulder points. The effect hinted at a bondage harness, while still giving her complete freedom of movement.

The panties had the same translucent plum-colored lace at the front, a tiny triangle that revealed almost as much as it hid, but the back was a series of open crisscross straps. There wasn't any real impediment to someone, say, bending her over and moving the straps aside so that they could explore her exposed pussy with deft fingers or an agile tongue.

Her reflection in the bathroom mirror was misty. She'd had a long, hot bath, and hand-washed a few pairs of her more everyday panties while she was at it. She trusted Manny would come up with a solution to the laundry problem, but she had to be practical. If she couldn't do laundry tonight, at least she'd have clean underwear tomorrow.

She shook her head in mock dismay at the panties looped over the heated towel rail to dry. "So sexy," she said. "What a temptress."

But she didn't think Manny would be put off by her bathroom sink laundry. She had the feeling her practicality was part of her appeal, given that she'd been able to turn him on by judging the provenance of a notebook. Practically, then, she belted her thick robe around her waist and headed downstairs.

The fire was roaring in the woodstove. She'd wanted the house heated to buck-naked comfort levels, so she'd trekked in armfuls from the woodpile and set them to steam and dry out in the basket next to the hearth. Over the last two weeks, she'd made the space more her own by putting away some of the innumerable knick-knacks and adding her own books to the shelves. She'd discovered a wealth of soft furs and loosely woven blankets in a chest and promptly draped them over everything, so that she was never more than two feet away from something snuggly. This part of the cottagecore vibe, she could thoroughly embrace.

Let's see. Dishes were done, bed was made, anything embarrassing or annoying had been hidden... She looked at the rug laid out on the wooden floor before the hearth, and pursed her lips. There wasn't quite enough room for any vigorous activity, but if she moved back those armchairs, and then laid the enormous pink faux-fur throw on top of the rug... There. Granted, the result looked like the part in a bad eighties movie where the femme fatale tried to tempt the hero, but the pink glowed in the firelight, and the rug's fur would tantalize sensitive skin.

Also, she really wanted to tempt the hero.

When the knock came at the door, she tossed the robe behind a chair, tousled her hair, fixed the positions of her many straps, and opened the door.

Frigid air and some snow blasted in, and she leapt back, instinctively wrapping her arms around herself.

Manny, wearing a thick coat and a plaid woolen hat with earflaps, gaped at her.

"Get in!" she squawked. "Get in and close the damn door!"

He startled and obeyed.

She sighed with relief as he locked the door behind him and stripped out of his top layers. Her nipples had gone stiff, and not with desire.

"You look incredible," he said.

"I'm sure I did for the split second before I turned into an icicle," she said ruefully. "This was supposed to be a sexy welcome."

"Didn't you say I was the one who was supposed to get naked first?"

"I'm not naked. Technically."

He looked her up and down, from the tips of her painted toes to her eyes, lingering on various places in between. "Technically, this may be the only thing that could make you look better than naked."

Cassie clapped. "Great complimenting, top marks."

"What's my prize?" Manny asked, and then shook his head hard. "Uh, okay, I want to rip all of that off with my teeth, but we need to talk first. Can you put something on so I don't lose my mind?"

Cassie raised an eyebrow, but turned her back and leaned over the chair to retrieve her robe. When she turned around, Manny's eyes had glazed over. "Sorry," he said hoarsely. "I just saw the back. Can we talk afterwards?"

Cassie dropped the robe. "Take off your clothes," she ordered.

Manny obeyed with alacrity, while she arranged herself on the fur rug. It tickled in distracting ways, but that was in the back of her brain. Most of her mind was occupied by admiring Manny's solid body, the slight curve of his belly, the dark blonde hair scattered over his chest and narrowing to an arrow pointing down. He shoved down his pants, jerked the socks off as elegantly as anyone could be expected to manage, and stood there, entirely naked.

His cock was already half-hard, rising from the thatch of golden hair between his thighs, and his hand went instinctively to steady it. "Don't," Cassie said. "You touched yourself plenty today. Do you want to watch me do the same?"

"Yes," Manny said, and Cassie wriggled her way into a comfortable position on the fur, sliding her hands down her body. Normally, when she got herself off, she went for the fast endorphins of a speedy orgasm, but now she took her time, deliberately sliding her fingers under the tiny panties and tracing slow circles around her clit.

"Mmm," she said, letting her head fall back. "Very nice."

"Can I touch you? Touch myself?" Manny asked, and she heard the implicit permission in the question.

"No," she said. "Just watch."

There was a pause, and she was about to drop out of it, about to ask if he wanted to set proper guidelines, and then she heard him say, "Yes, ma'am," a growl deep in his throat.

Cassie smiled, and brought her wet fingers up to her mouth, flicking her tongue over them, tasting herself. She heard the scrape of the chair as he sat down, and sat up on her elbows. He was sitting with his hands clenching the chair-arms. His cock was jutting out of his lap.

For a second, she contemplated whether she should drop the tease. She could just stand up and lower herself on all that lovely length. But her fingers did feel good, and Manny was watching her with such hunger, his knuckles white with the force he was exerting to not touch herself or him.

The little cottage was almost silent. She could hear the crackle of the fire, the occasional gust of wind outside, Manny's deliberately even breathing and her increasingly ragged gasps.

And the wet, sloppy sounds her body was making as she edged closer to her peak, her fingers moving faster and faster under her panties. The little scrap of fabric was holding up well, but she could tell it was shifting around, because Manny groaned every time he caught a glimpse of what was underneath.

"Cassie," he said. "Cassie, please. Please come soon."

"Ohhhhh," Cassie sighed, and rolled over, trapping her hand beneath her body, letting the fur tickle and tease her skin, shoving her hips down to get more pressure, more, more, until she came in a blinding rush of sensation that drew every muscle tight. The orgasm released her, limp and dizzy, and she sprawled on the rug, giggling quietly to herself.

"Cassie? Can I—?"

"All right, now," Cassie said lazily.

Manny jumped from the chair so fast it shot backwards. He grabbed at his discarded pants for a condom, and then he was on her from behind, lifting her hips with her dazed assistance until she was raised on her knees, face down in the fur, braced on her forearms. She heard the crackle of the condom wrapper, and then he slid between the open straps and into her in one deep, perfect stroke.

They groaned in unison.

"I'm not going to last," he said raggedly. "These panties, Cassie, holy shit."

"Go, go, go," Cassie chanted, moving her hips back in rhythm to the words. "Slow later, fast now."

"You got it," Manny promised, and then he was driving into her with flattering enthusiasm, and a satisfying amount of force. Cassie tried to match the rhythm at first, and then gave up and enjoyed the ride as he stammered filthy endearments and surged into her, over and over again. She was just wondering whether she might like to add a little hand action to encourage her body along when Manny unexpectedly dropped one of his own hands from where they were firmly grasping her ass, and slipped it around her body.

He found her clit at once, and stroked it three times with exactly the right amount of pressure. As astounded as she was impressed, Cassie found herself coming on his cock, clenching around him just as he draped himself over her back and choked out her name, his hips stuttering

Her knees gave way, and they both collapsed. Fortunately, they were low enough to the floor that it didn't matter. Manny withdrew and rolled onto his side to take the weight off, which Cassie thought was gentlemanly of him. She rolled as well, and took his hand when he draped his arm across her chest.

"I don't know about you, but I thought that was pretty excellent," she said after a long minute.

"I can't think about anything right now," Manny mumbled. "You blew my brains out."

"Well, not yet," Cassie said, mock-pedantic, and he growled in her ear, pressing close against her. "You know, this fur didn't provide as much padding as I'd hoped. I think my knees are going to be bruised tomorrow."

"Do you always talk after sex?"

"I talk in awkward situations. After sex is often an awkward situation."

Manny raised up on one elbow. "Do you feel awkward?" he asked, looking mildly concerned.

"Hm. No, actually." She idly stroked the thigh lying across her hips. "Didn't you want to talk about something, anyway?"

"Oh, shit," Manny said, and sat up. "Yes."

They'd already established this was the kind of conversation they needed to be wearing clothes for, so Cassie gave up on the afterglow and headed upstairs to get into her pajamas. A gift from Laodice, they were emblazoned with dancing, cartoon breakfast foods, and she eyed the slice of toast cartwheeling across her left breast, then shrugged. Manny hadn't complained about her clothing choices earlier, so he didn't have grounds to object now.

When she came down again, Manny was dressed and in his stocking feet, adding another log to the fire.

"Really leaning into the cozy lumberjack aesthetic," she said, and then saw the sober expression on his face. "Oh. Do I have to leave after all?"

"No," Manny said. "That, I hope I would have managed to tell you *before* sex. But that's about the only good news." He sat down in one armchair, and gestured her to the other. Then he told her, in simple, stark language, about what his father had done and what his mother feared.

Cassie sat quietly for a moment, digesting the news. "I'm so sorry," she said.

"Thank you," Manny said, and shook his head. "I honestly—I know everyone must think this, but I genuinely can't believe it. Dad adored Mom. I can't think of any secret bad enough that it would drive him to do that, knowing that she'd be the one to find him."

"Could your ancestors have enslaved people?" Cassie asked quietly.

"That's what I thought of first," Manny admitted. "But I don't think so—the Pelopsons didn't arrive until the 1830s, and slavery was illegal in the North then, right?"

Cassie grimaced, remembering the History seminar that had focused on the records of enslavement. And how weary her Black classmates had been at the shock of their white peers. "Not necessarily. The repeal of slavery was gradual, and in some Northern states slavery wasn't formally outlawed until the 13th Amendment in 1865. There are records of enslaved persons up here in the 1840 Census."

Manny stared at her. "That's horrible."

"Yes. The timing does mean it's less likely, but not impossible. The records of slave dealers in the area might tell us something too. Do you want me to put in a request to the National Archives?"

"Yes. Thank you." Manny rubbed his forehead. "What do people do, when they find out their ancestors were monsters?"

Cassie bit her lip. "A lot of them ignore it, or excuse it. Some add their voices to the national reparations movement. Some try to make private atonement, with scholarships or donations, maybe meeting their Black relatives. This isn't my area of expertise, but I can put you in touch with some people."

"But they don't—" Manny took a deep breath. "Kill themselves?"

"I don't know," Cassie said helplessly. "I'm not a psychiatrist."

"But there'd have to be something else too, right? Something underlying," Manny said. "Like depression, or psychosis. Something we all missed."

Cassie couldn't think of anything to say. She let her sympathy inform her face, and went to him, standing before his chair, offering silent comfort.

Manny leaned into her, letting his head rest against her belly and she stroked his hair. She expected him to weep, but after a long moment he straightened and looked up at her. "I'm sorry," he said. "You don't owe me anything. We've barely started... Whatever this is. No expectations."

"But we're friends too," Cassie said. "We are friends, right?"

Manny looked startled. "Yes," he said. "I guess we are." He smiled at her, and for a moment he looked much younger, a simple joy illuminating his face. "You're a good friend, Cassie Troiades. But I'd better get going."

Cassie nodded, and escorted him to the door. He pulled on his snow boots and outer layers and opened the door.

The light from the open door shone onto a whirling mass of snow. They both stared at that shifting wall of white, and then Manny shut the door. "Um, that's a snowstorm," he said.

"Holy shit," Cassie said, awed. "How did that happen so fast?"

"There was supposed to be one forty miles east of here. I guess the line shifted." He checked his phone and groaned slightly. "Yeah, the weather report updated an hour ago. Reduced visibility, travel warning, etcetera etcetera."

"Well, you can't go out in that," Cassie said.

"If Mom turns all the lights on, I can probably get line of sight to the big house," Manny began, but Cassie crossed her arms.

"Shouldn't you stay here?" she asked. "Everyone in Weeping Rock has told me horror stories about blizzards ever since I arrived."

"This isn't a blizzard. Technically it's only a severe snowstorm. And it's only a five-minute walk." His phone rang, and he winced, then held it to his ear. "Hello, Mother."

Cassie mimed zipping her lips and sat down cross-legged on the rug. The fire was in the red-ember stage, glowing brightly in the stove, and she gazed into it while, obviously, eavesdropping for all she was worth.

"Yes, I am," Manny said. "Mm. Yes. We talked about that. Really? I mean, okay. If you're sure. No, I didn't mean that you're not—Yes. Yes, Mother. I love you too. Good night." He hung up, and Cassie looked an inquiry at him.

"My mother just told me to stay with you tonight," he said, looking adorably baffled.

Cassie unfolded herself and stood up. "Are you going to argue with both of us?" she asked.

Manny's eyes crinkled with amusement. "I'm not that much of an idiot. Um, do you want your space upstairs? I could crash on the floor." He looked doubtfully at the faux-fur throw, which had definitely lost some zip in their tussle.

"Don't be silly," Cassie said, and held her hands out to him. "Come to bed."

He took her hands and leaned in to kiss her lightly. "Okay," he said, his voice low. "By the way, I like the pajamas. The dancing bacon is a nice touch."

"You be quiet," Cassie said. "Or I won't let you take them off in the morning."

***

Cassie let him take her pajamas off in the morning, and they made love under the covers in the snug warmth of her bed cave. When they tried missionary, Manny hit his head twice on the ceiling, and Cassie flatly refused to try getting on top herself, so they ended up side by side, facing each other as he thrust in shallow strokes. He could feel her breasts and stomach pressing against him as he moved, and her top leg was wrapped over his hips, her strong thigh clutching him close. He felt totally wrapped up in her, feverish with heat.

He would have been happy to stay there a long, long time, watching Cassie's beautiful face as they moved together. Her tousled curls bounced with the motion, her cheeks getting pinker and pinker. What had been teasing full sentences became urgent exhortations, and when she made a strangled noise in the back of her throat with no words at all attached, he grabbed her ass and yanked her hard against him. Cassie gasped, buried her head in the gap between his shoulder and neck, and clenched around him in shuddering waves.

And that, it turned out, he couldn't resist. With her gripping him tightly, inside and out, he came in a sudden rush that momentarily whited out his vision.

When he blinked the sparks away, Cassie kissed him, sweet and gentle.

Then she slid away and out of the bed and headed briskly to the bathroom, all her rosy flesh bouncing in a way that would have been incredibly enticing if he hadn't just thoroughly exhausted his ability to take advantage of it.

Manny flopped back and covered his face with his hands. That hadn't been just sex. He'd even *thought* "making love," like an idiot with no self-control. He wanted to sit with Cassie on the dock of Lake Lydia and tell her all his hopes and dreams. He wanted to hear all of hers. He wanted to tell her about Helen and how hard it was for him to trust, but how instantly he'd trusted *her*, and how this was surely a sign that they could be more than working friends with benefits, and all of this was a supremely terrible idea.

And not just because the dock at Lake Lydia would be covered in icy slush this morning.

He grabbed his phone and opened the file he kept in easy access. He'd used a throwaway email account when he'd written to Ask Cassandra, ashamed of his inability to leave Helen in the past. But Cassandra's response had been as bracing as seawater, and he didn't feel shame any more. She'd told him straight out. Helen hadn't been as kind as she should have been. He wasn't wrong or stupid to feel bad about what had happened. But if he wanted to move on, he had to stop telling the story of being the one left behind. He had to stop *performing* his shame, over and over, especially to people with whom he had a chance to tell a new story.

He read the email again, and deliberately put a cap on his emotions. There would be no impulsive revelations for Cassie. No spilling of his past trauma. He would keep things light and easy, or as light as they could be with the specter of his father and the possibility of terrible secrets haunting them both.

No expectations. No commitments.

When Cassie came back in, damp and clean from her shower, he gave her a friendly smile and got out of bed.

"Was I supposed to leave a tap dripping last night, or something?" Cassie asked, rubbing her hair. "I only realized when the hot water came on that I might need to worry about the pipes."

Manny shook his head. "There's heat tape on all the pipes here and in the big house." Not in the carriage house, though, so it was a good thing he hadn't turned the water mains on there yet. Another thing to add to his list.

"Heat tape?" Cassie said, and then waved at him. "Never mind, go take a shower and I'll look it up." She was already reaching for her laptop, so he got himself cleaned up and then wiped the condensation from the bathroom window to peek outside. Blue, blue skies, and white, white ground. It looked like about a foot of snowfall to his eye, though the weather app on his phone reported 10.5 inches. Either way, the county's snow ploughs would be getting a workout this morning.

But visibility was fine. He could walk back to the big house, at the minor cost of cold feet and waterlogged pants.

He'd left his clothes in Cassie's room. He slung a towel around his hips and went back in. Cassie was fully dressed, sitting on one of the two chairs and frowning at her laptop.

"Can't find heat tape?" he asked.

"Hm?" she said, and then closed the laptop. "No. Just doing some freelance work. I'm behind on a few deadlines. Want to stay for breakfast?"

Yes. He very much did. "I'd better get going," he said instead. "The vineyard will need hands today."

"I didn't even think of that. Is snow bad for the grapevines?"

"No, I don't think so. If there isn't too much in one fall, and if it doesn't stick around too long. Otherwise we'd never have been able to grow grapes here in the first place. I'm not really the expert, though, and I know Theo likes to clear the ground between the rows before they get too much meltwater. Endless water *is* bad for the vines." He dropped the towel and turned his back to put his clothes on. Cassie made appreciative noises and stood up behind him.

"What's this?" she asked, touching the white mark that covered much of his shoulder blade. "I didn't see that last night."

"No, I was the one looking at *your* back," Manny said, and grinned at her when she laughed. He threw his plaid on and buttoned it. "It's just the Pelopson birthmark. Dad had one too. So did our grandfather. It's not all of us—Theo and Augie don't have it—but apparently it's something we carried over from the old country."

"What was your grandfather like? I only know him as the man who liked green suede notebooks."

Manny sat on the edge of the second chair to put his socks on. "I didn't know him very well, but I remember him always being happy to see Augie and me. A few things my parents and Theo have said have made me think he might not have been as good a dad as he was a granddad." He looked at her. "Don't try to get to the big house until the snow's been cleared, okay? I'll borrow the vineyard tractor once we're done, and plough a track for you."

Cassie clutched her heart. "My hero."

She was joking, of course, but Manny experienced a treacherous up-swelling in his own heart. "Okay, see you later," he said, and pressed a deliberately casual kiss to her forehead.

***

Manny had expected Theo to be at his grouchiest, but in fact, he was jovial, joking with the permanent hands and clapping Manny on the shoulder when he turned up. "Told you he'd be here, Jim," he told the manager, and turned to Manny. "You're on shovel duty."

"We're digging out the vines by hand?"

"It's not so bad. There's less snowfall between the rows, and the two fields on the other side of the hill only got a light dusting. We won't bother with them."

Manny looked around the equipment shed. Jim and his men were all bundled up, nearly indistinguishable in their snow jackets, gloves and goggles. But he could clearly make out there were only four of them, plus himself and Theo.

Theo caught the look. "Don't look so worried. It's a snow day at the high school, so Jim and I have made a few calls to some of the townie kids."

"They'll be here once the highways are cleared," Jim said gruffly. He was a taciturn man who seemed just as unenthusiastic about Manny's ideas as Theo was, if much less vocal about it. But he was eying Manny with new interest, as if a puppy had just learned a new trick, and might turn out to be trainable after all.

"Sounds great," Manny said. "Do we have a standard casual labor contract? Do we just adapt the one for picking in summer?"

Jim grunted and turned away, but Theo laughed. "No, Manny. This isn't the city. We don't have to put them through an HR workshop or whatever. They turn up, they dig, they go home with fifty dollars each and a bottle of wine for their moms."

"Um," Manny said. "Can I talk to you in the office for a second?"

Theo rolled his eyes but came along. "Don't you tell me you need a contract for some kids to do some digging," he said. "Kids do this kind of thing for pocket money all the time."

"Sure, in their neighborhoods," Manny said, trying to keep exasperation out of his voice. "But this is a working farm. There are liability issues, we've got tax obligations—"

"*Taxes*? What, you want them to give us their social security numbers and let the IRS know about it?"

"*Yes*," Manny said. "I absolutely do, because that is the *law*."

Theo narrowed his eyes. "We've always done it this way. No contracts, no taxes, strictly cash only. Your father never thought it was an issue. Hell, you used to shovel snow yourself. You didn't have a problem with it then, you and Augie and your buddies."

"I was a teenager then, not a part-owner of the company," Manny said. "And now we're in the middle of probate. I just filed several federal and state tax returns on behalf of Dad and the estate. Theo, if we get audited..."

"We won't be," Theo said dismissively, but he dropped eye contact, shifting away. "Fine. I guess I'm just an old man who doesn't know shit about the business he's been running for nearly forty years."

"Theo, I only want to—"

"You draw up your contracts, you do whatever you think you need to do," Theo said, and then he stepped right up to Manny, his eyes glaring from his wrinkled face. "*You* can pay them, how about that? With the money you earned being the *manager* at your fancy hotel."

Manny could think of half a dozen reasons the IRS might take issue with that, too, but it wasn't worth the fight. "Sure, I'll make a transfer tomorrow," he said evenly. "Can I use your computer to create and print the contracts here?"

"No, you can't," Theo said. "Because that's only twenty-five percent your computer. It's fifty percent my computer, and twenty-five percent Augie's, and if I called him right now and said, Manny's throwing his weight around like a little shithead, he'd tell you where the fuck you should put your *contracts* and *audits* and *cellar door expansions*." He was practically vibrating with unconcealed aggression, and Manny was suddenly worried he'd throw a punch, or have a heart attack.

"Okay," he said, backing away. "I'll go back to the house and do it. I'll be back in an hour."

"You do that," Theo said, and he stalked out of the office, slamming the door behind him. Manny gave him a few minutes, and then followed. He wasn't surprised to see Theo had taken his shovel and vanished, along with the hands, but he was surprised that Jim had lingered.

The manager nodded at him, and Manny nodded back. "Sorry to disrupt your process," he said. He *was* sorry for the disruption. It would have been so much easier to give each kid they hired fifty bucks. Unfortunately, easy wasn't always better.

"He misses your dad," Jim said.

"So do I," Manny said. "But I'm less of an asshole about it."

Jim cracked a smile. "Well, Theo's got a head start on being an asshole. We'll see what you're like in your sixties. Anyway, point is, Arthur followed Theo's lead most of the time. Theo's got fifty percent ownership, sure, but he's been doing ninety percent of the work for years. He got to thinking of Tantalus as his baby."

Manny rubbed the bridge of his nose and stepped a little closer to the space heater. It was probably futile, given that he was going to have to trudge back to the main house in a moment. "I understand how he feels. I really do. But the truth is, Tantalus *isn't* just his baby. We've got a shared custody agreement. And he's pushing back on literally everything I suggest, even the things that I *know* make sense. The cellar door expansion, for example. Hospitality is literally my job. Hard as he might find it to believe, I do actually know what I'm talking about there."

Jim blew air out through his mouth, not disagreeing. "You want some advice?"

"Sure."

"He's protective of the vineyard in general, but the cellar door is his special toy. He came up with the idea, he managed, stocked and staffed it, did the advertising, took on the accounts, all of that. Only time I ever saw him really throw down with your dad was when Arthur suggested expanding the store and hiring someone to staff it during the summer, instead of Theo doing it all."

Manny frowned. "Why would he object to that? There's easily enough profit to justify hiring an attendant during the busy season, and it would free Theo up for whatever else he wanted to be doing."

"He claimed making changes could ruin a good thing," Jim said, and eyed Manny significantly.

"Sometimes change is necessary."

"I don't disagree. I took a look at those resources you recommended on organic growth. Might be worth trying."

Manny straightened from where he was holding his hands out to the heat. "Really?"

"Really. Can't claim I'm much of a hippie, but I can see the science works."

It was the first informed validation he'd had, and Manny felt the relief like a gust of wind blowing through him. "*Thank* you," he said, more fervently than he'd meant to reveal.

"Change isn't always bad. But Theo doesn't take it well. If you want him to take organic growth seriously, and I think I can probably get him there, my advice is to leave him something that's just his, you get me?"

"Leave him the cellar door?" Manny said.

Jim nodded. "Honestly, a lot of time I've gone by and seen him in there just reading a book by himself, no customers. I think he needs that."

Manny frowned. "Thanks for telling me."

"You've got your own project to worry about anyway. How's the carriage house going?"

"Good. Augie says he and the family can come up next month, and he'll help me clear the rest of the big stuff out. In the meantime, I've got Appleton Construction drawing up the plans and Simon at the Midas Bank is looking over the loan proposal."

"Sounds like a lot of spinning plates," Jim said. "Do you really need to be working on the cellar door too?"

Manny sighed. "Maybe not."

"Just something to think about."

"I will think about it," Manny said, and made good on it by mulling the idea over on his trudge back to the big house.

He didn't blame Theo wanting something for himself, but he could have gone after that in a dozen different ways. He could have picked up a million hobbies, like Arthur, or got a job of his own, like Aerope. Manny and Augie had both left Tantalus entirely. Theo didn't *need* to oversee the vineyard—that was why they had Jim in the first place.

Or maybe Manny wasn't thinking about it right. As far as he could figure out from his recent conversations with his uncle, Theo had never been encouraged to find his own passions. Even when Theo had moved out into his own place, far later than most of his contemporaries had left their childhood homes, it had been to a bachelor pad just down the highway. Perhaps Theo couldn't envisage anything for himself *but* Tantalus.

Manny remembered his uncle's face, staring into the dying sun as he spoke about his father's refusal to send him to college, the half-wistful, half-resigned twist to his mouth. Perhaps the cellar door was a way to tell himself that he was helping the family business, even as he carved out a place for himself. And he certainly wasn't *hurting* the family business—in the summer, especially, the cellar door made real money.

Manny didn't like it, but Jim was right. Maybe if he let Theo win this fight, he'd give way on some of the others.

"Let it go," he muttered to himself, and went inside to draw up the contracts.

***

The teenagers Theo had so cavalierly offered to hire comprised half the football team, a number of track and field stars, two competition swimmers, and one moody goth girl whose eyeliner turned into giant raccoon smears within ten minutes of sweating it out with the shovel. The kids had all signed their proffered contracts, looking a lot more cheerful about not getting paid in cash as soon as they realized that Manny was also offering them an hourly rate just over the state minimum wage. One of the boys had pointed out, in hushed tones, that they'd get a much bigger payday.

Theo had given Trace and her spindly arms a dubious look, but she turned out to be a tireless worker. She couldn't go at the speed Herc employed as he shoveled gigantic loads into the sled they were tugging along, but she was much more careful, following along behind him to clear snow closer to the vines, without risking any damage to them. Jim wanted them to keep a layer of snow untouched on top of the soil, so the work went much faster than Manny had anticipated—they were essentially just scooping off last night's fall, and that hadn't had time to compact down into hard ice.

"Why are we keeping some snow?" Manny asked quietly. He would normally have asked Theo, but he was at the other end of the field, setting a furious pace. Besides, he'd given his uncle enough opportunities to upbraid him for ignorance today.

"Insulation," Jim said, equally quietly. "A little snow is good. Keeps the soil hydrated, blasts the fungi and pests. If the soil has no protection, and there's a hard frost, roots might freeze. But if there's too much snow and we get a warm patch, then we're dealing with excess meltwater, and *then* we're dealing with rot and mildew." He gave Manny a curious look. "Didn't Arthur ever talk about this stuff with you boys?"

"Not really," Manny said. He was apparently even more ignorant than he'd thought. He probably *should* take a viticulture course, or at the very least, do some determined reading in the field.

Or ask Jim, who didn't seem to take questions as insults.

With the enthusiasm of the teenagers and the expertise of the hands, they cleared the vines by mid-afternoon. Jim offered the teens a trip back to the packing shed in the back of the vineyard truck, and a bunch of them crammed into the bed, chattering. Manny elected to walk, and arrived to discover that Aerope had also been busy. She'd set up a folding table, and covered it with a massive pot of chili and plastic containers filled with topping options.

Cassie was standing beside her, bundled up in one of Manny's old jackets, carefully putting hearty slices of cornbread in paper bowls before Aerope ladled chili over top.

The teens had descended en masse, and for a moment Manny lost sight of her.

Just as well, because that momentary glimpse of her had given him those inconvenient chest feelings again. By the time he got in line behind Herc Stormson, who was already going up for his second helping, Manny had gotten his brain back together. He smiled at her in a way that he hoped conveyed "thank you for your assistance" with a glint of "I hope to see you naked later." Absolutely no hints of "I think I'm falling for you," not here, no thank you, ma'am.

"I see you got dragooned," he said instead. He'd hoped his mother's attitude towards Cassie would have softened after the revelations yesterday, but if Cassie had been pressured into coming along, that was something else he'd have to deal with. The vineyard wasn't her job.

"I volunteered, actually," Cassie said, and tilted her head at Aerope. "I can't cook worth a damn, and the smells coming from downstairs were so good that I would have gladly traded more than help lugging things around for a shot at that chili."

"I'm grateful for the assistance," Aerope said, and to Manny's practiced ear she sounded genuine.

"Are there *animal products* in this?" Trace said, eying the chili askance, and Manny got out of the way while Aerope assured her that it was a four-bean chili, and that even the stock was a beef-like substitute with no actual cow in it. After that Trace devoured two bowls.

When Aerope produced two massive trays of brownies, with the twinkling air of a whimsical magician, she secured her place forever in the hearts of the youth.

"Thanks so much for this, Mrs. Pelopson," Herc said earnestly, then darted a glance towards Cassie. "Mrs. Pelopsons, I mean."

"Ms. Troiades," Cassie said, looking faintly alarmed.

"Oh," Herc said, and stared back and forth between Manny and Cassie, clearly confused.

"If you want to thank me, you can bring those overdue books back, Hercules," Aerope said, rescuing them both, and Manny let out a breath as Herc mumbled a promise to clean his room and find the books as soon as he got home.

"Thrace, dear, I got in that Interlibrary Loan about the Associated Daughters of Early American Witches," Aerope added.

The girl beamed at her. "Thank you, Mrs. Pelopson," she said, sounding suddenly very All-American.

"I thought her name was Trace," Manny confessed, once the kids had all piled into their various vehicles and driven off, with fervent promises to come back whenever Tantalus needed their services again.

Aerope wrapped foil around the last two brownies. "Well, I believe it was Tracey Hopkins originally. But she's been using Thrace for a while now, and I like to keep up with these things. Lovely girl. Very bright. Reads widely."

This, Manny knew, was his mother's highest compliment. He was trying to figure out a subtle way of escorting Cassie home without a chaperone, but Aerope piled the empty trays in his arms and nodded towards the ATV she'd commandeered to clear the road to the manor house. "You and Cassie head on home. I need to have a quick word with Theo."

Manny lost no time taking her up on the offer, enjoying the squish of Cassie behind him as she held on tight. The grumbling chug of the engine cut down on conversation, but he got to enjoy her arms around his waist all the way back to the guesthouse, where she jumped off the back of the ATV.

"I'm going to speed up the overall survey," she said. "Should be done by the end of tomorrow, and then I can start taking a look into…. Uh. Areas of interest."

Right. There was maybe something awful in the archives, and he'd set her to finding it. Manny's good mood soured a little.

"I'll need an early start," Cassie added. "I don't think we should do a sleepover tonight."

"Oh. Of course."

"So, do you want to come in now?" she said, her tone entirely matter-of-fact. She was wearing his old jacket with the patched sleeve, she had a hat jammed over her curls, her nose was red from the cold, and Manny was half-hard already.

He should say no. He should give himself some space. He should let the hormones settle down and think with his brain for a while.

"Yes, I do," he said, and followed her inside.

Chapter Eight

Over the next two weeks, Cassie called in a lot of favors from her peers, worked long hours examining and logging the earliest Pelopson records, and had a lot of very satisfying sex. Manny seemed preternaturally attuned to her body, able to tell when she was ready to climax almost before she was. They hadn't had sex in the attic again—by silent mutual agreement, sex during work hours was off the table—but getting eaten out *on* the table in the guesthouse was amazing, and so was riding him in the chair by her fireplace, and so was mutual masturbation in her bathtub, which was, after all, sized for two.

They couldn't do anything very athletic in the bed cave, so they mostly avoided it. And Manny seemed to prefer his own bed, since he didn't sleep with her again.

Once or twice, Cassie had considered asking him to stay the night. There'd been something so cozy about waking up beside him that first morning, something very sweet about the way he'd breathed against her neck while she wrapped her arms around him.

But no expectations, no commitments—that was the deal. He was keeping to his part of it, and she needed to stick to hers.

If only the work was as satisfying as her sex life. She'd started in the 1830s and moved forward in time, and in the process she'd actually uncovered quite a few unsavory secrets. The Pelopsons, it seemed, had been a contentious lot. There were a lot of shady land deals, and quite a few lawsuits that seemed more like petty feuding with their neighbors than a genuine need for arbitration. More concerning were the family members who just dropped out of the picture. There were traces of cousins who'd apparently quarreled with the various patriarchs and been more or less expelled from the family. They existed in records up to 1870 and 1903, respectively, and then there was nothing, not even a death certificate.

Prohibition had been an interesting time for wineries. Many had gone under, or banked on future liberty and consigned their grapes for raisins while they waited for Prohibition to lift. Tantalus had survived by being one of the very few vineyards allowed to produce wine for religious or cultural purposes, but when she compared yield data to official sales, there was a lot of wine unaccounted for. Cassie suspected that representatives of local and federal government might have ignored some late-night visits from shady characters. Some of the ledgers from the 20s were missing altogether, and the rest were scanty on detail.

She'd also found what she was positive were secret pregnancies. Two younger daughters, a generation apart, had been sent away to "convalescent retreats," returned six months later, and been married quietly off. The diaries of one girl's mother, Niobe, had recorded her fears about her daughter's condition, and concluded with the flat statement, "She leaves tomorrow. My husband thinks it best." The diary had made for tragic reading, even with the distance of years. Cassie had carefully turned each dry leaf of paper with her gloved hands, and blinked the tears away behind her glasses.

But all of it had happened long ago, and Manny's greatest fear, that his ancestors might have enslaved people, didn't seem to be borne out by the documentation. Not, Cassie concluded tartly, because of any great virtue in the Pelopsons. She thought they would have been just as likely as most people of their race and class to profit from slavery. But they'd arrived after the abolition movement had become stronger in the North, and she couldn't find any glimpse of enslaved people working on the estate, or investment in southern plantations or traders.

And while Aerope had been angry and upset about the cavalier treatment of Niobe's daughter, she didn't think that would have tipped her husband over the edge.

"Maybe I'm sending you on a wild goose chase," she told Cassie one Friday afternoon. Cassie had mentioned a new historical novel that she wanted to read, and Aerope had surprised her by bringing it triumphantly home from the library, her own name on the hold slip.

"I'm sorry," Cassie said. "Maybe I just don't know enough to recognize it, whatever it is."

"Or maybe there's nothing there," Aerope said. She wiped impatiently at the tears glimmering in her eyes. "And I was only hurting myself in search for an explanation. An awful secret would at least be a *reason*, do you understand?"

"I think I do," Cassie said. "I like certainty and order. Even if something terrible happens, knowing why is a little bit of comfort."

"Exactly." Aerope sighed. "I did think… Yesterday, when you told me about that poor girl. I thought, perhaps it was something like that, but closer to the present. But Arthur never had a sister. And Perry Pelopson wasn't the best father, but his wife was very family oriented. Damia wouldn't have let him send her daughter away."

They sat there for a moment longer.

"Did you find anything interesting today?" Aerope asked.

"Oh! Yes. A pocketknife. It's marked T. P. and I think the design on this sheath is Art Deco, so it might have been Theophilus Pelopson's." Cassie held up her hand, which sported a bandage on the thumb. "Whoever it belonged to took good care of it. The catch and blade were oiled before it was put in storage, and it's still sharp."

"Tell Manny about that," Aerope advised. "It's exactly the sort of thing he wants for the carriage house project."

"I will."

Silence fell again. Cassie was wondering if she should gently ask Aerope to go when the older woman cleared her throat.

"I must apologize again for how I treated you when you first arrived."

"It's all right," Cassie said. She'd said it a few times, meaning it more on each occasion. Aerope had been trying so hard to make up for it.

"You're really very good at this. And you and Manny seem to be getting along rather well."

"Um. I'd rather not...discuss any of that with his mother."

"As his mother, I'm merely looking out for his wellbeing. Given his past experience."

Cassie felt a spark of curiosity. What past experience? The ex-girlfriend Manny had referred to once? From his tone, she'd been *the* ex. But if Cassie asked, Aerope would take it as permission to pry further into her own intentions, and she didn't want to share. The plan was to leave and remember Manny as a fond interlude, but she couldn't see Aerope taking that well.

"Let's change the topic," she said brightly. "Do you like historical fiction yourself?"

"Yes," Aerope said. "But I'd rather discuss my son's future."

"I wouldn't," Cassie said firmly, and waited for the backlash.

But Aerope sat there for a moment, looking more pleased than not, and said, "Well! I'd better let you get back to work. Unless you want to read?" She nodded at the book she'd brought. "I must say I'd find it hard to resist. But perhaps you're more disciplined."

Cassie shook her head and got back to work. She had a feeling there was a double meaning in that.

***

Simon at the Midas Bank was probably just following procedure when it came to his loan application, but it felt to Manny like the man was moving at a snail's pace. So far, he'd resisted the urge to call and hurry him up, but as they inched closer to spring, the desire to just casually drop in on the man increased.

In the meantime, he was endearing himself to Jim and frustrating the hell out of Theo by trying to learn more about the vineyard business.

"Now, the shotgun," Manny said, and glanced at the weapon leaning casually against the wall.

"It's for the birds," Jim said patiently. "The noise scares them off the fruit." He grinned at Manny. "It's even organic."

Manny grinned back. "I mostly meant that we should put it in a locker or something. Having it in the office could be a safety issue, given that we don't even lock the door half the time."

"It's not loaded," Jim said. "And the shells *are* locked up in my desk. But I see your point."

"Okay, so next thing was that list of equipment we put together. Have you had a chance to think about how we should prioritize?"

"New destemmer," Jim said promptly, and scratched his beard. "And in frost season I'm basically up at 2am every night to check the temperature and get the burners on with the hands. I'm probably getting a little old for it and it costs a lot in labor."

"So these new cold-sensitive automatic heaters would be better?"

"Sure, if we could afford them."

"I'll run the numbers," Manny said, and turned as Theo came in.

"Aren't you two friendly?" Theo said.

Jim clapped Manny on the shoulder. "He's picking it up pretty fast."

"Watch out, next step is telling you how to do your job," Theo said, but it lacked some of his recent bite. "Soil has thawed, Jim, and some of the vines on the top field are bleeding."

Jim looked at Manny expectantly.

"Uh, the bleeding is sap coming from the pruning sites. That means bud break is soon, right?" Manny said.

Jim nodded. "And that means all hands on deck to protect the new growth from frost. You sure you can't get those new heaters this season?"

"I wish I could," Manny said, though he was pretty sure Jim was joking. "Maybe next year, if the cellar door sales are anything like last summer's."

Theo puffed out his chest. "I can practically guarantee it."

"We could think about expanding the cellar door space a little," Manny said tentatively, but he wasn't surprised when Theo bristled.

"What have I told you about messing with a good thing?" he demanded.

"Theo, can you put the shotgun in the truck locker?" Jim said unexpectedly.

Theo frowned at him. "Why? It's fine in your office."

Jim shrugged. "If we're getting more hands in, I don't want those kids to get their hands on it. They steal road signs. Might well think it funny to take a gun too, and then we've got a problem."

"Oh, fine, I'll do it now," Theo said, and Jim winked at Manny behind his back. "Manny, come and help me lay down that mulch we made."

Laying down the mulch took much longer than Manny had expected, and there wasn't time to go through the rest of his list with Jim after. He headed back to the house, and passed Aerope, who was just leaving.

"Are you off, Mom?"

"Yes," she said. "I'm going grocery shopping in Weeping Rock. And I'm having dinner with Beverley afterwards, so you'll have the house to yourself for *hours*." She gave him a significant look, one that was both knowing and encouraging.

"Uh-huh," he said.

"Cassie's still upstairs," she added. "You should go and say hello."

"Okay," Manny said, and escaped before she could start winking and nudging him. This was much better than open warfare, but his mother's eagerness was still disconcerting.

On the other hand, it might be nice to take advantage of his mother's absence and his own bed. True, his bedroom was less cozy than Cassie's, but it had the significant benefit of headroom. He mounted the stairs in good spirits, with a fair turn of speed, but stopped dead as soon as he saw Cassie.

She was sitting at her table outside the attic, archive boxes and various records piled around her, staring at a green suede journal.

She was too still, and her face was too serious.

His stomach dropped. "You found it," he said, and she raised her eyes.

"Yes," she said quietly. "I think I did."

***

Cassie watched the emotions pass over Manny's face—surprise, concern, wary interest. He settled on the last and pulled a chair over. "Okay. What did you find?"

"I can take you through it, if you like. It might be best if I go step by step instead of starting from my tentative conclusions."

"Yes," Manny said. "Yes, please, start from the beginning." He was looking a little shaky.

Cassie adopted her most professional tone and leaned over the records, hoping to give him some relief in her matter-of-fact account. "Your mom gave me the idea," she said. "She mentioned that perhaps I was looking at the wrong end of history, so I looked at the records closer to home, the things that might have directly affected your dad because he was alive when they happened."

"Right," Manny said. "That makes sense."

"So I started with my spreadsheet, just to get an idea of what there was, and that's where I started finding the gaps. Your grandmother Damia was an archivist's dream. She kept meticulous photo albums, one for every year, from the day she married your grandfather until the year she died. But there are two photo albums missing, from 1970 and 1973."

"She could have been too busy that year. Or they got lost."

"Very possible, but it made me think about that record book you found in the carriage house. I found the receipt for those in a pile of business expenses. Your grandfather ordered three dozen of those green suede notebooks in 1959."

"You mentioned that earlier."

"Yes." She pointed at two boxes. "So why were there only eighteen in the archives? He recorded the vineyard records in the front and personal expenses in the back, from 1960 to 1977. I thought he'd run out, because he used a different kind each year after that, but if he had eighteen more, why not use them until they switched to typed records?"

She picked up the notebook. "This is the one you found. That makes nineteen in total, which also doesn't make sense, because he ordered thirty-six. So I looked at it more closely. There *are* no vineyard records in this one. It's just what looks like personal expenses. Clothes, school fees, a payment for a summer camp."

"Stuff for kids," Manny said, with rising dread. "But... *Not* the stuff for my dad and Theo he'd already recorded in the other books. The expenses he didn't mind keeping with the vineyard records."

"Yes," Cassie said. "And when I went through page by page, I found this." She flipped to a point three quarters through the notebook, and showed him the page where the photo of the boy had been carefully taped in.

It was obviously a school photo, one cut from a grid of small wallet sized prints. The boy was sitting against a faded blue background and wore a white button-up shirt with a dark blue blazer, embroidered with a crest. He had a fluffy blond bowl cut, and a wide, crooked-tooth smile.

Cassie had carefully sliced one of the ancient pieces of tape, and now she flipped the photo over to show Manny the back.

The back had been inscribed in careful, round letters - not a child's writing, but someone who had taken their printing lessons seriously as a child. It read *Chris, 6th Grade, 1972*. The dot of the i was a tiny heart.

"That's not my grandfather's writing," Manny said.

"Or your grandmother's," Cassie said. "Or anyone else I could find samples for from that era."

"Right," Manny said. "Anything else?"

"Just this," Cassie said, and pulled out the photo that had been loose in the box on her very first day. The box that had been half-empty, although she was only now able to appreciate the significance of that. She pointed at the cluster of children on the dock of Lake Lydia, with the two adults in the center, and handed Manny a magnifying glass from her archive kit. "Do you recognize anyone in this picture?"

Manny squinted. "That's my grandfather, Perry, and my grandmother, Damia. My dad is there. He must be about fifteen, I guess, which would make Theo fourteen. There's Theo, off to the side." His voice went stiff. "And there's Chris, right in front of my grandfather." He put the magnifying glass down. "Okay. So. What does this add up to?"

Cassie's heart was breaking for him, because he was much too smart to deny what was coming next. "I don't think we could draw any definite conclusions yet, but—"

"My grandfather had another kid," Manny said. "I have another uncle. What else could it mean?"

"He could have been sponsoring Chris for another reason. Maybe he was a family member, but not that closely related. A descendant of one of your lost great-great-aunts."

"I don't think Granddad would have cared about that tenuous a connection," Manny said. "But eighteen missing notebooks. That would be eighteen years of expenses, supporting a child from birth to adulthood. And on top of that, we've got a school photo of a twelve-year-old with a strong family resemblance, who then shows up at one of Granddad's lake days for disadvantaged youth. Maybe more than one, if more than one photo album is missing. That's suggestive, wouldn't you say?"

"I would say it's suggestive. But not conclusive."

"And this is everything you found? A notebook and a loose photo?"

"That's all I've found this afternoon," Cassie said. "There might be more, if I dig. But I think your dad went digging before me. This box, the one with the photo in it, that was half-empty. Most of the other boxes are crammed so full the lids barely fit. I think the missing photo albums were in there, and they were taken out. This photo might have fallen out then."

"Dad found out he might have another little brother." Manny dropped his head into his hands. "Shit. I still don't think he would have… But that might have done it. I don't know."

Cassie abandoned her pretense of professionalism. Without even thinking about it, she was walking out of her chair and hugging him. "I'm sorry," she said fiercely. "Manny, I'm so sorry."

"Do we know who Chris *is*? Do you think Dad looked for him?"

"I don't know if he could have found him with this. It's a common first name. And without a last name or a solid date of birth, I don't have much to work with. We've got an approximate birth year, though, and that's not nothing. If his mother was local, there could be birth records. But I was thinking that if your dad *did* find more evidence, maybe he put it somewhere in his office, or another storage area."

"Right," Manny said, looking more invigorated. "Right, he could have done that. The office is a dump. I've barely looked at anything except the vineyard records or the carriage house blueprints since I got here. Or maybe there was more in the carriage house—that filing cabinet didn't have anything else in it, but there are still hiding places in there. I'll take a good look when Augie and I finish clearing it next weekend." He paused. "Don't tell Mom or Theo yet," he said, with sudden decision. "And I won't tell Augie, either."

"I got the impression your mother would welcome a little clarity," Cassie said cautiously.

Manny waved at the paltry evidence she'd gathered. "You said it yourself, this isn't conclusive. I want to *give* her clarity, if I can."

Cassie nodded. "Your call, boss," she said, hoping to make him smile.

He didn't, not quite, but his eyes crinkled at the corners, and he looked ruefully at her. "And here I was planning to ask if you wanted to check out *my* bedroom while my mother's in town."

"With an actual bed?" Cassie said, just a little too eagerly.

"Yeah, that was my thinking too," Manny admitted. He looked at the notebook. "For some reason, I'm not really feeling it at the moment."

"Wow, weird," Cassie said, and kissed his cheek. "In that case, I've got a couple of hours free. Want me to help you turn the office upside down?"

Manny's eyes softened. "You don't have to do that."

"I want to," Cassie said, and found herself meaning it. Even if it wasn't for the mystery, she would have wanted to help Manny. He was taking so many blows, and he just kept going, trying to make things better. Even more impressively, he didn't ignore the impact of those blows. He wasn't shoving his emotional reactions down, so they could surface in some huge unpredictable explosion later. He let himself feel what he felt about the problems, and then he started looking for solutions.

That was a guy you could trust. That was a guy you could rely on.

That might be, if you were absolutely honest with yourself, a guy you could develop inconvenient feelings for.

Not that she would, of course.

It would be such a terrible idea.

Chapter Nine

M anny couldn't find anything in the office.

Well, that wasn't true. He could lay his hand on anything he wanted within a few seconds, because he'd spent nearly a week cleaning and organizing the space. He hadn't had much else to do, while the Midas Bank kept dithering on the loan and Appleton Construction finalized the plans. Aerope approved of his work, and when he was done, he had a beautiful, airy space that felt like *his* office, not his father's.

He'd put most of his own possessions in storage when he'd sublet his apartment in the city. Now that he was staying—and it definitely felt like he was staying—he could see about getting them moved. Perhaps he'd wait until he found a place here, though. He loved his mother, but he wasn't positive he wanted to live where he worked. Maybe Theo would be interested in moving back to the main house? They could be company for each other.

In the meantime, he'd found absolutely nothing more about the mysterious Chris. There were no photo albums or records in the office, not even a loose document. He'd gotten really excited when he'd found the desk had a hidden drawer, but when he'd pried it open it had contained a 1998 *Playboy* and half a pack of mints. Cassie had been trying her best with what she had, but without a last name, and with Manny's wish for discretion, she'd been limited to searching local birth records. A few Chrises *had* been born in Weeping Rock at around the right time, but she and Manny had been able to rule them all out. *Their* Chris had been born somewhere else.

If the missing records weren't in the office, Manny couldn't figure out where his father would have put them. His parents' bedroom might have been a possibility, but his mother obviously knew nothing of what her husband had discovered. Manny didn't think Arthur would have hidden anything in a place he shared so easily with his wife if he meant to keep it a secret.

His phone rang. He glanced at the name and then lunged for it. "Simon! Hello!"

"Hi, Manny," Simon said affably. "Sorry for the time it's taken, but I'm happy to tell you that Midas is prepared to sign off on the loan."

Manny let out an explosive puff of breath. "That's great."

"There are a few things to talk about, so if you wanted to come in some time, perhaps next week…"

"How about today?" Manny said instantly. It was Thursday afternoon. He didn't want to waste another minute, much less a whole weekend. It took a minute of gentle pressing, but he finally got Simon to admit that he didn't have any appointments for the rest of the day. Simon sounded disappointed—he'd probably been planning to leave work early. Normally Manny would have been sympathetic, but not today. He promised to be there in twenty minutes, grabbed his coat and keys, and hurried outside.

Twenty minutes later he was shaking Simon's hand and sitting down in his office. Simon was a tall, skinny man a decade or so younger than

Aerope. He looked like he was built for speed, all sharp angles and taut muscle, but he moved—and spoke—like molasses.

"Now, I don't mind telling you this was a little complicated," Simon said, shaking his head conspiratorially. "Those accounts you gave us, whew."

"Yeah, sorry about that," Manny said. "The bookkeeping got a little lax sometimes. But my projections are solid. The comparative analysis of similar proposed business ventures—"

"Yes, that all checked out," Simon assured him. He rummaged around his files, taking twice as long as Manny would have liked, and produced a red folder, embossed in gold with MB. "But we've got a few limitations, some conditions we'd like you to look over." He looked hopeful. "Perhaps you'd like to take the contract away and consider it? Speak to your uncle and brother?"

"They've given me carte blanche on the carriage house project, including the financing," Manny said, and flipped the folder open. "I can look at it now."

Simon sighed in gentle disappointment, and Manny ignored it. A shorter loan term than he'd like, and the interest rate had moved up a few fractions. The repayment schedule was still well within his profit projections, but it gave him less leeway if something went wrong. And... He looked up. "You've removed the overdraft facility."

"Yes. You'll be able to draw down the full amount of the loan, of course, but you won't be able to go beyond that without approval of an additional loan."

"Uh-huh. And am I likely to get that approval?"

Simon looked at his desk succulents, then played with his pen for a minute. "Well..."

"I see."

"I mean, if you mortgaged some land, or perhaps the manor house, I'm sure the bank would be more than willing—"

"Not an option," Manny said firmly. Aerope might be willing to approve it, but there was no way he was risking the Pelopson family home on this venture. Even the surest of sure things could go to hell in the wrong circumstances, and there were always unforeseen risks in hospitality.

Okay. This was tighter than he'd like, but it was still doable. He'd budgeted for a construction cost overrun of twenty percent, and this would still cover that. His alternative was going to another bank, which would start this whole process again and delay construction to the point where he wouldn't be able to open for peak tourist season this summer. Or he could ditch the entire project, but quite apart from the sunk cost of the time and money he'd already put into it, his predictions for the future of Tantalus hadn't changed. If they kept going as they were going, no one would risk money with them, no matter how immaculate the bookkeeping.

"Fine," he said. "Do I just sign and initial? And you can make the loan available today, so that I can get Appleton their construction deposit, right?"

"Er, well," Simon said, and Manny ruthlessly bullied him into admitting that yes, they could do that, a little unusual, they usually *preferred* to wait three business days, but Manny was quite right to point out there'd already been some delay—unavoidable, but understandably frustrating—so perhaps he could hurry things up just a little...

Manny left with an impressive addition to the bank app on his phone and strode into the late winter sunshine, feeling good. The truncated payment schedule was something of a concern, but not a big enough one to smother his growing sense of triumph. He headed towards the car, then hesitated. Appleton Construction's main office was just down the street, and he could drop in and arrange the deposit in person. Maybe take possession of the plans, if they were ready.

"Mr. Pelopson!" he heard, and for a moment it didn't register as his name. Mr. Pelopson was his father, and occasionally his uncle. But Herc Stormson was rushing up to him, all ruddy good health and wide shoulders, and Manny resigned himself to feeling old for a minute.

"What can I do for you, Herc?" he asked. For once, Herc wasn't accompanied by his shadowy girlfriend, and he looked oddly unbalanced without her.

Herc beamed at him. "Did you maybe need more help at the vineyard?"

"Jim Stevens is the man to talk to, but yes, probably, especially during vintage." He saw Herc's confusion. "Harvest. Grape-picking season. Are you looking for work?"

Herc nodded. "I need to make some money for college. And you paid pretty well for the snow day, so I was hoping..."

"Your dad told me you had scholarships," Manny said. He'd had a beer with Tyron Stormson just last week, and Tyron had bragged about it, in his quiet way.

"Oh, yeah, I got full ride offers from sports schools. But I only got a partial scholarship to Asclepius. I need more to cover the gap."

Manny paused. Asclepius specialized in the sciences, and while their pre-med program was renowned, he'd never heard anything about their sports teams. He'd imagined Herc going to Eleusis or Nemea instead.

Herc caught his look and said, "Thrace is going to Asclepius." He sounded half-proud and half-defiant, probably already anticipating Manny's reaction.

"Ah," Manny said, and resisted the urge to explain that following your high school sweetheart to college wasn't necessarily a good idea. No doubt many people had already pointed that out to Herc, and anyway, who was he to give anyone romantic advice? His most meaningful relationships were a disastrous engagement to his sister-in-law's sister and… Well. And whatever he was doing with Cassie.

"Thrace is really smart," Herc said, in a tone that verged on worship. "I mean, I do okay, Cs and Bs, but she's like an actual genius. She's going to be a research scientist and invent drugs that cure cancer and heart disease and stuff. She got a full scholarship, all four years. She's a really good musician, too, and she could have gotten music scholarships for cello, but she wants to help people and do good for the community."

Manny pictured the gothic teenager who'd faced him down when he'd caught them stealing road signs and tried to picture her as an altruist. "Does doing good for the community include stealing the community's property?"

"Um," Herc said, and then his mouth twisted. "Can I tell you something? If you promise not to tell my dad?"

"I am not promising to keep anything from the chief of police," Manny said, alarmed, but Herc looked so downcast that he relented and added, "I promise to use my discretion, how about that?"

"The road signs thing was a challenge from the football team," Herc said, talking fast. "Like a quest, you know? Last year's seniors got fourteen signs without getting caught, and they were like, no one will ever beat this record, so this year me and the guys were aiming at twenty-five.

We took some other stuff, too, like those orange cones, and those bird decoys the town puts out to scare birds away from new lawn planting. Nothing *expensive*, nothing, like, really important."

Manny thought of Cassie, hopelessly lost on her first day, and briefly closed his eyes. "We might have a different standard of important, here, Herc."

"Right, well, Thrace thought the whole thing was stupid, and she told me so, and she only ever went with me to be a look-out, so I wouldn't get caught. And after you *did* catch us, she researched how much replacing those signs actually cost and it was nearly four hundred *dollars. Each.*"

"Yes, Herc," Manny said. "That's been mentioned several times in the many stories the local newspaper has run on sign theft."

"Newspaper?" Herc said, as if Manny had suggested he take a quick trip to a cave system to examine the drawings marked there in charcoal and ochre.

"Never mind."

"Anyway, we didn't realize it was that much. Like, twenty-five signs would be ten thousand dollars! So we stopped, even though we only had twelve and couldn't break last year's record. And I'm trying to figure out a way to give them back without my dad noticing."

"A heroic sacrifice."

Herc nodded, taking him at face value. "Yeah. I should have known it was a bad idea from the start. The very first sign I took was the night your dad died. Afterwards Thrace told me it was an *omen*."

Manny winced. "Omen might be a bit ghoulish. I would have said a coincidence."

"I nearly got caught then too," Herc confided. "It was the middle of the night, so I thought I'd be safe, but the truck from your vineyard barreled right past me, and I was sure Mr. Stevens must have seen me. I nearly pissed—uh, I was surprised. But he never said anything, so I figured he was a good guy. Or maybe he just didn't notice me up the step-ladder with the hacksaw."

"Are you sure it was Jim Stevens?" Manny asked. From Jim's complaints about getting older, he hadn't thought he was much of a night owl.

"Sure. Pickup with a painting of grapes hanging over a lake, right?"

"That's the vineyard truck," Manny said, and then frowned. "Wait, you were nearly caught in the middle of the night, so instead you started trying to steal signs in the middle of the day? That *is* what you were doing when I caught you, right?"

"That one was kind of an impulse decision," Herc confessed. "Trace and I were going for a drive and I saw the sign, so I pulled over. Um, do you have any ideas about how I could give the signs back? Trace said I should dump them somewhere and make an anonymous call, but I don't know."

"Tell your father," Manny said firmly.

"He'll be pretty mad. I, uh, kind of lied to him about it already."

"Then he deserves to be mad, wouldn't you say? But coming clean will help. You *don't* want one of your buddies to let it slip and for it to get back to him anyway. Tell him, and deal with the consequences."

"Are *you* going to tell him?" Herc asked, already looking betrayed.

"Not yet," Manny said. "I'll let you have a shot at it first.

Herc winced.

Thrace was coming out of the library, weighted down by her selections, and she eyed them suspiciously.

"Let me take those, babe," Herc said quickly, and took the books from her. "Uh, thanks for telling me about the work, Mr. Pelopson."

"You're welcome," Manny said meaningfully, and left them there.

Appleton Construction's yard was on the outskirts of Weeping Rock, but Petra Appleton maintained an office in town, where she met clients and did most of the design and budgeting work. Her older brothers, who seemed to enjoy being ruthlessly managed by their little sister, ran a solid construction crew, and Manny had confidence in their work.

Petra was a short woman with flame-red hair, and an old acquaintance from high school. She'd run the student council with the same neat efficiency she now applied to the family business, and Manny knocked on her office door with a smile.

"Sorry, reception was empty," he said.

Petra's face went from stern attention to her work to bright anticipation. "Chloe leaves at three for the school pickup. Can I take it you come with good news?"

Manny grinned at her. "Loan officially approved, and I can get you that deposit right now."

"Fantastic! Well, in that case..." She got to her feet and pulled a long roll of paper out of a filing shelf. "These blueprints are all done. I've blocked out the schedule. We can do the initial assessment on Monday, and if all goes according to plan, we'll finish cleanup by the first of June."

"What if it doesn't go according to plan?"

"It will," Petra said, as if she wouldn't allow the universe to get up to any tricks. She extended the roll of blueprints to Manny. "These are your copy."

"Thank you," Manny said, feeling the relief settle through his bones. Petra would make the redesign work. And after that, he could handle the rest.

Petra smiled at him. "Planning to celebrate?"

He *should* celebrate. He hadn't taken the time to acknowledge a major milestone like this in a long time. His mind went, immediately and inevitably, to Cassie. She was planning to spend the weekend with Steph again, tactfully getting out of the way as his brother's family descended on them, but she'd probably be free tonight. He'd been promising to cook something for her. Maybe that, and a couple of beers, a movie on her laptop while they sat by the fire... Maybe he'd have the guts to ask if he could stay the night.

"You could celebrate with me," Petra said, unaware of his train of thought, and he blinked at her. She was smiling at him. "I could buy you dinner. What do you say?"

Oh. *Oh.* "Um, thank you so much," Manny said. "But I'm kind of seeing someone."

"Are you?" Petra said, and her eyebrows went up. "That hadn't hit the grapevine yet."

Because he and Cassie had spent most of their time having amazing sex and trying to work out mysteries, Manny realized. They hadn't been on a public date that would ping the radar of the Weeping Rock gossip network. Which made sense, because they weren't really dating.

Would she even say yes, if he asked?

"It's pretty new," he said.

Petra shrugged. "Okay. Figured I'd take my shot. But we can keep it professional. Let's talk schedules."

Ten minutes later they'd arranged a meeting at the carriage house for first thing on Monday, and Manny was back out on the street, trying to struggle through his whirling emotions. Petra was pretty and smart as hell, with the edge that he'd acquired a taste for after Helen. She was exactly who he'd normally be interested in. But she wasn't Cassie, and that was starting to become more and more of a factor.

Okay. If he wanted to date Cassie, for real, he'd better let her know about it. They had an agreement for no expectations—but they also had an agreement for honesty. And he honestly wanted to start expecting. It was time to take his shot.

Ask Cassandra

Dear Cassandra

I wanted to write in with an update, because I'm pretty sure you saved my relationship.

A few months ago, I told you about my wonderful boyfriend who was totally perfect, except I worried that he was keeping secrets from me. He seemed to have more money than a copywriter should have. When I told my sisters about some expensive jewelry he gave me, they encouraged me to snoop, telling me that I deserved to know the truth about who I was sleeping with.

I was right on the verge of breaking into his email accounts or stalking him around the city when I wrote to you.

Instead, I followed your advice. I sat him down and told him about my concerns. I told him that I understood if he wanted to keep some things private, but that I was starting to lose trust in him, and that was going to poison what we had. It was the hardest thing I've ever done, but I said I was prepared to walk away when things were still good between us, rather than wait until doubt had made me bitter.

You could have knocked me over with a feather when he laughed and told me the truth.

He's not a copywriter. He's a bestselling romance novelist!

I won't name names, of course, but he writes a few series under a couple of super-secret pseudonyms. They're very popular and really saucy, and his income is over seven figures yearly. He was on the verge of telling me anyway, but his mom was telling him he shouldn't trust me, because I was acting shady—because I wasn't sure I could trust him!

That's the last time I'm gonna let my sisters give me advice on my relationship!

Talking to each other cleared everything up, but I don't think I would have gotten there without your advice, so thank you so much. We're both living in bliss, now that he can spoil me as much as he wants to and I know that he's locked away on deadline and not a secret monster with another girlfriend.

Plus, I've gotta say, it's really fun to help him research and plot the sex scenes!

Yours,

(Formerly) Psycho Psyche.

Dear Psyche,

Thank you for writing in! I'm so glad you were able to clear things up with your boyfriend. I am, of course, in my group chat right now trying to figure out if I've read any of his books, but the field is so huge that I think his secret is safe.

Enjoy that research!

Yours,

Cassandra.

Chapter Ten

Cassie dropped by Manny's office on her way downstairs, but he wasn't there. She stifled the pang of disappointment, and let herself out just as Aerope arrived. She'd obviously gone shopping right after work, hauling gigantic paper bags of groceries towards the kitchen.

"Can I help with that?"

"Oh, thank you, dear," Aerope said, and Cassie grabbed the last two bags. Fresh produce, cheese, artisan breads; Aerope clearly meant to get busy in the kitchen for her family visit.

"There's enough here to feed an army," she said, as she deposited the bags on the table.

"My grandchildren *are* an army," Aerope said from the fridge, where she was moving things around to make room for a giant rack of spare ribs. "Manny did mention that Augie and his family are coming up tomorrow evening?"

"Yes, he said. Steph Marshall offered to have me over this weekend, so I won't be in your way."

"Oh," Aerope said, and there was a moment's silence. She emerged from the fridge, looking distracted. "Well, that's very thoughtful of her. Of both of you. Lovely girl, Steph."

"She mentioned that you'd helped her out a lot, when she was a teenager."

Aerope snorted. "Katherine Tannock—Katherine Marshall now—was always good at ignoring reality that didn't suit her desires. She was very put out when Steph made her listen to a truth she didn't want to hear."

"Do you know everyone in town?"

"Oh, goodness, no, Weeping Rock isn't quite *that* small. But you do get to know the library patrons, and we're better funded than the high school library, so a lot of students use our collection. And while a lot of them leave for school or work, many come back here eventually."

"Like Manny."

"Like Manny." Aerope paused. "It's a lovely place, Weeping Rock. Prettier in the summer, of course. You're not really seeing it at its best."

"I like what I've seen of the town," Cassie told her. "And the people, too." Isaac Corey most definitely excepted. Steph had promised to introduce her to a few people at the Black Cat on Saturday evening, and she was looking forward to that.

"It's a wonderful place to bring up a family," Aerope said. "That's why many people move back."

"I bet. I liked the kids from the school, too. Thrace seems like a livewire."

"She certainly is. Well, let's see. I'd better start the marinade for the ribs, and figure out something for dinner tonight."

Cassie's phone vibrated against her thigh, and she pulled it out to look at the text. "Manny's offered to buy me dinner in town," she said, surprised and pleased. "He can pick me up in an hour."

"*Really*," Aerope said, but by the time Cassie looked at her, alerted by the tone, Aerope's expression was placid. "In that case I'll have a poached egg on toast, perhaps a light salad."

"If you had something planned, we could always eat here," Cassie offered, feeling bad for her, but Aerope shook her head, smiling.

"No, no, you two enjoy yourselves," she said. "You'll probably want to wash up, hm?"

Which was probably a gentle hint that Cassie was covered in attic grime. She texted Manny a reply, then went back to the cottage and opted for a quick shower. The little stall wasn't nearly as comfortable as the deep claw-footed tub, but the luxury of a bath every day was starting to feel a little indolent. She took the time to wash and blow-dry her hair instead, scrunching the serum Laodice had snagged for her into the curls. They were getting a little longer than she liked. Maybe Steph could recommend a good stylist. Back in the bedroom, she opened her wardrobe and paused.

She'd meant to put on clean jeans and grab a fresh sweater, but a deep red gleam had caught her eye. She pulled the dress out and laid it over the chair, considering. It was the dress she hadn't chosen to wear for her one-and-only date with Isaac, a red chiffon swing affair, with long, transparent sleeves and a hem that cut off just below the knees. After a moment's contemplation, she hunted out black tights and gave her black T-bar heels a quick polish. Her puffer jacket would have to go on top, and that wasn't a great match, but at least she'd look good once she took it off.

No need to think too hard about why she wanted to look good. She climbed into her red silk lingerie set before she got dressed, and applied lipstick of the same shade. A quick coat of mascara, and she was ready for...whatever this dinner was.

Nervous despite herself, she ran downstairs when the knock came on her door, and zipped up the puffer before she opened the door.

Manny was waiting outside, looking unfairly debonair in black slacks and a sweater over a shirt open at the collar, all of it visible under the open front of a long grey coat.

"This is nice," Cassie said, reaching out to touch the lapel. The wool felt soft and warm under her fingers. "I haven't seen it before, have I?"

"I mostly wore it in the city," Manny said. "Thought it was time to pull it out." His eyes snagged on her mouth, and took in the tights and heels without comment, but he opened the passenger door in silent tribute to her efforts. Cassie accepted the gesture and settled herself on the seat.

"Ooh, butt-warmers," she said, snuggling in.

"I like a little luxury, now and then."

"I appreciate it. Where are we going? The Black Cat?"

"I thought maybe we'd try somewhere else, if you don't mind. How was your day?"

"It was good. Although I can't claim to have made much more progress on discovering who and where Chris is. Without a surname, I think I've done as much as I can for now."

"It was a big ask," Manny said. "I guess the next thing is to tell Mom and Augie and Theo after all. They might have some ideas. Theo might even remember more from that day on the lake." He sighed. "I just wanted to have more to show them. Maybe I'll wait until Sunday night. We might as well enjoy the whole weekend before I drop a bomb on them."

"I think that's really kind," Cassie said. "A couple more days won't matter."

"Yeah," Manny said, and perked up. "The loan came through today."

"Oh, great! You can start work on the carriage house soon."

"Monday." Manny hesitated, so briefly she could have imagined it, and added, deliberately, "That's why I thought I'd ask you out tonight. To celebrate."

Cassie looked at his nice coat, then down at the hem of her dress, poking out from under her jacket. "So this is a date."

"If you want it to be," Manny said. "Otherwise it's two friends with benefits getting dinner."

Cassie felt a spike of alarm, all the things she'd been carefully not thinking about immediately rising to the surface of her mind. "I don't mind if it's a date," she said, after a minute. Because who was she fooling, anyway? Before this, she hadn't put on lipstick in weeks.

Manny cleared his throat. "Good. I'm glad."

And then they both shut up until they got to the restaurant, a small place in town on the third floor of a wooden building, with a narrow set of stairs that reminded her of the attic. She almost wished it *was* the attic. They'd never been awkward in the attic, and now she had no idea of what to say or how to behave.

Manny helped her off with her coat, with the same ingrained courtesy that had opened her car door, but his automatic manners stuttered when he got a good look at the dress.

"Wow," he said.

Cassie smiled, feeling better. "Like what you see?"

"If I'd seen it before we left, we might not have gotten this far."

The hostess showed them to their table, one of only six in the smallish room. Four of the others were occupied by people paying very close attention to their plates.

"I appreciate the effort, but I want you to know I would have been happy with a pizza and a good beer."

"That was my first impulse. And maybe a movie by your fire."

"Not a bad idea at all." A plate went past her, covered in tiny gleaming balls of gel, sitting on a wide black cracker so thin it looked like lace. The rich, nutty scent of warm sesame oil drifted in its wake, and saliva suddenly flooded her mouth. "Wait, no, I take it back. This is perfect."

When she turned back, Manny was looking at her. "Yes," he said quietly. "I think you're right."

As she should have expected, Manny had excellent taste in fine dining. They chatted between courses, but otherwise she directed most of her attention to the food and its layers of texture and flavor, each bite a revelation. Manny wasn't drinking, but Cassie had elected for the wine pairings with each dish, and by the time she'd finished the meat course, a tender nugget of lamb topped with a rosemary-potato mousse, she was feeling pleasantly fuzzy.

"Thank you so much for bringing me here," she said. "It's amazing."

Manny cleared his throat. "We could do things like this more often, if you like," he said.

Cassie laid her fork down. "You mean...more dates?"

"Yes." Manny was looking at her, his eyes blue and honest. "I'd like to go on more dates with you. I'd like us to be dating."

"Right," Cassie said, trying to catch her breath. "I'm not opposed, in theory."

"But in practice?"

"In practice, I can see so many ways it would go wrong," Cassie told him. She had an entire inbox of examples, people who had pledged themselves to lovers, only to be ripped apart when their lovers turned on them. Emotional abuse, financial disaster, sometimes physical danger—she read about it nearly every day. She thought he was a really good guy, trustworthy to the bone, not a single red flag flapping in the breeze. But everyone in her inbox had thought that, once. They'd been blind to those red flags because the rest of it felt so good.

And she couldn't tell Manny she was cynical about commitment because she gave advice to people for whom the good had inexorably turned into something terribly wrong.

"Can I think about it?" she asked.

"Sure," he said, which was another green flag, and they devoted themselves to the salad course. Cassie crunched through delicately bitter endive leaves and thought.

Not *all* the relationships that turned up in Ask Cassandra had unhappy endings. *Agora* had just published that update from the formerly psycho Psyche, who'd taken her advice and spoken honestly to her boyfriend. Cassandra had truly—and cynically—expected that relationship to go up in flames, but Psyche had been brave, and been rewarded with a hot boyfriend who made bank writing hot romance novels.

Maybe, if Cassie was brave and honest, she'd get a hot boyfriend who knew where the best restaurants were.

"I haven't done anything serious for a long time," she said. "I really like you. But I'm a little scared."

"I haven't either. I'm scared too. But I'd really like to try."

"Okay," Cassie said. "I'll think it over this weekend, then, while I'm hanging out with Steph and you're hanging out with your family. And then… Maybe we can be scared together." She looked at him. "I'm really happy you brought me here. And not just because the food is amazing."

"One of our local secrets," Manny said.

A man in chef's whites was coming out of the kitchen with a tray of dainty treats arranged on a single piece of chocolate bark. He set the tray down before them, and then straightened, glaring at Manny.

"I want to be solvent, not secret," the chef said severely. "Tell your friends, review and rate."

"This is Jacques," Manny told Cassie. "He runs this place. We went to school together."

"Your food is amazing," Cassie said sincerely. "I'll tell everyone I know."

Jacques unbent enough to smile at her. "Your taste in women is getting better," he told Manny.

Manny raised his eyebrows. "You realize there's no good way for me to respond to that, right?"

Jacques shrugged. "Enjoy your dessert." He walked away, with Manny still frowning at his back, and Cassie took advantage of his distraction to take the first treat, something that tasted like a lemon cream suspended in a dark chocolate globe.

"Oh," she said. "Oh, wow."

Manny turned back and glanced at her face. "Okay, I have to try whatever made you look like that."

"I think I ate the only one," Cassie said, with zero remorse. "Don't worry. I'll make it up to you later."

***

Manny walked over to the big house the next morning feeling pretty damn good. "I'll think about it" wasn't a yes, but it wasn't a no either, and when Cassie said she'd think about something, she meant it. Last night, she'd invited him in "for a drink," taken that incredible dress off, put a cushion on the floor to pad her knees, and given him the most spectacular blow job of his entire life. The sight of her red-painted lips sliding around his cock was going to stay in his memory for a long, long time.

Unless he could replace it with new, even better memories, like the moment he'd woken up in bed with her this morning. He'd wriggled under the covers, and licked her with slow and lavish attention, until her quivering thighs had clamped around his head and she'd chanted his name as she shook against his eager tongue.

He hadn't even asked to sleep over. Cassie had asked *him* if he'd like to. He thought that gave him grounds for optimism on the topic of dating.

He opened the back door, stepped into the kitchen, and found himself nose to nose with his mother, fully dressed and with her most no-nonsense expression.

"Manny, I need to talk to you," she said.

"Why does that never precede something good?" Manny asked, making a beeline for the coffee pot. If he was going to be lectured, he wanted to be caffeinated for it. "'Manny, I need to talk to you. I've just found a million dollars in a neglected bank account, and I want you to help me spend it.'"

Aerope did not appear to appreciate the levity. "Did you suggest to Cassie that she make herself scarce this weekend?" she asked severely.

"Of course not," Manny said. "She and Steph Marshall were planning a Saturday girls' night, and she figured that Augie's visit would be a good time to do that, and then Steph offered to host her for tonight as well."

"But I wanted her to meet the family! Better that she knows what she's getting into."

Manny heard alarm bells. "It might be a little soon for that, Mother. I like Cassie a lot, but I'm not sure how this is going to pan out. As far as I know, she's still planning to head back to the city in a couple of months."

"That's just silly," Aerope said. "She's wonderful for you. Aren't you even going to fight for her?"

"What happened to 'I can't believe you slept with that woman?'"

"Obviously, I was wrong," Aerope said, unperturbed. "I like Cassie. She's very bright. Perhaps even brighter than Ness, and much less abrasive."

"I thought you and Ness were getting on better these days."

"Well, I wish she and Augie wouldn't fight so much, but I can't claim he doesn't give her cause," Aerope said. "But Cassie doesn't fight with you. And you're obviously sexually compatible."

Manny sputtered on his coffee. "This is *not* a conversation I want to have with my mother," he said firmly.

"See, she said exactly the same thing last week. You're perfectly matched."

"Mom!"

"Helen would never dream of telling me to butt out," Aerope said. "She would clam up or make an excuse to leave, or just pretend that she'd never heard me in the first place, but she didn't push *back*. And you didn't used to push back either, Manfred, but you've learned how, and you need a woman who can do the same. I think it's Cassie."

Manny squinted. "So the solution to our family being bad at respecting boundaries is to bring in someone who's good at setting and enforcing them? As a role model?"

"It couldn't hurt, surely."

"Mom, why don't you just work on your own issues around boundaries?"

"What makes you think I'm not?" Aerope demanded.

"The part where you're trying to pimp me out to a prospective daughter-in-law, *right now*."

Aerope folded her arms. "One day you'll see I'm right. I only hope it won't be too late."

Manny bit down hard on the impulse to tell her that Cassie was *thinking about* dating. He could just see Aerope trying to seal the deal, and while Cassie didn't scare easy, his mother's enthusiasm might be even more intense than her fear had been. "Well, at that point you can tell me you told me so."

"Don't think I won't," Aerope sniffed, but she softened and poured him another cup of coffee. "I just want my children to be happy. Is that wrong?"

"Nope, but you can't *make* it happen."

"Hm," Aerope said, in a tone that indicated she wasn't quite ready to believe that. "Well. We'll see."

***

He was on guard against his mother sneaking up to the attic for the rest of that Friday, but when he kissed Cassie goodbye before she left for Steph's, she didn't mention any motherly ambushes. At least Aerope had respected his wishes that far. Or perhaps she'd been too busy. The kitchen had been a source of tantalizing smells all day as she cooked in a nurturing frenzy.

Augie's family arrived too late for dinner, which didn't prevent Aerope from trying to feed them anyway. The meal was a frenzy of conversation, hugs, and observations on how much various grandchildren had grown. Little Chrys, his youngest niece, was obviously up way past her bedtime, and so exhausted that she threw a tantrum at the thought of sleep. Geni, the eldest, was able to calm her down with the promise of three full stories at bedtime and carried her off, while Electra and Orestes, engaged in some complicated private game, nobly suffered ten minutes of attention from their uncle and grandmother before sneaking away to entertain each other.

"Four of them," Ness said, sitting down heavily at the kitchen table. She was a beautiful woman, dark-skinned and full-featured, with long, relaxed hair and huge eyes, but at that moment she looked more tired than stunning. "Why did we have four?"

"I wanted two," Augie reminded her, and Ness sat up straight.

"Excuse me? Who watched Orestes graduate kindergarten and asked if I couldn't be talked into another?"

"You gave in pretty damn easy," Augie said, and Manny could see the shape of the fight taking place before his eyes.

Except Aerope cleared her throat and said, "If you two don't mind, I have something to discuss."

"Oh," Ness said. "Of course, Aerope. Go ahead."

"As you've probably noticed, I haven't been doing very well after Arthur's death," Aerope said.

"It's been hard on everyone, Mother," Augie said, in a tone that probably didn't mean to be quite so patronizing.

"It's not a competition," Manny said mildly, and his mother flashed him a grateful look.

"I spoke to Doctor Olsen, and he referred me to a lovely specialist, who says I probably have situational depression," she said. "I just wanted you all to know that I have a diagnosis and I'm getting treatment. So there's no need to worry, but, well. There it is."

"What?" Augie said, and then Ness elbowed him and he went to hug his mother, still looking slightly baffled, but at least doing the appropriate thing. "Uh, I'm glad you're getting help, Mother. Would you like to stay with us in the city for a while?"

"No, dear, don't be silly. I have work."

Ness's lips tightened and she closed her eyes in a slow blink, but she didn't say anything. Manny eyed his sister-in-law with some surprise. There would have been a time when Augie making such an offer without consulting with his wife would have precipitated an instant screaming match, but perhaps they were all growing up.

Augie was certainly looking older. Still burly, still boisterous, but his hair was thinning, and as he released Aerope, Manny had a sudden inkling of what he'd look like as an old man. What they'd both look like, come to that, given the strength of the family genes.

For the first time, he wondered if the mysterious Chris had kids. Did Manny have cousins he didn't know about, more distant branches of the Pelopson tree? Did Chris know about his heritage, or had it been kept secret from him as well?

"You okay?" Ness asked, and Manny blinked.

"Yes, thanks. Just tired. How are you? How are your family?" He'd always gotten on well with Helen and Ness's parents.

"They're fine," Ness said by rote, and then she looked uncomfortable, an expression that was so strange on her that Manny was actually alarmed. "I've been meaning to tell you. I don't know if you've heard, but Helen and Paris had a little girl. They've named her Hermione."

"Oh," Manny said, and waited for the familiar sting.

It didn't come.

"Good for them," he said. "And congratulations on being an aunt, Ness."

"Thank you," Ness said, looking gratified. "I hope I can do it as well as you do."

"Manny's an excellent auntie," Augie said, and tried to ruffle Manny's hair, which ended in the usual scuffle. Manny got away easily, surprised at his own strength. The work he'd been doing in the vineyard was evidently paying off in more than one way.

"Stop it, boys," Aerope said tolerantly. "I'm sure we could all do with a glass of wine."

Manny nursed a beer instead and watched his family talk at and around each other. Being the quiet one in the corner was an easy role for him to fall into. Cassie wouldn't be quiet, if she were here, but she wouldn't be loud, either. She'd be amused by Augie's occasional blustering and unintimidated by Ness's sharp tongue.

Was Chris quiet or loud? Were his imaginary kids? Did *they* have kids, more cousins for Augie's brood?

When Aerope and Ness both declared themselves ready for bed, Augie offered to wash the wine glasses, and sent his brother a sidelong look, inviting him to linger.

"Are you really all right?" he asked Manny, rinsing the soap off. "I thought... It was a big thing you did. Giving up your job to come up here. Especially if Mom wasn't doing well."

With a start, Manny realized his brother was feeling guilty. "It's okay. I like it."

"Really?"

"Really. The loan has been approved, I got the carriage house designs yesterday, and I've been learning more about the vineyard. Jim's a good teacher."

"Who?"

"The foreman? The guy who's been in charge since Granddad died?"

"Oh, right," Augie said. He made a face. "I thought Theo would be trying to teach you."

"Well," Manny said, and cast around for a diplomatic way to put it. "He is trying, in his own way. But he's also going through the grieving process."

"I don't think there's such a thing as being a situational asshole," Augie said, and Manny snorted in agreement.

"You and Ness seem to be getting on well," he ventured.

Augie looked bashful. Which was almost as bizarre as Ness looking uncomfortable, and just as alarming. "We're trying." He rubbed a glass that Manny suspected was already very clean. "I, uh...haven't looked at anyone else for a while. And neither has she."

It shouldn't be shocking when your nominally-monogamous brother admitted he *wasn't* having an affair, but nevertheless, Manny was shocked. After a moment, he said as much, and watched Augie turn dull red.

"It wasn't—" he said, and then, "It's not like I ever stopped loving *her*. It was just, you know, the *temptation*."

"Which you gave into," Manny pointed out. "A lot."

"So did she," Augie protested, but it was automatic response rather than the injured spite he used to employ. "She, uh, we talked at New Year, and she said that as far as she could tell, we had three options. We officially opened the marriage, we divorced, or we committed to monogamy, for real."

"And you chose option C," Manny said. He was trying very hard not to sound dubious. Augie making emotional revelations of any kind was rare, and he didn't want to make him feel bad about that. Even if he, once again, failed to understand his brother's choices.

"Yeah," Augie said, looking defensive. "We're going to counseling, and it's—Like I said. We're trying." He scrubbed the back of his head. "Anyway, Mom said you were fucking the help, so—"

"Mom did not say that," Manny said, resisting, with some effort, the urge to smack his big brother in the nose. "She might have mentioned that I am seeing Cassie, who is the archivist working in the attic."

Augie grinned. "But she's working for *you*, right? You dog."

"We've got an agreement," Manny said, and then when Augie's grin widened, "No, not like that. Stop it."

"Archivist," Augie said, rolling the word around his mouth like a hard candy. "Sounds like a sexy secretary type to me. Does she call you sir?"

"Good night," Manny said, and walked out of the kitchen before Augie could say anything worse. His mother was right. He *was* better at pushing back.

He was on the defense against further innuendo in the morning, but Augie had apparently decided they'd come to a truce. With Theo's help and the forklift from the vineyard, they got the last heavy pieces out of the carriage house and onto the vineyard truck. Manny kept an eye out for green suede record books and missing photo albums, or even the brown archive boxes that crowded the shelves upstairs, but nothing came to light.

"You don't have to check every armoire," Theo said, but it was friendly enough. He kept slapping Augie on the back and making awkward jokes, as good-humored as Manny had seen him since the funeral.

"Did you get much hunting in this season?" Augie asked, gesturing at the gun locker.

Theo shook his head. "Too busy. Shame you can't stay longer. Water-fowl season's over, but we could bag some squirrels."

"Take Manny," Augie suggested, and they both turned to grin at him.

Manny rolled his eyes. "You know I can't shoot. No one bothered to teach me."

"That's because you cried the first time I came home with game," Augie said.

"Cried like a baby," Theo confirmed.

"I was *eight*," Manny said. "I *was* a baby."

Augie's grin sharpened, but Theo nodded. "Fair enough," he said. "I'll teach you, if you like."

"Oh," Manny said. He wasn't at all sure he wanted to learn, but he *was* trying to encourage Theo to give him more opportunities. Anything to make his uncle take him seriously. "Yeah, thank you. That'd be great."

"You're not taking all this stuff to the dump, right?" Augie said, his eyes moving over the furniture and machinery.

Manny shook his head. "No, we got rid of the trash already. These are the pieces we can restore. I'm just moving them to the vineyard warehouse so we can start construction on the suites."

"Who'd you get for that?"

"Local firm, Appleton Construction. They've promised to get it done by June."

"Nice girl, Petra Appleton," Theo said. "She was asking about you the other day, Manny."

Manny flushed. Fortunately, neither of his male relatives noticed. Augie was looking up the prices of vintage armoires on his phone, and Theo was eying a badly scratched table with a wobbly leg.

"Can I have that for the cellar door instead?" he asked.

"Sure," Manny said, with perhaps too much enthusiasm.

"I can put a display on it," Theo said. "Make some changes, in my own way." He glared at Manny, but it was half-hearted.

"I'm going to ask Ness if she wants this armoire," Augie said, and walked away to make a phone call.

"Are you coming over for lunch tomorrow?" Manny asked Theo. "Mom's planning to break out the grill and spoil the grandkids. She's already marinading the ribs."

Theo grunted. "Can't. I'm opening the cellar door tomorrow. First Sunday of spring." He gave Manny a steady look. "It's tradition."

"Of course."

"Jim got me to take another look at that organic stuff. I guess it's worth thinking about for planting next year."

"*Thank you*," Manny said. Jim had been right, it seemed. All Theo had needed was time, and the assurance that not everything would change.

"And you're sticking around," Theo said, with only a faint question.

"Yes," Manny said. He looked around. "I'm here to stay."

"Your dad would be proud of you," Theo said gruffly, and clapped him on the shoulder before he moved away, pretending not to see the tears that had sprung to Manny's eyes.

Manny had never doubted that his father was proud of him, wherever he was and whatever he was doing. But he couldn't help thinking that Theo was right, that Arthur would be especially proud Manny had decided to put down roots in their family's land, using his talents and experience to support the family business. He took a deep breath of air no longer frozen, but merely cool. Some invisible wound was healing inside him.

And there was someone he wanted to thank.

<h1 style="text-align:center">Ask Cassandra</h1>

Dear Cassandra,

It's been over a year since you wrote to me, and I'm not sure if you'll remember me. I'm the guy whose new wife ran away with someone else, six hours after the ceremony. When you first replied, you asked me to keep you and your readers updated. I didn't, because even though your response was exactly what I needed, I was also deeply ashamed when I realized how much of my life I'd spent telling myself the story of being left just after the altar.

I followed your advice. I got therapy. I stopped telling women the story of The One Who Left, and at first I was actually surprised when I got to go on more dates, and they were more fun for everyone.

I mean it, I really was surprised. But since not telling other people the story helped, I stopped telling myself I was the one left behind.

Now I don't even think of myself that way. I think of myself as starting a new chapter in my story. My life has changed a lot since I wrote to you, for both good and bad. But the good things have been pretty good. I left my job, I moved, and I'm working on several new and interesting projects. At first they felt like pushing a boulder uphill, but now I wake up every day excited to get to work.

And I've also met someone I think could be the real deal. It's maybe too soon to say for sure (and too soon to tell her about The One Who Left—see, I've learned!) but she's incredible; smart, funny, amazing in bed, and kind. Genuinely kind, the type of kindness where she doesn't keep things from me because they might hurt my feelings, but acts with honesty because she trusts and respects me.

I don't know if we have a future (there are a few complications) but I do know I want to explore the possibility of one with her. Without your advice, I might never have gotten here, so thank you.

Seriously. Thank you so much.

Yours,

Looking Forward (formerly Left Behind)

Chapter Eleven

"What are you grinning at?" Steph asked. She put a tall glass of hard cider in front of Cassie and sat down in the booth, taking a sip of her own drink. Cassie very much approved of the local hard cider.

"I got a nice email from a former client, thanking me for my help," Cassie said. Her *Agora* editor had forwarded the letter to her with, "Just came in! Love it when this happens. Give me a response and we'll post next week." Isobel had a terrible habit of working through the weekend, but Cassie couldn't complain too much when it came with this kind of pick-me-up.

"I wish I got thank you emails," Steph said. "Not that people aren't grateful when you fix their cars, but they don't write follow-up notes."

Cassie grabbed a napkin and a pen from her purse and scribbled, "thank you for fixing my car xoxo." "There you go."

Steph eyed the crumpled napkin. "Thank you. I'll treasure it always."

"Put in your scrapbook," Cassie suggested. She surveyed the Black Cat, which was in the middle of the Saturday night flow. As far as she could tell, the crowd was evenly split between tourists and townies, who mostly kept a polite distance from each other. They'd been seated in the

"

locals section, so Cassie could only guess that Steph's presence lent her legitimacy.

"Is there a reason most of the locals are sitting further away from the band?" she asked. The band, who were setting up for the advertised 8:30 show, were two men in their thirties and a woman who looked barely old enough to drink.

Steph took a long pull on her drink. "You'll see. Oh, hey." She half-stood and waved at a short red-haired woman in an impressive mini-dress who'd just entered the bar. "Petra! Over here!"

The redhead came over, giving Cassie an inquiring look.

"Cassie Troiades," Cassie said, holding out her hand.

"Petra Appleton," the redhead said, and shook, looking thoughtful. "Yeah, okay, I get it."

"Get what?"

"I asked Manny Pelopson out the other day, and he said sorry, he was seeing someone. So I asked a few questions and found out you'd gone to Pie in the Sky on Thursday night."

"Wow," Cassie said. "I don't know if I'm more impressed or intimidated."

Petra shrugged. "Small town gossip is no joke."

"Petra, don't freak her out," Steph said.

"I'm not freaked out," Cassie assured her. "I'm professionally nosy. Out of interest, what else do you know about me?"

Petra ticked items off her fingers. "You went to Maenad College for undergrad, Steph fixed your car your first day here, your last job was down south, you normally live in the city, you make good cornbread, you have two younger sisters and a younger brother, and you told Isaac Corey where to stick it. About time. There's a rumor that you and Steph are hooking up, but I figured that was just wishful thinking from my informant."

Cassie laughed. "I didn't make the cornbread, only served it, and I'm not hooking up with Steph. Otherwise, completely accurate."

"I'm trying to make it with one of her sisters," Steph said helpfully. "Cassie says neither one's available, but I live in optimism. When are you going to invite them up here?"

"I...wasn't planning to," Cassie said, but now that she thought about it, it wasn't a bad idea. Laodice would swoon over the romance of a small town in spring-time, and Xena was always on the lookout for good locations to shoot content. Tantalus could certainly profit from the publicity.

"You should definitely invite them up for the carriage house opening," Petra said.

"Oh, you're that Appleton! Manny said you'd done an amazing job on the bid."

"And it's going to come with a fat bonus for finishing by the end of May," Petra said, looking smug. "So invite your sisters up in June."

"That sounds good," Cassie said, and caught another thoughtful look from Petra. "Is there something on my nose?"

"Nope. Okay. You seem like an upfront kind of person, so I'm just going to ask straight out. Are you planning to stick around?"

"It's a three-month contract," Cassie said.

"So you're going back to the city?" Petra persisted. "Are you and Manny going for a long-distance relationship, or is this a short-term thing? Don't get me wrong, I don't hit on people who are taken. But the pickings are kind of slim around here and Manny's a great guy. I don't want to miss my shot if I have one."

"Petra!"

"Steph, we're grown-ups. It's a reasonable question."

"Okay," Cassie said, and put her hands flat on the table. "Give me a minute to think about this."

Petra stayed quiet as Cassie organized her thoughts, which won her a few points. Steph watched apprehensively, obviously regretting waving Petra over.

"Right," Cassie said. "The answer is, that *isn't* a reasonable question. Because you want to go out with Manny, not me, but you're asking me, not him, which is kind of going behind his back, and also implies you think he wouldn't react well to the question. And people aren't library books or restaurant tables. You can't call dibs on the next turn. If Manny and I stop seeing each other, that'll be between us. If you and Manny start dating after that, that'll be between you. You can't triangulate with me for a green light. Okay?"

"Huh," Petra said. "Yeah, okay." She sat quietly for a moment. "I'm sorry."

Cassie nodded. "Okay. What are you drinking?"

Petra looked taken aback, but pleased. "Vodka soda."

Cassie scooted out of the booth and started towards the bar. Behind her, she heard Steph's voice go sharp, and smiled. Petra probably deserved a talking-to, but she didn't want to be the one to deliver it. And it spoke well of the woman that she'd listened to what Cassie had to say, and then apologized.

Also, Manny had one hundred percent not mentioned that a hot and forthright woman had asked him out, and Cassie was trying to sort out her own feelings about that. He'd turned her down, so it didn't violate their agreements about not cheating or dishonesty, but it turned out it was something she would have wanted to know.

Did she *want* more with Manny?

When she listened to herself, she had to conclude that the answer was *yes*.

Ugh. She was going to have to be *brave*.

This was the problem with being an advice columnist. She was almost obliged to act on the advice she would have given herself—although, as Steph had so astutely pointed out, that advice would have begun with *don't sleep with your boss*.

Honestly, the part where she was starting to fall for him probably served her right.

The bar was crowded, and it was a minute before Laura could take her order. "Sorry," she said, wiping her hands on her apron. "What can I get you?"

"Two vodka sodas and two ciders, please," Cassie said. If the wait was any indication, they'd all be better off with double orders. She tipped Laura, and gathered the drinks, watching her step as she started back towards the booth.

The singer let out an unearthly wail.

Cassie jumped, but didn't drop her burden. She did wince when the guitarist came in with a discordant tumble of harsh notes, but by the time the drummer joined him, she'd braced herself against further surprises. The townie reluctance to sit near the band was explained.

A few claps and whoops were starting near the stage as some of the out-of-towners moved in, apparently specifically there for whatever this was. The tourists who'd come for a drink or two shared startled glances. Those with seats near the stage started looking behind them.

Cassie walked carefully, but she didn't have eyes in the back of her head, so when someone walked right into her from behind, she stumbled heavily. The glasses didn't fall and smash, but most of the liquid jumped out of them, tipping directly down her front.

"Hey!" a masculine voice said. "Watch where you're going!"

"*Excuse* me?" Cassie said, and turned on him. "You walked into *me*."

And then she froze, because the face glaring at her was directly from her nightmares.

The year before, Cassie—or rather, Cassandra—had answered a letter from a woman in serious distress. She was accidentally pregnant, but had decided to have and keep the child, partly because she'd believed herself in love with the father. The second she'd showed him the positive test, he'd proposed. She'd said yes. He'd showered her with attention, encouraged her to quit her job, and promised to take care of her.

And then he'd changed. His rich grandfather wasn't pleased that his only grandson had knocked up a stripper, but he was clearly equally unwilling to miss out on a possible heir to what turned out to be a very impressive fortune. The fiancé, she thought egged on by the grandfather, had tried to get her to sign a terrible prenup that would give her no support and limited custody in the event of a divorce. He'd sulked for days when she refused to sign. When she'd mentioned at a family dinner that she meant to study and look for work in a new field after the baby was born, the grandfather had been patronizing, then furious. Apparently, mothers in his family didn't work.

She'd told him that the mother in *her* family would.

Then things got stranger. Her phone wasn't always in the same place she'd left it. She'd started wondering if she was being followed in the street. She wanted the fun boyfriend back and a loving father for her baby, and maybe it was all just pre-wedding weirdness, but she was seriously starting to question the wisdom of the marriage. What should she do?

Cassandra had told her to dump him, immediately and unequivocally, with some harsh words for both the fiancé and his grandfather. Cassie had been personally worried as the weeks went by without any response, but eventually she'd received another email from the young woman, who'd just walked out of her rehearsal dinner. The grandfather had made a threat that implied she was an obstacle who could be removed, and she'd left. She had no job, no support, she was just a few weeks from giving birth and had no idea of what she'd do next, but she was still grateful to Cassandra for the advice.

The next day, the society pages had been full of the broken engagement of Cressida O'Brien to millionaire playboy Dammond Argive. And some enterprising internet sleuth had drawn parallels between that dramatic exit, and the *Agora* column of a few months before.

Dammond had tried to sue—first Cassandra directly, then Olympus Publishing when he couldn't find out who "Cassandra" was. He'd demanded that at the very least, the columnist should be fired.

Cassie had never been so relieved to be anonymous, but she'd fully expected to lose her job. Instead, the newly-appointed CEO of Olympus Publishing had gone into bat for her. Hera Rheczack had not only protected Cassie's identity, but her only steady source of income.

And now Dammond Argive was inches away, glaring at her. He was tall and well-built, with an expensively "casual" haircut and crafted stubble. If not for his reputation and the permanent sneer stamped upon his finely chiseled features, she might have thought he was handsome.

As it was, she froze. The singer wailed again, in an odd echo of her internal alarm.

"You stopped right in front of me," he snapped.

She hadn't. She'd been moving slowly, because of the drinks, but she had been moving. Evidently, it hadn't been fast enough for him, because he'd ploughed right into her back.

"I—" she said. "No, I didn't."

"Whatever," Dammond said dismissively, and she could see him getting ready to shove past her. Then his eyes moved over her shoulder and stopped, arrested.

"You okay, Cassie?" Petra said, and Dammond's face flipped from surly to charming in the second it took him to assess the diminutive redhead.

"Your friend and I bumped into each other, but it's all okay," he said smoothly. "Here, let me buy you new drinks."

"No, thanks," Petra said, taking two of the glasses from Cassie so that she had more freedom of movement. Cassie was beginning to recover from the original shock. Dammond had no idea who she was. Not only was he ignorant of Cassandra's identity, but Cassie Troiades was a complete non-entity in herself.

"I insist," Dammond said. "Can't have you going thirsty."

Petra ignored him, which instantly gained her more points, and looked at Cassie instead. "Oh damn, girl, you're soaked."

Cassie looked down at her splashed sweater. She liked clothes that made the most of her curves, but the wet wool clinging to her skin was both uncomfortable and unflattering. "I think I'd better visit the ladies room."

"I'll send a bottle to your table," Dammond said, still very obviously talking to Petra. "Or maybe you'd like to come drink with me?"

"Maybe another time, Dammond," Petra said. She put the drinks down on a nearby table, and hustled Cassie into the bathroom.

The spill didn't look any better under the brighter lights, and Cassie was beginning to smell like a distillery. She stripped down to her bra and dabbed herself mostly dry with paper towels while Petra attended to the sweater.

"Do you know that guy?" she asked, hoping she sounded casual.

Petra rolled her eyes. "Dammond Argive. Rich asshole from the city."

"He wasn't talking like he knew you."

"Oh, we've met three or four times. He just hasn't bothered to remember my name. He hits on me every time he sees me and then forgets I exist."

"Uh, wow. I've known you five minutes, and you're not exactly unmemorable."

"Sure, but you're not Dammond. There are babies with a better sense of object permanence. I'm not sure he grasps that other people are real when he's not around."

"Damn," Cassie said mildly.

"Sorry. He just pisses me off. We get a bunch of obnoxious trust fund kids every summer, but Dammond's always been the worst. A few years ago he started coming first thing in spring instead. He claims Weeping Rock is better without the tourists, and is totally oblivious about the part where he is one." She brightened. "On the other hand, he probably has sent a bottle of the good stuff to our table. Here you go, I think this is as dry as I can get it."

Cassie took the sweater, which had gone from dripping to merely damp, and struggled back into it. "How long do you have to live here before you're not a tourist anymore?"

"Three generations or so," Petra said. She looked thoughtfully at Cassie. "Unless you marry in."

"Okay," Cassie said. She wasn't sure whether Petra was warning her off or encouraging her, but either way she didn't want to have that conversation. "I think I'm good to go."

Dammond *had* sent the bottle, and Steph had already poured them all a glass of something that tasted like liquid sunshine. The band was playing a new song, something less shrieky, though there were still weird harmonies and dissonant chords. Every now and then, the listeners at the front would whoop or clap at something musically significant, although Cassie couldn't figure out what they were responding to. She began paying more attention, and blinked at a sudden moment of convergence, where the singer's voice shimmered above and through a complicated guitar glissando, like the moon passing behind thin cloud.

"Wait, are these guys actually good?" she said, taken aback.

"Yes," Petra said promptly, just as quickly as Steph said, "No."

Cassie laughed.

"Well, they're geniuses," Steph conceded. "Lexie who runs the music department at the high school explained their music to me once, and it all made sense while she was talking, but it turns out I still don't like the sound."

"My cousin might like them," Cassie said. "She's a musician." Paris and the Archers made most of their money at corporate gigs, playing while people ate canapes and hobnobbed, but Paris's own tastes were more wide-ranging. She'd taken teenaged Cassie to more than one baffling jazz show before Cassie had been forced to admit that when she'd said she liked jazz, she'd meant the popular big band songs, not avant-garde improvisation full of musical references and jokes she couldn't even recognize, much less appreciate.

She leaned out of the booth and snapped a picture of the band's poster, helpfully on display, and sent it to Paris.

"Heads up," Steph said, and Cassie leaned back just in time for Dammond Argive to show up again. This time he had an entourage, two men about his own age who had the same air of unthinking entitlement, and an older man in a dark suit who was practically screaming "bodyguard" with every sweeping glance around the bar.

"So," Dammond said, smiling at Petra. "Are you enjoying the champagne?"

"Yes, thanks," Petra said, and her voice was cool and unconcerned, but Cassie could feel her leaning further back into the booth.

"And my sweater isn't damaged beyond repair," Cassie said helpfully, and angled her body to block Petra more thoroughly. "Apology accepted!" She was ignoring the part where Dammond hadn't actually apologized.

Dammond's eyes flicked over Cassie, paused a moment on her breasts, and then went back to Petra. "Have we met before?" he asked. "You seem so familiar, but I'm sure I would have remembered *you*."

"I like *your* sweater," Cassie said, and leaned into him with clumsy enthusiasm. "And your tie! Cool crest thingy!" She flicked the knot of his tie.

"It's my old school tie," Dammond said, looking more irritated than smooth. "So, I was wondering…"

"Oh my gosh, *vintage*! I love vintage, don't you?" Cassie beamed up at him, letting her eyes go slightly unfocused behind their glasses. "This place has just the *cutest* antiques."

The two younger men were exchanging smirks, and Dammond was clearly aware of it. He was wavering, trying to figure out if the potential of hooking up with Petra was worth the annoyance of dealing with this drunk airhead. Petra was silent, and Cassie caught the movement as the redhead started scrolling through her phone, apparently bored.

Dammond looked thwarted, but he might need a push.

"Where did you go to school?" Cassie said, and tapped the tie again. It was... Wait, it was familiar. Hot damn. "I went to Maenad for college, but before that I was at Wilios High. Charge, Stallions, charge! Did you play football?"

"Lacrosse," Dammond said, and pulled back from her waving hand. "At Argos Academy."

"I bet you looked cute in the uniform," Cassie said, and watched Dammond realize, with some outrage, that *she* was hitting on *him*.

"Okay, so...have a good night, ladies," he said, and walked off. One of his friends was barely concealing a snicker, and the other wasn't bothering to hide it. The bodyguard gave Cassie a cool look and she shivered—that man hadn't been fooled by the bubbly idiot act—but followed Dammond back to his own booth.

"That was amazing," Steph said. "It looked like all your brains had fallen out the hole in the back of your head."

"Kill 'em with kindness," Cassie said, and took another sip of her champagne. It tasted like victory. Dammond's party were gathering their things and moving out of the bar, loudly declaring it to be lame.

"I owe you one," Petra said, and Cassie shook her head, dismissing the offer.

That crest had looked *really* familiar. She wasn't positive it was the same one, but it had reminded her of the crest on the blazer of twelve-year-old Chris in the school photo, carefully taped into the back of Perry Pelopson's secret record book. She flicked out her phone and looked up Argos Academy.

A private prep school, of course, from K-12, promising graduate success to the children of the well-heeled. She looked carefully at the crest emblazoned on the front page. She'd have to check the photo, but she thought it *might* be the same. And schools meant records. Schools meant yearbooks and alumni registries and possibly current and up-to-date contact details for their graduates. They wouldn't want to give Cassie most of that, but at the very least she could probably get a last name, and if she was lucky, and it wasn't Smith or Jones, she could start trawling social media and public records. She had a subscription to a database a lot of freelance archivists found helpful, and if that didn't work, she could ask Laodice a few questions, because Olympus had access to a *lot* of databases.

She could do this. She could find Manny's uncle, and maybe put Aerope's fears to rest.

She looked up, once again aware of herself and where she was, and blinked at her companions, who had clearly been politely ignoring her while she dove down the research rabbit hole.

"Sorry," she said.

"Whatever that was, it looked intense," Petra said.

"Dammond Argive doesn't know it, but he just did me a massive favor," Cassie said. "I feel like celebrating. Who wants to get drunk?"

***

Jim and Theo were right; the thaw was here. Manny looked at the crisp blue sky and huffed a plume of visible breath into the cold late morning air.

"Are you a dragon?" Orestes asked.

Manny looked at his nephew. Orestes was eight, old enough to know dragons were make-believe, but maybe young enough to wish otherwise.

"No, of course not," Electra said, with all the confidence of ten. "Dragons aren't *real*."

Geni came out to join them on the back patio, blowing on her hands. "Mom says that if you guys are going to run around outside, you need to put more clothes on."

"Okay," Orestes said.

"*I'm* not cold," Electra said. "Besides, Uncle Manny's setting up the grill, and that will be warm, so there."

Geni rolled her eyes. "I'm just telling you what Mom said."

"Orestes can go and get his coat," Electra said magnanimously, and watched avidly as Manny filled the grill with charcoal and set it alight. Manny kept an eye on her. Electra wasn't always the best at risk management.

After a while, she tucked her bare hands into her armpits. "Do you miss Grandpa?" she asked.

"Every day," Manny said.

Electra nodded. "I don't miss him every day, but I think my dad does."

"That's sort of how it works," Manny said gently.

And Electra turned horrified eyes on him and said, "One day my dad will *die.*"

Manny instinctively looked back through the patio door, but he was the only adult in sight.

"And then *I'll* miss *him* every day," she continued, looking aggrieved. "That's not fair!"

"No," Manny said. "It's not fair."

Electra stared at him, jaw set stubbornly, and he had the absurd feeling that he might offer to fight death for her, or something equally impossible and stupid, just so that she'd never have to deal with this stuff.

"It won't happen for a long, long time, long after you're a grown-up," he said instead, but that wasn't much better, because he was an adult, and so was Augie, and their mother was older than both of them, and they were all still having a tough time with bereavement. "I—Do you want a hug or something?"

"No," Electra said, and then she darted in and hugged him anyway, her skinny little arms barely making it around his body, and her face pressed against his side. Manny patted her springy curls. He felt completely helpless, but apparently this was enough, because after a moment Electra let go.

"I'm going to help Orestes find his coat," she announced, and ran back inside.

Manny wondered if he should be following to give one of her parents a quick update on the conversation, but he heard an engine and the crunch of gravel, and a second later, Cassie's car parked in the back parking lot.

She got out and turned towards the house, then looked at the guesthouse. Then back at the big house again, indecision clear on her face.

Manny realized that she hadn't spotted him yet, standing still on the patio, and waved. "Hi," he called, and she spun and waved back.

He covered the distance between them at a quick walk, happy to see her in a way that felt both completely natural and utterly terrifying. Closer up, she looked a little rough, her eyes bloodshot and her hair less bouncy than usual.

"Good night?" he said, grinning.

"Oh yes," she said, her voice a little husky. "Steph introduced me to Petra Appleton. Damn, that woman can drink."

"Petra? Uh, did she happen to say—"

"—That she'd asked you out? Yes." Cassie coughed, and reached back into her car for a water bottle. "It's cool. I have been given provisional approval." She drank thirstily, and Manny watched her throat bob. "You haven't spoken to your family yet?"

"Not yet, no."

"Okay, good. I didn't mean to come back before this evening, but last night I came across something that might be helpful for our investigation, and wondered if I could check the archives. Is that okay?"

"Sure, it's fine," Manny said, more curious than anything else. He rather liked the sound of *our* investigation. "My niece just had the epiphany that all mortals must die. Nothing else can be even a little bit inconvenient for at least ten minutes."

Cassie laughed, and then winced.

"Not that you're inconvenient," Manny added. "Just how hungover are you?"

"Someone is ringing a bell in the back of my skull," she said mournfully.

"Then I'll have mercy," Manny said, and snuck her through the house without trying to introduce her to any of his louder family members. Chrys and Electra were discussing the rules of a game at the top of their lungs, and Cassie winced again as they passed the living room.

Once they got to the attic, she went straight into the archive room, and came out with the now-familiar green record book, opening it to the page where the twelve-year-old Chris beamed from his school photo.

"It *is* the same crest," she said, comparing the photo to something on her phone.

"I think you're going to have to take me back a couple of steps," Manny said, and Cassie explained.

"Oh hell, I've met Dammond," Manny said. "He's a good customer, unfortunately—buys a lot at the cellar door."

"Well, he did us a favor. A first name and a birth year isn't much, but a school is a *lot*," she said. "I'll drive to the city tomorrow and see what I can get out of the Argos Academy."

"In person?"

Cassie nodded. "No school administrator worth their pay is going to give me anything over the phone or via email, but you'd be surprised what I can charm out of people one-on-one."

"No, I wouldn't," Manny said, and Cassie smiled at him.

It was an amazing smile, *she* was amazing, and he couldn't help but lean over the table and gently press his mouth to hers. She kissed him back, her lips soft and her breath minty. Manny melted into her for a moment then pulled back, resting his forehead on hers.

"I don't think we're a ten-week fling," he said quietly.

Cassie's cheeks were stained pink. "I don't think so either," she said. "We should probably talk about that."

"Yes. Tonight?"

Cassie nodded, still blushing. Manny grinned at her, delighted by how shy she suddenly was, by how much he liked her, by the bubbles of joy rising up in his throat. She liked him too, and they were going to talk about making this real.

"Come and meet my family," he said, and Cassie tucked the record book into her bag and came downstairs with him without protest.

Most of the family were gathered on the back patio, where Aerope was guarding the grill against Augie's attempted incursions.

Augie stopped trying to tell his mother what to do as soon as he saw Cassie, shaking her hand with firm bonhomie and sneaking Manny sly looks he obviously thought were subtle. Chrys hid behind her father's leg, and Orestes and Electra were politely puzzled by the appearance of this strange grown-up, but Geni had obviously put a few things together, and she shook Cassie's hand with solemn good manners and said it was very nice to meet her.

Ness came out of the kitchen then, carrying a tray of bread rolls in one hand and an enormous salad bowl in the other, and she gave Cassie a raised eyebrow as she set them down. "Hello," she said.

Cassie was looking faintly puzzled. "Hello," she said. "We've met, haven't we?"

Ness frowned. "You do look familiar."

"Oh!" Cassie said, and snapped her fingers. "Yes, you're Ness Laconia, aren't you? You work at Olympus Publishing? Your sister Helen is married to my cousin Paris."

Ness's eyes went wide. "Your cousin is Paris Chen?"

Aerope dropped the tongs.

"Yes. She introduced us when she played at the Winter Ball last year." Cassie looked uncertainly at Ness, and then at Manny.

Manny stared back at her without a single useful response forming in his brain. There was a distant ringing sensation in his ears.

"It was a brief introduction, no reason you'd remember," Cassie said. "And of course I'm not wearing a ballgown right now." She plucked at her coat and made a deliberately rueful face, trying to smooth over the awkward moment. Manny's heart hurt for her.

"My sister works at Olympus, actually. Laodice Troiades? She works in the Bridal—" Cassie stopped and looked around. "Okay, what's going on? What did I say?"

Augie took a step forward, his face dark, and that shook Manny out of his trance. He had to speak up before Augie could say anything awful, because Ness would defend Helen, and Augie would rage about Paris, and this was not the first impression he'd wanted Cassie to have of his family.

"Ness's sister was engaged to me first," he said. "Helen left me for Paris. Your cousin?"

Cassie looked taken aback. "I'm sorry," she said tentatively.

"Oh, that's the nice version," Augie said, his face like a thundercloud. "Paris eloped with Helen, six hours *after* she'd married my brother."

"Be quiet, August," Aerope said sharply.

"Aunt Helen and Uncle Manny were *married*?" Electra asked, and Manny could have felt sorry for his brother at the moment where he realized he'd just shared an inconvenient truth with his children, but his own brain was still buzzing.

"Nice, Augie," Ness said bitterly, and she turned on her heel and went inside the house.

"Really married?" Electra asked.

Aerope bent down by her granddaughter. "Only for a little while, a long time ago," she said reassuringly. "Before you were born. Shall we go inside and play a game?"

"But I want to know about the wedding," Electra said, twisting to look at Manny.

"Go inside with your grandmother," Augie said flatly, and handed Chrys to Aerope. Geni took Orestes's hand and tugged, and Electra gave her father a dubious look and followed them all inside, looking over her shoulder.

"I didn't know," Cassie said faintly. "Neither of them ever mentioned it."

"Well, they wouldn't, would they," Augie said, sneering. "Helen strung Manny along like a dog on a leash, and then Paris snapped her fingers and Helen wrote him a Dear John note on the back of a receipt. She ran away still wearing her wedding dress. Not the kind of thing you brag about if you've got any decency at all."

"Augie, please," Manny said.

"No!" Augie wheeled on him. "You're my little brother, and that was supposed to be the happiest day of your life, and they fucking *ruined* it. You *hired* Paris for that wedding band gig. She knew whose wedding she was playing at and she knew she should have said no. Helen had every damn opportunity to tell you, and she wrote you a shitty—" He broke off. "You're not like me," he said, almost plaintively. "You're *good*. You didn't deserve that."

"It wasn't about what I deserve," Manny said, touched despite himself. Augie had been very, very angry that night, but Manny had thought it was wounded familial pride. That Augie had been upset *for* him was a new revelation.

"When did all this happen?" Cassie asked.

"Over a decade ago," Manny said wearily. "It's okay. You didn't do anything wrong. I just wasn't expecting that connection."

"Over a decade," Cassie repeated. Her face went smooth, hiding some reaction he couldn't read. "I see. Well. I think I'd better head to the guesthouse after all."

"No, don't go," Augie said gruffly. "I'm sorry I yelled. Manny's right, it's not your fault."

"Still," Cassie said, and took off at what was very nearly a run.

"You should go after her," Augie said, and Manny turned to look at him.

"That's what you said about Helen," he said. "Have you ever thought about what could have happened if we'd actually found her?"

Augie frowned. "She owed you more than a note."

"A truck full of half-drunk idiots after two women, Augie," Manny said. "No matter what she owed me, that was a spectacularly bad idea."

"We wouldn't have—"

"How would you feel if it were Geni?" Manny said, and he could see that hit home. Augie's frown deepened.

"Well," he said, sounding less certain about it. "You're just one guy now. And Cassie probably thinks we're all mad at her."

"I'll give her some time," Manny said, and went back inside, climbing the two flights of stairs to his office, feeling as if concrete had been poured into his bones.

Theo had been wise to skip the family barbecue after all.

***

Cassie had half-expected Manny to follow her, but she'd been grateful he hadn't. She needed time to process all that information—the revelation about Helen and Paris, and her own realization that Manny had to be Left Behind, the guy she'd so blithely advised to *not* tell women about Helen.

She had to consider her options and her own next best steps.

And most of all, she'd needed to get away from that stricken look on Manny's face.

She'd felt sorry for Left Behind, but she *knew* Manny. She knew how loyal he was, how kind-hearted, how endlessly willing he was to sacrifice himself to help his family. Helen's betrayal must have struck him deep in all his most vulnerable points.

Was it better or worse that she knew exactly how badly that betrayal had hurt him? Was it better or worse that she knew he was trying to move on?

Huddled by the fire, she read over the email her editor had forwarded last night until the words imprinted themselves into her memory. *I've met someone. Could be the real deal. She's incredible. A future.*

He'd written *she acts with honesty. She trusts and respects me.*

She hadn't known, before. Hiding behind the anonymous shield of "Cassandra" had been all right when it kept her safe and protected her from people like Dammond Argive.

But keeping that part of herself from Manny, now... That would be an act of deception. He thought she was honest. She had to respect his right to know he'd revealed himself to her. She had to trust he'd keep her secret.

Cassie tried to plot out the conversation in her head, find scripts for what she wanted to say, pinpoint the possible pressure points and awkward moments, but it was all an impossible whirl of fleeting thought and heightened emotion in her head. She couldn't give herself the advice she needed. For once in her life, she had no idea of what might happen next.

What happened next was that in the late afternoon of the first Sunday of spring, Manny knocked on her door.

"Hey," he said, looking tired. "I wasn't sure if you still wanted to talk. Feel free to tell me to get lost."

"No, come in," Cassie said. She heard the awkward formality in her own voice and hated it.

Manny seemed equally awkward. He took his time taking off his boots, arranging them neatly under the coat hooks in the entrance, and then sitting carefully in the armchair by the wood stove that had become *his* chair. "So," he said. "I guess the good news is that the working relationship wasn't actually the problem,"

Cassie tried to smile. It felt fake. "This sucks," she said. "I can't believe your ex betrayed you for my favorite cousin."

"Paris is your *favorite* cousin?" Manny shook his head. "Sorry. Never mind."

Cassie steeled herself. "And actually, the work thing is kind of a problem. Except it's my work thing. Okay. I'm going to tell you something that only five other people know, and trust that you understand why that is."

"Okay," Manny said cautiously.

"You know I do freelance writing sometimes?"

"You've mentioned it."

"Right. Well. One of those jobs is actually under a pen name. I write for a popular advice column in *Agora* called—"

"No," Manny said, and he was so *smart*, she could see him leaping to the correct conclusion and working through the implications.

"Yes," she said miserably. "I'm Cassandra."

Manny took a deep breath in through his nose and sat very still for a moment. "So you… Right. I wrote to you. And you know that. Now that you've *heard* the story, you know I'm Left Behind."

"I figured you had to be. Something like that can't have happened to too many people."

"I meant to tell you about Helen tonight," Manny said. He covered his face with his hands. "I would have told you before! We both would have known everything, long before this. But you—Cassandra you—told me *not* to."

"I know*!*" Cassie said. "It feels like one of those awful prophecies that come true *because* of the prophecy. Like a king hears that his son will kill him and marry his wife, so he exposes him on a mountain top to die, and twenty years later a boy raised by shepherds accidentally kills a strange man on the road and goes to a city and marries the newly widowed queen. But the king would never have exposed the prince in the first place if it hadn't been for the prophecy."

The fire popped and crackled in the silence. Cassie kept her eyes trained on her hands, lightly linked in her lap.

"Okay," Manny said. "Well, on a base level, I'd say that infanticide is never a good idea."

Cassie tried to smile at the joke, but it felt feeble.

"But *your* advice was actually good," Manny continued. "The real prophecy was that if I stopped telling myself and others that I was left behind, I'd stop building my life around that story. And I have. You were right."

Cassie looked up. Manny was looking at her steadily.

"Did you already know that?" he asked. "I sent a follow-up email yesterday. Did you—Does an editor screen those or, or is it sitting unopened in an inbox somewhere, or—"

"I've read it," Cassie said. "My editor passes on the good follow-ups as soon as she sees them. She knows they cheer me up. I *was* cheered up."

"Well, that's just fine," Manny said, sounding frustrated. "You now know all my secret feelings. Okay. Cassie, I like you a lot. Do you want to be with me? I'm staying here, and I know your job involves a lot of travel, but we could try long distance, or commuting or… We could work something out, if we wanted to. Do you want to?"

"I don't know," Cassie said. "I like you too. Yesterday, I would have said yes. Today… Knowing this now makes me uncertain." She scrunched up her face. "And I'm really not good with uncertainty. I don't handle things well when I'm not *sure*. That's my baggage, not yours, but it makes things harder for both of us."

"I don't want to stop seeing you because my ex married your favorite cousin," Manny said.

"Your ex *ran away* with my cousin. It's a big deal." She frowned. "And by the way, how come you never mentioned how beautiful your ex was? I've *met* Helen. She's drop-dead gorgeous. If you'd said something like, *my ex is the most beautiful woman in the entire world* I might have worked it out a lot earlier."

"I guess I got used to it," Manny said, and she tilted her head at him. "Okay, fine, yes, she's stunning. But it's always the first thing anyone ever says about her, and usually the last. It used to drive me crazy, all the people who stopped there, like her beauty was the *only* thing about her worth noticing. After a while, I sort of made a point out of not saying it. Besides, she's beautiful, but she's not you."

"Oh," Cassie said helplessly. How was she supposed to *not* fall for him, when he said things like that? "But wouldn't it be awkward? The cousin thing?"

"It's already about as awkward as it can be," Manny said wearily. "My brother is married to Helen's sister. Paris and Helen are aunts to my nieces and nephews. We sort of dodge anything where we might spend the holidays together, and Paris is never going to be *my* favorite relative, but I promise, being with you wouldn't add much to that awkwardness. At least, not on my side."

"Right," Cassie said. "But doesn't it feel like a fundamentally terrible idea? It's so complicated, there's so much history..."

"If you want out, say so," Manny said. His voice was steady, where hers wobbled.

"I—" Cassie said, and then stopped. She *didn't* want out. She just didn't know if she was brave enough, solid enough to see it through. "I think I need more time."

"That makes sense."

"I'm going to the city tomorrow anyway." She stuck her jaw out. "Because I'm damned if I'll let our personal drama get in the way of solving this mystery."

Manny's smile was fond. "You wouldn't be you if you did."

"So I think, while I'm there, I'll stay with my sister for a few days. I might call my cousin. And I'll do some thinking."

Manny nodded. "Of course, you'll want to check my version of events."

"No," Cassie said. "I trust that you told me the truth. But I do want to know their perspective." She looked miserably at Manny. "I'm sorry. I know this isn't what you were hoping for. I wouldn't blame you if *you* wanted out."

Manny reached across the space between them, and she gave him her hand. He ran his thumb over the inside of her wrist, and she remembered all the other times he'd touched her, in desire, in comfort, in grief. Remembered the way he'd panted her name in her ear, curled behind her in the dark bed cave, driving her wild with his hands, his mouth, her name on his lips.

He'd said her name like it was something precious.

"Cassie," he said now, and she nearly broke, because even when she was pulling away, she couldn't help but be drawn back in. "I'll give you time, if you need it. I can't say I'll wait forever. But I can wait a while. Because you told me to stop telling the story of being left behind, and I did, and now I'm ready to let it go for good.

"I mean, yeah, Helen did something shitty. I reacted badly. It was all a big fucking mess. But it was years ago, and she's happy, and now I can be happy for her. And I want to find that kind of happiness for myself. I want a new story, Cassie. Or at least a new chapter. And I want to write it with you.

"So take some time. I'll be here when you decide. Whatever you decide."

Cassie's vision had gone blurry. She blinked hard, and felt the moisture spill onto her cheeks. "Thank you," she whispered. It wasn't a strong enough phrase. It didn't do enough to convey her gratitude, or her regret for her own cowardice.

They stood up and went to the door together, still holding hands, and Manny kissed her cheek before he left.

Cassie didn't kiss him back. If she had, she might never have had the strength to go.

Chapter Twelve

Manny had been looking forward to his meeting with Petra that Monday morning. He needed a way to occupy himself while Cassie did her investigation in the city, and focusing on the renovation seemed like the best possible distraction.

Unusually, Petra was late.

By the time half an hour had gone by with no word, Manny was seriously concerned. He took his phone to one of the better reception spots and checked it. There was a terse "on my way" text from five minutes ago, which meant Petra was going to be nearly an hour late.

So he was already braced for bad news when she drove up in her cherry red Prius and hurried across to him, her face grim.

"I'm sorry, Manny," was the first thing she said.

"Just tell me."

"I went to put the order in for the steel girders you'll need, and our supplier informed me they were raising their prices, as of today."

He flinched, and Petra scowled. "I tried to check in with another vendor, and they said they couldn't help me. Then I started calling around to check on the other materials—that's why I'm late—and it turns out a lot of suppliers are raising their prices today."

"It's April," Manny said, feeling dazed. "The financial year—I should have guessed."

Petra was looking murderous. "But they shouldn't all be doing it at the same time, across the same materials. I think there's been some collusion on prices, and that means there's probably a massive antitrust suit coming from the big construction companies—but that doesn't help us, or you."

"What's the increase?"

"Across your budget? 12.4 percent."

"*Shit*," Manny said. "I budgeted a twenty percent blow-out, but if a chunk of that is already taken by material increases…"

Petra grimaced. "Twenty percent should have been plenty. We've got a solid long-term crew, so we don't deal with much in the way of labor shortages or new hiring costs. I can usually keep blowout down around twelve percent, the best you'll find anywhere around here. But that puts you at just under a twenty-five percent increase on project costs. And I can't guarantee material prices won't increase again."

They shared a look of complete understanding.

"I'm fucked," Manny said.

"Can you talk to the bank?" Petra asked intently. "Simon dragging his feet on the loan agreement delayed you long enough for that price change to kick in."

"I'd like to wring his neck, but no, I don't think Midas will take that into account. They were pretty clear there was nothing else there for me."

"Another bank?"

"Maybe." Manny scrubbed at his face. "Shit. Sorry, Petra, I have to think about this. Run some numbers."

Sympathy looked strange on Petra's sharp features, but she clearly meant it. "We can refund your deposit. Or hold it in escrow while you come up with solutions. Maybe you could try for a more low-budget refurbishment?"

"There are plenty of low-budget places in town," Manny said. "I'm aiming for a specific demographic, and they won't be happy with anything that looks economical. But I'll take another look at the plans."

Petra nodded. "Okay. Well, let me know." For the first time, she took a look at the carriage house exterior, at the sturdy walls and dark wooden windowsills. "What a shame. It would have been amazing."

"That it would," Manny said. He saw Petra off and went back to his office, mind grinding on the problem. What could he do to save the dream?

***

The drive into the city hadn't been too bad, except that it left Cassie with far too much time to think. She parked in the visitor's spot at Argos Academy and tried to pull herself together.

At least she looked like someone who knew what she was doing. She'd taken some care with her hair and makeup this morning, and deliberately gone for a more formal look. Her blazer and skirt weren't a matched set, but they at least suggested a suit, and she'd ditched her comfortable snow boots for the dark tights and T-bar heels again.

She checked her lipstick, smoothed a couple of flyaways, and walked into the school reception as if she had every right to be there.

"Hello," she said, leveling her best professional smile at the receptionist. "I'm researching some Argos Academy alumni for a story about the school's history, and I'm hoping you can help me."

Ten minutes later, she was tucked into a back room in the school library with decades of yearbooks and a cup of coffee the receptionist had eagerly brought in for her. Sure, she'd lied just a tiny bit, but her press credentials were real, and who knew, she might actually turn some of this into the puff piece she was hinting at.

She found what she was looking for almost immediately. Chris Ipith smiled up at her from multiple pages in the 1972 yearbook. He'd won several science prizes that year and played soccer in what appeared to be a non-competitive but truly adorable junior team. She went back through the years, and found that he'd been enrolled in the school from kindergarten on. Perry Pelopson might not have openly acknowledged his son, but he hadn't skimped on his education. She jumped forward, looking for the spiel about his next steps in the senior yearbook. If she could get a college, that would make her search even easier.

He wasn't listed among the graduating students.

Cassie frowned, and went back to the yearbook of his junior year, and Chris's face sprang out at her among the head shots. With the loss of his rounded features and baby fat, he had a much stronger resemblance to those old photos of Theo and Arthur. Perry wouldn't have risked inviting him to the lake again, where comparisons could have been drawn between his boys.

She opened the senior yearbook again, this time skimming through the photos. He was there in a few of them, carefully measuring something into a beaker, playing chess with a bespectacled freshman, sitting in the quad beside a dreamy-eyed dark-haired girl. They were gazing at each other with the intensity of the truly besotted. There was no caption for that photo, but Cassie found the girl again in the sports team photos, neat and pretty in her field hockey uniform, her hair parted neatly in the middle and ironed straight. She was identified as Julia Simmonds.

Cassie flipped to the list of senior graduates again. Julia Simmonds wasn't there.

"Oh, hell," she said softly, staring at dreamy Julia and bright-eyed Chris. "Tell me you didn't."

She took photos of the relevant pages, skimmed through the rest of the yearbooks to make sure there wasn't anything else there, and delivered the coffee mug back to the receptionist.

"The headmistress is in a meeting with the International Institute of Academies, but she said she could slot you in for an interview later tomorrow," the receptionist said helpfully.

"Thank you, I'll check my schedule," Cassie said, because there was no point in turning down a potential lead. And because if she decided *against* dating Manny, she might have to quit her job to stick to it, and a few extra freelance pieces wouldn't be a bad idea.

The receptionist beamed. "Did you find everything you need?"

"I've made a good start," Cassie said, feeling just a little ashamed of herself. "Could I call you if I think of anything I might have missed?" She was hoping that she could track Chris down without having to ask for anything obviously suspicious, like, oh, his current address, but if she had to, this very friendly woman would be a great place to start.

"Absolutely!" the woman said, and Cassie thanked her for the help and the coffee, marched down the granite steps, and found herself caught in the chaos of the school run pick-up. One of the long-legged girls floating effortlessly out of the gates looked familiar, and after a moment

Cassie placed her as Leia Graham, the kid Hera Rheczack and her partner had adopted. Laodice had talked about the romance of Hera and Don Kronion for a solid week after the Winter Ball, until Xena and Cassie had declared a group chat veto on the topic.

Actually, there was a thought. As she waited for the shiny SUVs and town cars to clear out, she tapped Laodice a quick message.

[Cassie] You in the office?

[Laodice] yes?

[Cassie] Can I drop in? Got a couple of research questions.

[Laodice] Sure!! We still on for tonight?

[Cassie] Yes, unless you want me to get a hotel?

[Laodice] don't be dumb

Okay, then. She pulled out cautiously into traffic and made her way downtown to the monument of glass and steel that was Olympus Publishing.

***

Cassie's freelance credentials were enough to get her past the security guards and into the elevators, but she had to wait for Laodice at the reception of the floor dedicated to the Bridal section of Olympus. Cassie was lucky this receptionist hadn't been at Argos—she'd never have gotten yearbook access from this sharp young woman, who kept an eye on Cassie the whole time she was waiting, presumably in case she tried to pluck flowers from the orchid arrangement on the coffee table, or run away with the display copies of *Goddess* and *Bliss*.

Fortunately, Laodice hurried up in a few minutes. She was looking particularly bridal herself, wearing a long, fluttery pink dress with dramatic, full sleeves and lace detailing at the neck. Her long, dark hair was up in a loose French twist, her makeup was fresh and dewy, and her wide smile for her sister was extremely welcome.

"You look gorgeous," Cassie said, and hugged her.

"So do you!" Laodice said, and held her out at arms length to survey her outfit. "Very professional. Love those T-bars! They're kind of naughty librarian."

"I was a little naughty in a library today," Cassie confessed, and Laodice led her past the suddenly-interested receptionist and down the labyrinthine halls of Bridal to the office she shared with the other writers. It was largely empty, except for a dark-haired man typing steadily at a desktop computer, who didn't even look up when they came in. Laodice ignored him just as thoroughly and sat Cassie down by her own desk.

"Have you seen Xena's new video?" she asked.

"No, I've been driving or working all day."

Laodice cackled. The man's shoulders shifted, a flicker of irritation passing across his face.

"It's on breast checks," she said, and clicked to a tab on her laptop. The vertical window sprang to life. Polyxena was mid-sentence, wearing a sports bra and bike shorts, arm in the air to expose her neon-green pit hair.

"—really got to get into the armpit, because those lymph nodes are a danger zone," she said, pressing enthusiastically. "Okay! No bumps or lumps there! Now, I can't demonstrate the visual examination, because apparently cis female nipples are lewd content and against the app rules, but weirdly! Cis male nipples are fine! So here's a handy cis male, my brother Iulus—"

"Oh no," Cassie said, as the camera tilted to show a shirtless Iulus, grinning bashfully at the camera under his mop of tangled reddish curls.

"Oh yes," Laodice said, as Xena pointed at Iulus's chest and talked about the importance of noticing any discharge, dimpling, scaly skin, or unusual nipple inversion. "Mom's going to have a meltdown."

"Male breast cancer is often delayed in diagnosis," the man in the corner said suddenly, without looking up from his computer.

"Um, did anyone say it wasn't?" Laodice said.

"I'm saying that however hilarious you find him, your brother might well be saving a life."

"We're not laughing at *Iulus*," Laodice snapped. "Mind your own business, Telfer."

The man muttered something and went back to typing. Cassie blinked at her sister, who returned to her usual sunny tones without skipping a beat. "Anyway, I'm guessing Mom hasn't seen this yet, because I don't have any missed calls, but I'm just waiting for my phone to blow up."

"Thanks for the heads up," Cassie said, as Xena finished drawing helpful arrows on Iulus's chest with a Sharpie and slung her arm over his shoulder.

She grinned at the camera, her expensive dentistry gleaming in the ring light. "Thanks for helping out, Iulus, and everybody, don't forget to check your breasts! XO, Xena!"

The video looped back to the beginning and Laodice clicked it off. "Can you believe she earns more than both of us put together?" Despite the words, she sounded proud.

"Oh, easily ten times that," Cassie said. "This has only been up for a couple of hours, right? Look at that engagement. I bet that sports bra is sold out already."

Laodice sighed enviously. "I wish we could get those kinds of numbers for *Goddess*."

The man in the corner—Telfer—had turned around and was looking thoughtful. "Would your sister be interested in a collaboration with Olympus?" he asked. "We could draw in more wedding vendor advertising dollars if we offered access to influencers they might not otherwise be able to target."

Cassie laughed. "Maybe? I mean, Xena's been dating the same guy for two years, but she's not exactly the fairytale romance type."

"Unusual young women get married too," Telfer said crisply. "And they're less likely to pick up a bridal magazine at a newsstand."

"*Unusual?*" Laodice demanded, but Telfer was already on his feet and heading for the door, pausing only to sling his Italian suit jacket around his shoulders. "Ugh, I'm sorry. That guy only thinks about the bottom line."

"Where is everyone today?" Cassie asked. The last time she'd visited Laodice at work, the office had been bustling.

"It's Bridal Week," Laodice said. "Everyone who can write 50 words about a gown is at the shows, filing their stories in the cab to the next one. Telfer and I are supposed to be holding down the fort while designers and vendors suck up to our editor in person. But of course everybody who's anybody in the bridal world is *also* at the shows, so there's not much to do here except proof and edit the copy and throw it on our digital channels as it comes in. Okay. Tell me about Manny."

"That might be over," Cassie said, and got up to close the office door.

"Ooh, secrets," Laodice said, and then listened intently as Cassie told her the story of Helen and Ask Cassandra, and the messy, messy consequences of Manny's very short marriage.

"Well, that sounds like Paris," Laodice said.

Cassie blinked. "Wait, really?"

"Yes? Paris, our selfish cousin who only ever talks about herself and what she cares about?"

"I've never thought of Paris as selfish."

"That's because you're her favorite," Laodice said, with no bitterness. "I don't think she's ever asked me a question about my life that went any deeper than 'how are you?' Forget it. I don't see why Paris and Helen should come between you and the man you love. And so what if he asked you for advice without knowing it was you? Sounds like you gave him the right advice."

"Oh, so now I love him?" Cassie said. "And you've just decided that for me?"

Laodice waved at the office, which was decorated in pale pink and cream. Framed portraits of women in wedding gowns covered an entire wall. On Telfer's desk were glossy brochures advertising wedding expos, caterers, planners, and a dozen other services. Beneath the next desk was a collection of bejeweled tiaras, haphazardly sticking out of a plastic tub. "You can't deny I'm an expert."

"Really? How did things go with that barista?"

Laodice's eyes narrowed. "He wasn't the one. But Manny could be your one. I have a good feeling about him."

"I think you might be biased," Cassie said, looking around the office again. "You spend all day thinking about weddings and writing about weddings, and then in the weekends you go to other people's weddings and write profiles about them. You're predisposed to believe in happy endings."

"Cassie, please," Laodice said. "Half the couples I write about aren't going to make it. Twenty-two percent of first marriages end in divorce within five years. Manny's first marriage ended in *six hours*. I believe in unhappy endings too." She rolled her eyes at Cassie's surprise. "I'm not *stupid*."

"I've never thought you were stupid," Cassie said, stung.

"No, just way too romantic and silly. Obsessed with love, that's what you and Xena say."

"We don't want you to get hurt," Cassie said weakly.

"I'm afraid that's inevitable, when you're looking for love," Laodice said. "Love is painful. And magnificent and consuming and... It's wonderful, Cassie. Of course I'm obsessed with it. I love being in love. And, sure, it hurts when it ends, it hurts when a guy is like, you're too much, I don't feel the same way, I have to go. But chances are, one day, it won't end. One day, I'll find someone who thinks I am wonderful."

"You are wonderful."

"I know! That's my point! All the guys I've loved so far—they weren't right. But how would I know they weren't right if I didn't try? And it hurts, but that's okay, because one day, I will love the right guy. That's worth a few aches and pains. I worry about *you*, because you *don't* take the risk of getting hurt. Do you love Manny?"

"I don't know," Cassie said. "I like him a lot and the thought of leaving already hurts like hell. I was already thinking about how we could negotiate something long distance."

Laodice looked satisfied. "And the sex?"

"Oh, incredible. Sometimes, in the middle of sex, I think I love him. And then I come out of it and I'm like, Cassie, that's just the oxytocin speaking. Simultaneous orgasms are not true love."

"Simultaneous orgasms? Really?"

Cassie grinned. "Nearly every time."

"Wow," Laodice said. "Does he have a brother?"

"Yes, but he's married, and kind of a dick." She gave Laodice a stern look. "Also, I cannot underline how much I do not need further family entanglement in this mess."

Laodice laughed again, her unrestrained cackle ringing out as Telfer re-entered the office, looking triumphant. "I got five minutes with Hera and she gave me the go-ahead," he announced.

Laodice frowned at him. "On what?"

"On the influencer advertising integration. Pending Miriam's approval, of course."

"Did you put that together just now?" Laodice asked.

"Yes," Telfer said, looking pleased with himself. "Hera's asked me to prepare a proper proposal and present to her and Miriam next week."

Laodice folded her arms. "So you're just going to leave all the Bridal Week office work to me?"

Telfer looked around the empty office, then pointedly at Cassie, clearly there for non-Bridal Week purposes. "I guess I am," he said. "Have fun."

"Unbelievable," Laodice muttered and sat upright as notifications started flooding her laptop screen. "Oh, damn. Cassie, I have to get to this now. Naeem Khan is doing something exciting with feathers."

"I actually need to do some research," Cassie said quickly. "I was hoping I could get your login access to Archives." Laodice was already typing, her tongue stuck between her teeth, and if she got really intent she wouldn't even be able to hear Cassie.

"Sure, use my desktop," Laodice said absently, and before Cassie could say that she really meant that she wanted to ask Laodice the questions and Laodice could search up the answers, which felt much less ethically dicey, Laodice had swung around, typed in her password, opened the Archives database search engine, and shoved the keyboard in Cassie's direction.

"Um, okay," Cassie said, staring at one of the best media databases in the world, with digitized records of Olympus Publications going back nearly a hundred years. Even better, she now had access to the Municipal Office Births, Marriages and Deaths Registry.

From across the room, Telfer swung around in his chair to look at them, looking dubious.

"I'm a freelancer," Cassie told him, and he made a doubtful noise, but went back to his computer. Laodice hadn't noticed the byplay. She was scrolling through runway pictures and descriptions of women in white gowns, with feathers trailing out at the end of enormous trains, or edging sleeves, or wrapped around the model's shoulder in a fluttery stole.

"Thanks," Cassie said.

"Mm," Laodice said, and then made the satisfied sound that meant she'd spotted a rogue semi-colon.

Cassie had already tried "Chris Ipith" on normal search engines, and despite the unusual surname, nothing had come up. "Julia Simmonds," on the other hand, was too common. She'd found dozens of social media profiles and websites, and while she could go through them one by one—and would if she had to—she was hoping to jump around that obstacle. For that, she needed serious research power.

And now, she had it.

She crackled her knuckles, and got started.

Sometime later, Laodice put her hand on her shoulder. "Cassie," she was saying. "Cassie, did you hear me?"

"What?" Cassie said, and blinked back to reality. The office was lit by bright fluorescents now, the city lights glimmering in the twilight. The notebook she'd brought with her was half full of scribbles she didn't even remember making. Telfer was still there, hunched over his computer, but now a hand-scribbled diagram with arrows and boxes was tacked above his desk, and he was scrolling through his phone with earbuds in, stopping every now and then to take a note. "What time is it?"

"Time to go home," Laodice said cheerfully. "Although we should stop for takeout first, I don't have a thing in the fridge. Unless you want to take your chances with last week's fried rice?"

"No, thank you," Cassie said. Her mouth was dry. There was a half-drunk coffee in a paper cup beside her. She vaguely recalled Laodice setting it down some time ago.

Laodice frowned at her. "Are you okay? You look like someone died."

"Someone did," Cassie said. She lifted her glasses and wiped at her eyes. "I'm sorry, I can't stay tonight after all. I have to go back to Tantalus."

Chapter Thirteen

Manny took another swig of cold coffee and grimaced at his spreadsheets. No matter how he massaged the numbers, he couldn't make them work with the new budget. If he kept the plans as they were, he just couldn't afford the new material prices. If they lowered the luxury level on the carriage house rooms, he'd have to charge less for renting them. But the maintenance and staffing costs would be nearly identical, so the profit margins would be much lower. And since the bank had given him a shorter term on the loan, he couldn't even guarantee they'd be able to keep up with the payments at that lower income level.

He'd explained it all to his mother at lunchtime, who, for once, hadn't blithely assured him she was sure he could handle it. She *had* indicated that she was going to have a sharp word with Simon at Midas the next time she ran into him, and Manny hadn't tried to stop her. Simon really deserved it. That two-week delay had blown the whole project out of the water.

Manny rubbed the bridge of his nose. Hours ago, he'd looked at the dimming sunlight and contemplated a run, only to be swallowed by yet another idea that hadn't panned out when he iterated it. He was starting to fuzz and lose focus, and it was probably time to stop. He started when the doorbell rang, echoing in the otherwise empty house, and went down the stairs in a rush.

It was Theo, hovering on the doorstep, looking unaccustomedly bashful.

Manny blinked, wondering why he hadn't just used his key. "Is something up?" he asked.

"Your mom told me about the trouble with the carriage house plan," Theo said, shifting from foot to foot. "I wondered if I could help."

"Oh," Manny said. "Well, if you wanted to take a look at my figures, you'd be welcome." He couldn't do any harm, at least, and there was an outside chance he'd come up with *something*.

"No," Theo said. "I mean, help out with the money. I live pretty frugally, and I've got a fair amount in savings. It'd be a gift, not a loan."

Manny stopped. "Did Mom tell you how much of a gap we were looking at?"

"Yes," Theo said steadily, and named the number. "I can cover that."

Manny had to grab the doorknob to stop his knees from giving out. "You have *that* much in savings?"

Theo's eyes were gleaming in pleasure at the surprise. "That won't even clean me out," he said. "Doesn't touch my retirement accounts, either."

"Theo, I don't know what to say. That's incredibly generous. But I don't know if I should let you do it."

"Look, I don't have kids," Theo said gruffly. "Everything I have is eventually going to you boys and Aerope anyway. Arthur would have wanted me to take care of you." He shoved his hands deep into his pockets, looking defensive. "Just take the money, okay?"

"Come in out of the cold and we'll talk about it?" Manny said, and then they both turned at the sound of a car coming down the driveway, slowly appearing out of the dark.

"That Cassie's car?" Theo said.

"Yes."

"Huh. Thought she was going to be away for a couple days."

"Maybe she forgot something," Manny said. His heart was thumping unpleasantly hard. If Cassie had come back to tell him whatever she'd found in person, it couldn't be good.

Theo gave him a conspiratorial look. "Maybe she did."

Cassie jumped out of the car. She was wearing some kind of suit, with tights and high heels, ridiculous in this weather. She walked towards them as if the cold was the last thing on her mind, the lights from the house casting refracted shadows behind her. She spared Theo a smile, but her eyes were serious and intent on Manny. "Do you have a moment?" she asked.

"Thanks, Theo," Manny said. "I mean it, really, thank you so much. Can we talk about it in the morning?"

"Sure, sure," Theo said. "You kids have fun." He clapped Manny on the shoulder, and Manny held the door open for Cassie and didn't even wait for Theo to turn away before he closed it behind her.

"Is Aerope here?" Cassie said immediately.

"She's having a girls' night out with Beverley and Marie, and staying in town tonight," Manny said. "She says you inspired her."

"Okay," Cassie said, and rubbed her hands together nervously. "Okay. I'll tell you and then you can decide whether I tell her, or you do, or both of us."

"It's bad, isn't it?"

"Pretty bad," Cassie admitted. "I didn't think I should tell you over the phone. And I thought about texting to say I was coming back and needed to talk, but then I didn't want you to worry for three hours while I made the drive, and then the whole way home I kept thinking I should stop and text you anyway, but it just seemed easier to keep going. I haven't eaten anything. I might not be thinking too clearly."

Manny wasn't distracted enough to miss that she'd absently called Tantalus "home". But now wasn't the time to point that out. "Do you want dinner first?" he asked instead.

She shook her head. "No, I've got to get this out. Do you still have those protein bars in your office?"

"You got it," Manny said, and as they went up the stairs he tried to steady his hands, which kept being annoyingly shaky. Cassie demolished two protein bars and downed most of a root beer, and then pulled her notebook from her bag.

"Okay," she said. "First thing. Chris's full name was Chris Ipith, born to Augusta Ipith, and he did indeed attend Argos Academy until mid-way through 12th grade. Then he dropped out before graduation."

"Why?"

"He had a girlfriend, Julia Simmonds, and she got pregnant. They both left."

"Oh," Manny said. "I can see why she left, but why would he?"

"I don't know," Cassie said. "He might have been expelled for conduct unbecoming of a student or something. Or he might have left in protest when she did, because I'll bet you anything *she* was expelled. I don't think Argos in the seventies would be very accommodating for a pregnant teenager." She snorted, sounding much more like herself. "I'm not sure they'd be accommodating now."

"So he stuck with her?" Manny asked, feeling better about it.

"Yes. That's how I was able to confirm the pregnancy. They got married in February 1978, Julia moved in with Chris and his mom, and in May they had a baby named Gus. Reading between the lines, Julia's family were not happy that their little princess got knocked up to a nobody, and they might have cut ties for a while. I think Gus was named after Chris's mother, Augusta. They lived with her until she died in 1989, and she left them the house."

"What did Augusta do?"

"She was a legal secretary. I couldn't find out much about her—most of the records from her time aren't digitized. As far as I can tell, she lived in the city her entire life and mostly worked for a firm called Gortyn, which is a name that appears on a lot of vineyard paperwork from the 50s and 60s."

"Right. So Grandad Perry meets her then, and they conduct an affair in the city. Accidentally or on purpose they conceived a kid, and Perry felt he has some responsibility towards him."

"I can't confirm any of that, because Chris's birth certificate doesn't name the father, but it's plausible," Cassie said. "Augusta must have been a tough lady. Even if Perry was helping her out financially, that was not a good time for professional single moms."

"You sound like you admire her."

"I kind of do. She supported her son and daughter-in-law through a difficult time. I don't think the affair with a married man was a good idea or anything, but you might be surprised by how common it is. I get a lot of letters from people who have fallen in love outside their marriage and agonize about it."

Manny thought uncomfortably about Augie and Ness. "People have affairs for less noble reasons."

"They do," Cassie agreed. "I like Julia too. She kept her own name, and Gus was hyphenated Ipith-Simmonds, which was pretty radical in the 70s."

Manny mouthed the syllables. "Well, that's a searchable surname, but I bet it got him into strife at school."

"Maybe. He went to Westfield High, a public high school. No Argos Academy for him."

"Gus," Manny said, trying it out. His cousin, Gus, who was...let's see, forty-six now. Eleven years older than him, nine years older than Augie. "Are Chris and Julia still together? Do they live in the city? Were you able to get an email address or phone number?"

"No," Cassie said, and her eyes were huge and dark and full of sympathy. "Chris and Julia are dead."

"Oh," Manny said. This, somehow, wasn't a possibility he'd considered. Chris was three years younger than his father, and Arthur hadn't even hit seventy. He felt grief claw at him, mostly for his father, but also for these two strangers, the uncle he'd never known, and his high school sweetheart wife. Even Augusta, his grandfather's mistress, sounded like an interesting person. He would have liked to meet her too. "You're right. That is bad."

"It gets worse," Cassie said, looking grim. "Chris was murdered."

"*What?*"

"The death certificate said homicide, gunshot wound, so I looked into the newspaper coverage. There was a lot of it. Chris Ipith was shot in his own home, in August 1996. There apparently wasn't any sign of a struggle or break in. Nothing was taken, so it probably wasn't a burglary.

My guess, and I think it's what the police were thinking, is that either he let the killer in or they already had a key."

"You're saying *they* like you don't know who it was," Manny said.

"No one was convicted," Cassie said, and swallowed hard. "Julia was visiting her family in the Hippocampus, but Gus was in the city. He was eighteen. He said that he came home from a walk and found the body."

Manny was momentarily dizzy with horror. He took a deep breath and put his head down, and Cassie's hand came down on the back of his neck, cool and soothing. He looked up into her eyes. "Did the police think it was Gus?"

Cassie sat at his feet, tucking her legs underneath her. "Yes," she said quietly. "I think they did. With a domestic murder, they always look at the family first. And Gus and his father had argued, earlier that day. There's an interview with a neighbor who said she saw Gus storm out before noon, but she didn't see what time he came back. Gus said he just walked around the city for hours, getting all his frustration out, before he came back and found his father lying dead on the kitchen floor. He said he was already cold." She paused. "Is this too much? Do you need a minute?"

"No," Manny said, squeezing his eyes shut. "Keep going."

Cassie took him at his word, and he heard the sound of flipping pages as she went back through her notebook. "He also said that when he left he saw a strange man in a car he didn't recognize, parked around the block, but no one seems to have taken that seriously. There's a perfunctory call for anyone who has any information about the man in the car to come forward, and a lot of talk about Gus helping the police with their inquiries. The papers are all leaning pretty heavily in the direction that he did it, but in the end the police can't have had a strong enough case, because he was never charged. But the suspicion must have been terrible. He and Julia moved out of the neighborhood a year later. There's a brief story, interviewing the same neighbor, and I was able to confirm it in the deed records."

"His mom didn't think he did it, then."

"I guess not," Cassie said.

"She died too? But not murder, right?"

"No, no," Cassie said hurriedly. "She died five years after that, in 2001. Skin cancer. Sad, but unrelated."

"And what happened to Gus?"

"There was no death certificate in any of the databases I could access, so chances are that he's still around. But 1996 is really pre-social media. It's pre-Google. If he had any presence online then, a GeoCities account or something, it's been wiped. And there's no Gus Ipith-Simmonds anywhere online now. I think he might have changed his name, maybe even left the country. Julia's family were wealthy, and by then it looks like they'd reconciled with their daughter and grandson. They could have helped him disappear."

"Fuck," Manny said. "Well, I mean, I would. Either he'd killed his dad, or he hadn't, but nearly everybody thought he had. I'd want to run from either of those things as far as I possibly could."

"That's what I figured," Cassie said, and sighed. "I'm sorry. I really wanted to bring you better news."

"I didn't think you would, given how Dad reacted," Manny said. He was picturing his father discovering all this; finding the records that pointed at another little brother, then the horror of what had happened to that brother. Murdered, perhaps by his own son. And then... What? What had prompted the suicide? Dwelling on this terrible history, maybe. Thinking about all that death. Waiting until his wife left home, then—

"Wait," Manny said. "Wait. Chris died alone at home, when his wife was out of town and his son wasn't there?"

"Well, claimed he wasn't there."

"Assume Gus didn't do it. Chris let someone in, someone he trusted. And then that person killed him, and someone else got the blame."

Cassie sucked in a breath. "Manny."

"I don't think my dad killed himself," Manny said, reality twisting into a new shape. "That's the part that's never made sense. The doctor said that maybe he'd forgotten he'd taken some pills, and swallowed more of them, but that didn't make sense either. They weren't even his pills, and he'd never taken them before. He'd never had any issues with addiction or depression. Mom said he hadn't said anything and he didn't leave a note. He just went quiet, that's the only thing she noticed. And he might have gone quiet because he'd discovered the existence of his half-brother." The words kept coming out of his mouth, faster than his brain could keep up.

"You think finding that out might have triggered an attack?" Cassie said.

"I don't know." Manny's head pounded. "Herc Stormson said he saw the vineyard truck on the road the night that Dad died. I didn't think anything of it."

"Who uses the truck?"

"Jim, mostly. Theo or one of the hands, sometimes."

"Did Jim have any reason to want your father dead? Did he inherit anything?"

"Nothing big," Manny said. He swiveled to his desk and yanked open a desk drawer, pulling out his copy of his father's will. He'd been using it to finalize probate, and now he flipped through, looking for Jim's name. "No. He left Jim a bottle of aged whiskey, that's all."

"Was it expensive whiskey?" Cassie asked intently. "Rare bottles can go for hundreds of thousands at auction."

"Seriously?"

Cassie nodded. "Is the specific bottle named in the will?" Manny told her and she looked it up, then shook her head. "It's nice whiskey, but not that nice. I don't think that's a motive." She paced around the room, floorboards creaking. "Maybe it was something else. Maybe when your father found out about Chris, he stumbled across a motive for *that* murder."

"When was Chris killed again?"

"September 7th, 1996."

Manny's spine went cold. "That's the year my grandfather died. Jim was working for us then."

Cassie sucked in a breath. "When exactly did your grandfather die? Before or after Chris?"

"I don't know, I was six! Hang on." He pulled out his phone and pressed his mother's name on the contact list. It went to voicemail. "Mom? Can you call as soon as you get this? I need to know what date Grandad Pelopson died. It's important, thank you."

Cassie had stopped walking, arrested in mid-step. "What about your *grandfather's* will?" she asked. "If his death was the trigger..."

Manny rose from his chair. "Do you have it?"

"It's upstairs." She went for the door and he was right behind her when she stopped dead. "Theo," she said, her voice flat and strange.

"What about—" Manny started, and then he saw what Cassie had seen.

Theo hadn't gone home. He'd used his key to come inside after them, crept up the stairs, and along the hallway, and listened to their conversation.

And now he was standing in the doorway, blocking their exit, with his mouth in a grim line and the shotgun the vineyard used to shoo birds away held steady at his hip.

"Theo," Manny said. At first, he couldn't comprehend what was happening. This didn't make sense, his uncle pointing a gun at them, his uncle eavesdropping as Cassie told him the terrible story of this branch of the Pelopson family tree.

And then it all exploded in his brain at once, connections sparking off each other like fireworks. "Theo. *You* killed Dad?"

"You evil son-of-a-bitch," Cassie said, her voice absolutely level.

Unadulterated fury boiled through Manny's veins and he made an aborted motion forward. Theo swung his gun up, pointing the muzzle straight at Cassie's chest. "Don't," he said, his voice husky. "Don't make it worse, Manny. Where's your phone?"

"There," Manny said, pointing at the desk. The screen was still unlocked, from his last call to his mother.

His mouth went dry. Unless he was misinterpreting this completely, that voicemail was going to be the last words he ever spoke to his mom.

"Good. Now you get your phone out," Theo told Cassie. "Slowly, now."

Cassie complied, glaring at him.

"Put it on the floor and kick it down the hall."

Cassie did, looking like she wished she could be kicking Theo instead.

"Let her go," Manny said.

"I can't do that," Theo said. He gazed sadly at both of them. "Why couldn't you two just leave well enough alone? I never wanted to do this. I thought I'd cleared out those fucking files."

"*You* took the records about Chris," Cassie said. "We thought it was Arthur."

"It *was* Arthur," Theo said. "Him and his damn hobbies." He gestured with his head, but his eyes never left them, and the muzzle stayed steady. "We're going upstairs, folks. Start moving."

Manny could see his own tension mirrored in Cassie's stance, the muscles in her broad back rigid. Either one of them could be stronger than Theo. Two against one and he wouldn't stand a chance.

But not as long as he had the gun.

If Manny were by himself, he might take the chance. Theo was probably going to kill them anyway, he told himself harshly. He should at least make an attempt to get the gun off him.

But if Theo shot, and missed Manny, but hit *Cassie*...

He glanced at Cassie, and saw something similar flash across her face. "Please don't hurt us," she said. "Theo, Manny's your *nephew*."

"I know that!" Theo snapped. "Get up those stairs, now!"

Cassie gave Manny a single agonized glance and stepped into the hallway. Manny went after her, hoping for a chance, but Theo kept his distance, his eyes careful. "I'm not going to hurt you," he told them. "Cassie's going to find something for me, and then I'm going to lock you in the attic. Your mom will be back tomorrow, Manny. You won't come to any harm. I just need a head start."

Manny desperately wanted to believe him.

***

They went up the stairs and into the attic. Cassie moved as slowly as she dared. There were plenty of hiding places in the attic, plenty of potential weapons or places to take cover, but the problem would be getting away in the first place.

Cassie didn't think she could outrun a shotgun. She didn't know much about guns, which was starting to feel like an important knowledge gap, but she had a vague impression that your aim didn't need to be too good. Still, as she went to the heavy table she used as a desk, she slowed down even more.

"Don't," Theo said flatly. "Manny, you stop there."

Cassie turned around, and saw Manny was several feet behind her, several feet in front of his uncle. Too far away for him to lunge at Theo. But much too close for Theo to miss.

Theo watched her register all of that and looked satisfied. "Cassie, you go into the archive room and bring out my father's will. If you do anything I don't like in there, or try anything stupid when you come out, I'll shoot Manny in the knee. He'll probably survive, but he won't like it much."

Cassie didn't bother to assent. She went into the archive room, her brain working furiously. Finding the will would take her seconds, but Theo didn't know how good her system was. He'd never bothered to come up here. And now his view of her was partially blocked. It wasn't much of a chance, but it was *something*, if she could only think it through.

What could be useful in the archives? There were heavy ledgers that might make decent weapons, but they'd be immediately obvious. What they needed was something small but helpful, if one of them could get close enough. Her eyes caught on a box at the back, marked "Sundry miscellaneous, c. 1920s", and she squeezed through the shelves towards it.

"What's taking so long?" Theo called.

"I'm trying!" she called back, trying to sound terrified—which she was—and not so angry that it was taking all of her common sense not to rush straight at him, which she also was.

"Is this how you got Dad to take the pills?" Manny said conversation-ally. "Held a shotgun on him and made him swallow them?"

Oh, bless him. He couldn't know what she was doing, but he was trying to distract Theo while she worked.

"Sit down," Theo said after a moment, and Cassie grimaced, even as she reached into the box. Reducing Manny's maneuverability was smart of Theo, and bad for them. But what choice did Manny have? She caught movement from the corner of her eye, and heard him shuffle down. From the position of his torso, he was kneeling on his haunches, not sitting cross-legged. He'd still have some lunging power, if they could draw Theo closer...

Her questing hand found the pocket knife in its leather embossed sheath. Heart pounding, she unsnapped the pouch and fumbled the folded knife out, levering the blade open with her thumb. Bless whoever had oiled it—it came out as smoothly as it had the day it had cut her, and this time she avoided the jab.

"Cassie, have you got that will yet?"

"I'm looking," Cassie said, deliberately breathy. "There's a lot in here."

"What does the will say?" Manny asked. "Did Grandad leave something in there for Chris? Is that how you found out?"

Theo laughed, a harsh crack of sound without any mirth, and Cassie used the moment to turn away from that box and to one on the next shelf, the box that held Perry Pelopson's will. The knife was pressed flat in her palm, and she held it firmly against the sheaf of paper.

"Cassie!" Theo said. He was beginning to sound angry.

"I've got it," she said and reappeared in the doorway with the will in her hands. "Please, Theo. Please, let us go."

"Theo, tonight you offered me enough money to fix the carriage house," Manny said. "Did you mean it?"

"Of course I fucking meant it," Theo said gruffly. "Do you think I wanted to hurt your dad, Manny? I loved my brother, damn it!"

"Then *why*?" Manny's voice broke on the word. Cassie thought it wasn't a delaying tactic, but a sincere and anguished demand for answers, and her heart ached for him.

"Read it," Theo said, nodding at the pages in Cassie's hands. "Top of the second page."

Cassie kept her right hand under the paper, and turned the top page over with her left. Manny knew she was right-handed. His eyes caught the movement.

"To my son Arthur I leave my house and chattels. To my son Theodore I leave fifty thousand dollars. The Tantalus Vineyard land, business, debts, chattels and all other goods I leave to be divided evenly among my sons." The implications washed over her even as she said it out loud. She looked up. "His sons."

"Yeah," Theo said. "Not named. Just there, if you knew. Three sons, divided evenly. A third of the family business to someone who'd never been part of the family."

"And you already knew about Chris," Cassie said.

Theo's weathered face was caught in an ugly sneer. "The old man wrote me a letter, to be opened in the event of his death. He wasn't man enough to tell me about his third kid in person. He did it in writing."

"That must have been hard," Cassie said. It was too much for her to sound sympathetic to this murderer, but she could manage acknowledging that he had been placed in a shocking position by his father.

"He had the fucking gall to ask me to break it to Mom and Arthur. Asked me to get in touch with that guy and tell him who he was, where he was from. Can you believe it? Chris didn't even know who his dad was. I burned that letter, and I promised myself I'd never say a word. Let it all die with the old man."

"And then you heard the will," Cassie said. "And you thought, wait. What if my dad wrote more letters. What if Chris gets curious and hires a private investigator. What if, somehow, he finds out he's got a family, and his father's will says he has one third of a business worth hundreds of thousands of dollars."

Theo glanced at Manny. "She's smart."

"Yes, she is," Manny said. "And so you went to Chris yourself. Did you tell him you were his brother, before you shot him?"

Theo didn't say anything for a moment. He was taking labored breaths, his chest heaving. "He went to that fancy private school," he said. "Dad paid for that. He got into some colleges, and Dad would have paid for that too. But instead he got that girl pregnant and dropped out, and everything still turned out peachy keen for him. He had the kid and the wife and the townhouse and his happy little life.”

Cassie watched the color in his cheeks bloom and fade. If she was going to use the knife, she needed to get closer to him, and that wouldn’t happen while he was watching her. She widened her eyes slightly at Manny.

And he caught her signal and kept talking. “And meanwhile, you’d been working at Tantalus.” He was better at sounding sympathetic than she was. “You never got to college. Grandad spent the money on Chris instead.”

“He was happy,” Theo said again, and his eyes were blank. He wasn’t even looking at Manny anymore, though the gun stayed steady. Cassie edged forward, a miniscule motion that was barely a step. But it was something.

“I didn’t even tell him about the will,” Theo continued. “I told him I was a representative of his father, and he got excited. He let me in and asked if we were family. Like it meant something, like he was really my brother. Arthur was my brother. This guy wasn’t anything, but he let me into his house and I looked at his family pictures and his kid’s report cards on the fridge, and when he turned away to get me a drink I shot him in the back.” His eyes focused on Manny again. “I waited until his kid walked out. There wasn’t any reason to kill the kid.”

“No,” Manny said. “You just framed him for his father’s murder.”

“I didn’t know he was going to get the blame,” Theo said sharply, and Cassie took another step. “How could I know that? He took a good look at me when he walked past my car, the little punk. It would have been safer if I’d waited and got him too. But I’m not a monster.”

From the way that Manny's mouth twisted, Cassie was pretty sure he'd had the same thought she had about Theo's monstrousness. But his voice stayed soft and understanding. "Dad found out, though. And you had to be safe."

Theo nodded. "Arthur didn't tell me right away. I don't know how he found anything in this dump, but he collected a boxful of stuff—photo albums, a couple of Dad's old record books, some information about those lake days for the underprivileged. He asked me over to dinner while Aerope was away. I didn't even want to go, but he said it was important, said I'd be glad I'd came. So I came on over after I finished a few things at the vineyard. And then he pulled out this big box like it was a birthday present, and said he'd found us a little brother."

"He didn't suspect you'd murdered Chris?"

Theo snorted. "Arthur hadn't even realized he was dead." He looked at Cassie. He didn't appear to notice that she'd got much closer to him, nearly level with Manny. "Bet you're wishing you were a little less good at your job."

"You killed Dad because he learned Chris existed at all?" Manny said, drawing Theo's attention back to him.

Theo got the lost look again. "I didn't know what to do. He was going on and on about how we could reach out and make a connection with this guy, except he was worried about whether his *feelings* would be hurt. He had plans to hire a private investigator, plans for family mediation. He didn't mention the will. I don't think he'd realized what it meant. But he was up in those archives every day. He would have found it soon."

"And even if you'd had a gun with you, shooting him would have been messy," Manny said. "The police always look at family in those cases."

For the first time, Theo looked ashamed of himself. "Yeah. But I remembered your mom's sleeping pills. She had nearly a full prescription."

"Yeah, you really lucked out," Manny said, disgust leaking into his voice.

Theo glared at him. "I loved my brother, Manny. I knew him my whole life. But if he started sniffing around, if someone noticed the dates, the police could reopen the case. That kid saw me. It didn't matter when no one knew about the connection, but if they found out, they might take another look. So I sat down with my brother to talk things over and we had a couple of whiskeys. After the first two glasses, Arthur got confused and sleepy, and I told him to take the rest of the pills. And he did."

"Because he trusted you," Manny said. "And you put him to bed, and Mom found him, and for the last eight months she's been thinking it was her fault. You killed your brothers and you ruined my mother's life, because you're a selfish son of a bitch and you didn't want to share. You didn't have to kill Dad, Theo. You could have confessed what you'd done, actually taken responsibility for your crime. Dad would have *helped* you. He would have got you the best lawyers, negotiated a plea-deal."

Theo looked blank, as if that had never occurred to him. "But they would have looked into Tantalus. Bad enough to have you poking into everything and checking the accounts for probate and insisting we file everything with the IRS. Casual hires on contracts! Who does that?"

"Why would looking into Tantalus matter?" Cassie asked. It was the first time she'd spoken in a while, and she regretted it immediately. Theo's face closed up, and she had the unnerving sensation that she'd just walked into a trip wire.

"It wouldn't," he said brusquely. "Put the will on the table and go back into the archive room. You too, Manny."

Cassie didn't move. "What are you going to do, Theo? You can't just shoot us. That looks too messy. They'll investigate the archives, and then you've got the same problem again."

"Yeah," Theo said heavily. "The archives are a problem. I got rid of everything Arthur showed me, but you still found more. No, I think there has to be a fire."

Cassie looked at Manny and saw her horror reflected in his eyes. She swallowed it down.

"Are you going to lock us in the archives and burn us to death?" she asked. "That's not quick, Theo. You made it quick for Chris and easy for Arthur. You owe your nephew better than that."

Theo glanced sidelong at Manny and frowned. "I don't like it either. Got another suggestion?"

"You could just run," Manny suggested. "Clear your accounts and go somewhere else, set up another life. I promise we wouldn't look that hard." He sounded sincere. Cassie would happily break that promise for him, but if they could just get Theo to *leave*... The seed of another idea began to sprout. Getting any closer to Theo herself would be tricky, but maybe she could get him out of the attic.

Theo looked taken aback. "Leave Tantalus?" he said. "No. Some things you can't run from."

"I have another idea," Cassie said, keeping her voice easy and her body language relaxed. She was slipping into advice mode, where you assumed the case as it was laid out, and offered the best solution to the writer's problem. "When a woman is murdered, the first person the cops look at is the boyfriend. Everyone knows Manny and I have been dating. You could make it look like he shot me, then himself."

"Manny wouldn't do that! No one would believe it," Theo said. He sounded honestly offended, and it was so ridiculous that Cassie almost laughed in his face. The whole situation was hideous. Theo had murdered both his brothers, and was about to kill them, but he baulked at impugning Manny's reputation?

"I don't know," she said instead. "Thirty minutes ago, I wouldn't have believed you could do it either."

"I guess it'd be faster," Theo said doubtfully.

Theo had killed his younger brother when his back was turned, and Arthur hadn't known what was happening. Cassie wasn't positive he could look his victims in the eye. Setting a fire and leaving it to roast them alive sounded horribly possible.

"You wouldn't want us to suffer," Cassie said, making it sound like a given. "And maybe Manny sets a fire, tries to burn everything before he gives up and dies. Then you could use accelerants and turn off the alarms, and that wouldn't look suspicious." *Go*, she thought. *Leave us here, and go get gas or fire starters or something*. "Manny would have to be alive to set the fire, though. If you set it up after he died, the forensic examiners would know." She wasn't actually sure how much evidence forensics could get out of a burned body, but it sounded plausible, and that was all she needed right now.

"Is that so," Theo said, and Cassie realized the flaw in her reasoning the moment he swung the muzzle towards her. She'd argued that *Manny* had to be alive, but the story she'd plotted for him hadn't accounted for her.

"Wait," she said, stepping backwards even though it was totally useless, he was going to shoot her, she was going to die, her last word was going to be *wait*.

With a shout, Manny lunged to his feet and staggered in front of the gun.

"No!" he said.

"Get out of the way, Manny," Theo said irritably, as if he were standing in front of a cabinet Theo wanted to reach into.

"No," Manny said, spreading his arms wide. Cassie gasped for air, and then stepped up behind him, trying to hide behind his bulk. Theo looked mad enough to try the shot anyway, and she didn't want to present a tempting target. "You can't shoot her yet. You need her as a hostage to make sure I build your fucking fire. Otherwise I won't do it. You'll have to shoot me first, and there goes your perfect set-up."

"What difference does it make?" Theo said. "Now or later, Manny, why does it matter?"

"It matters to me," Manny said, and turned around to look at Cassie. He looked as shocked and terrified as she felt. "Every minute she's alive matters to me."

Cassie stared at him. "This is an insane time to realize I love you."

"Stress and proximity will do that," Manny said, and she felt a smile tremble on her lips.

"I could do with a little more proximity," she said, and went up on her tiptoes, mashing her mouth against his.

He was unresponsive at first, understandably uninterested in a make-out session in front of his murderous uncle, but Cassie shoved the will flat against his chest, and he stopped hesitating when he felt the hard lump of the pocket knife. He opened his mouth to her, and put his arms around her in a convulsive movement that handily disguised her scrabbling at his chest. She fumbled the knife into his inside jacket pocket. He winced, and she thought she might have cut him a little on the way, but there was no help for it. If he was leaving with Theo, she wanted him armed, even with such a trifling weapon.

Manny's hands tightened on her back, and the kiss was abruptly real, all of her terror and grief transmuting momentarily into passion. She clung to him and felt desire zing through her body as if every cell had suddenly woken to the possibility of impending death, and was frantically trying to grab after life instead.

"Damn it," Theo said as they broke apart. Manny was looking at her with dazed joy, but that broke the spell. He flinched, and she saw him subtly shift his shoulders, feeling the weight of the knife.

Theo gestured with the shotgun. "Cassie, give Manny the key. Manny, lock her in and throw me the key. If you try anything, even if you get away, I'll come right up here and shoot her, and figure out the story later. You got me?"

"Crystal clear," Manny said. He kissed Cassie again, hard and brief, and then she walked into the office and heard the chunk of the lock. After a moment, Theo tested it, but Manny must have anticipated that, because he'd played fair and really locked it.

The men didn't talk to each other as they left. Cassie waited for the footsteps to die down, and then strained her ears. She thought they might have gone outside, but at the very least, they were out of easy earshot.

Holding her breath at first, and then moving with more speed and confidence as no running feet came up the stairs, she cleared a bottom shelf of boxes. Then she started kicking the wall, which was not only the smart move, but a deeply satisfying outlet for her rage.

The archive room was only drywall slapped up over some wooden framing, and she was already making some impressive dents. She was pretty sure she could squeeze through the frame, and then it would be time to call the authorities.

Even more importantly, if Theo came back, she didn't intend to be there.

***

Manny hoped he'd been reading Cassie right. He was fairly sure she had some kind of plan in mind that required being left alone.

Ideally, he figured, she'd wanted him to be with her. But at least this way, they'd cut Theo's targets in half. And he had the knife, if that might help.

Theo had ordered him out into the yard, and their breath plumed in the air as they walked towards the truck, still parked where Theo had left it. Manny altered his gait once as an experiment, but Theo kept the same cautious distance. "Don't do that again," he said.

"What is your next move, out of curiosity?" Manny said. "Once I'm dead and buried, that is."

"I don't have any next moves," Theo said. "I'll keep running Tantalus, like I have since Dad died. Burning the archives should tie up any last loose ends. I doubt Augie will make himself a nuisance like you did. I'll send him the profits every year, and he'll put his kids through college."

"There won't be profits, if you keep going the way you have been."

"Yes, there will," Theo said, and what Manny had been regarding as a stubborn resistance to reality suddenly sounded like confidence based on information Manny didn't have.

"How? Where's the money coming from?" He paused. "How did you get that much in your savings account, Theo?"

"You don't need to worry about that," Theo said. "You won't need to worry about much anymore, Manny. Cassie made a good case for shooting, so as long as you don't give me any trouble it'll all happen fast. I didn't feel great about leaving you to burn."

"Yeah, your feelings are important here." Manny stopped by the truck. "What now?"

"Get the gas container and siphon tank," Theo said. Manny didn't feel like pointing out that using the vineyard's tools would mess with the story of Manny acting alone. If he and Cassie did end up dead, he definitely wanted Theo to get caught.

He reached for the empty gas container, and used the movement and shadow to conceal reaching into his jacket pocket for the knife.

Theo had come closer, looking jittery. "Don't forget, if you run, I'll shoot her," he warned.

"I remember," Manny said, and swung the gas container down and around, tossing it directly at Theo's face. Theo ducked instinctively, bringing up one arm to fend off the missile, and Manny lunged forward. He didn't have the slightest idea of what he was doing, but the blade had his momentum and weight behind it, and he felt it sink deep into Theo's arm, grating on bone.

Theo screamed, jerking the blade out of Manny's hand. Manny jumped back, instinctively diving for cover underneath the tall truck. The gun went off with a shattering roar, and something sharp stung his leg and hip, but he kept rolling, and sprang to his feet on the other side, sprinting away into the dark. Another shot behind him, and he remembered to zig-zag. Whatever Cassie was planning to do, he hoped she'd had time to do it, but all Manny could do now was get to a phone, and there was one in the office at the winery.

He risked a glance behind him, and Theo had stepped around the truck, taking aim again. He was yelling something, his face contorted in fury. An engine roared and headlights swept over the scene, a spotlight on Theo and the gun.

Theo barely had time to look around before the car hit him, with a meaty, unpleasant thud.

Theo went flying in a tangle of limbs, to land in a limp, unmoving pile on the driveway. Manny stared at him, the blood roaring in his ears, and then turned to look at his rescuer.

"Oh no," Aerope said, tumbling from the driver's seat. "Oh no, it was Theo! I hit Theo!"

"No, Mom, you did great," Manny said. The shotgun had gone flying when Theo did. He retrieved it gingerly, keeping it pointed down. He had a vague idea that you kind of broke it in half to take the shells out, but he wasn't sure how to do that, and he didn't want to mess with it. Keeping it away from Theo and not pointing it at anyone else seemed like a good start.

"I didn't know he was Theo! I just saw someone shooting at you!"

"He killed Dad," Manny said, distantly wishing he could have softened the blow. "He was going to kill me and Cassie. Call the police."

"I got your call," Aerope said. "And you said it was urgent, and you sounded odd, but you didn't pick up, so I told Beverley I had to go home."

"The police, Mom," Manny said, and tilted his head to the side as sirens began to sing through the night. "Wait, did you call them already?"

"I did," Cassie said, and he spun around to see her behind him, holding her retrieved phone to her ear. There was white plaster dust in her hair and all over her black tights. She'd discarded her jacket at some point, and one of her blouse sleeves now featured a long tear. She looked tired and pissed off and incredibly beautiful. "Um, is that thing still loaded?"

Manny looked at the gun doubtfully. "I don't know. He shot it twice, I think. How many bullets do they have?"

"Goodness, Manny, give me that before you hurt yourself," Aerope said. She took the gun, turned it over, and began popping the cartridges out, her hands sure and confident.

"Huh. You don't break it in half," Manny said, feeling a bit dazed. The moment of crisis had sparked an adrenaline rush, but it was rapidly fading, and taking the last of his energy with it.

"Sit down and put your head between your knees if you feel woozy," Cassie said, and she knelt beside Theo, feeling for a pulse, and then checking his airways. "I think he's alive."

"My womenfolk are very practical," Manny said, sitting on the cold ground to take Cassie's advice. She gave such great advice.

"If you ever call me your womenfolk again I'm going to rethink this whole being in love with you thing," Cassie said, without looking up.

"Oh, *good*, you've both worked that out," Aerope said, and then her hands paused in their efficient action. "Wait, Manny, did you say Theo killed Arthur?"

"You can't shoot Theo in front of the cops," Cassie said. "Besides, we need him alive to confess."

"Hm," Aerope said, her eyes fixed on Theo.

"There's already too much murder in this family, Mom," Manny said.

Theo chose that moment to groan, and Aerope put the gun down as the red-and-blue lights flashed down the driveway. The first vehicle was an ambulance, and the EMTs took over from Cassie.

She sat by Manny, and he linked his arm in hers, taking her hand.

"In love with me, huh?" he said.

"You realize you still haven't said it back?" she said, staring at their joined hands. "I fessed up in the attic *and* in front of your mom."

"I love you too," he said. "Do you want me to announce it over the police radio? Maybe stand on a table in the Black Cat? Because I totally will."

"That won't be necessary," Cassie said, and relaxed against him.

Tyron Stormson crunched over the gravel and leaned down over them, the lights flashing over his badge. "Sorry to interrupt, Manny. I'm going to need you to explain why Theo's the one who's been stabbed and run down, but your mom thinks I should be arresting him."

"Well, let's see," Cassie said. "Manny and I are both witnesses to his confession of the murders of Arthur Pelopson and Chris Ipith. That second one's a cold case, by the way, but there's probably an independent witness formerly known as Gus Ipith-Simmons, if you can find him. I've already gathered a lot of circumstantial evidence for motive. Oh, and Theo shot at Manny, which should be easily corroborated by fingerprinting and a ballistics analysis."

Tyron stared at her. "Do you listen to a lot of true crime podcasts or something, ma'am?"

"No," Cassie said. "I'm an archivist."

"Cassie, this is Tyron, Herc Stormson's dad," Manny said. He was feeling lightheaded again, but this time with joy and relief. "Tyron, this is Cassie Troiades, my girlfriend. She's a genius."

"We haven't discussed labels yet," Cassie muttered, but she snuggled closer to him, and he tucked his arm around her.

It was going to take an act of divine intervention for him to ever let her go.

Chapter Fourteen

By the time Cassie was finally able to relax, she was too exhausted to enjoy it.

Manny had some scrapes from rolling under the car, and he'd been hit by the gravel that had ricocheted away from Theo's shots. Those wounds had needed to be debrided. Cassie had sustained a few injuries herself that she hadn't really noticed at the time, mostly self-inflicted. Walls weren't quite as easy to break through as it looked in TV, as she'd tried to explain to the nurse.

Was it ironic, that they were being treated in the same hospital as the man who'd tried to kill them? She'd asked the nurse that too, and been gently informed she was experiencing psychological shock.

Cassie would have argued, but instead she'd gone into a full-body sobbing fit for ten minutes.

Once their injuries had been treated, they'd had to speak to the police, though Tyron had let them be the ones to tell Aerope the full story, while he listened closely and took more notes. Aerope had asked only a few questions, more subdued than Cassie had ever seen her. Her husband's murderer was a man she'd known for most of her adult life, a member of her extended family, and Arthur had been ultimately killed for such spiteful, petty reasons. But on the whole, Cassie thought, she'd taken it pretty well. When Manny had told Aerope about Chris and Julia, and the crime Theo had been so eager to conceal, she'd sat there for a long moment, and then said, "Oh, but Manny. We must find that poor boy."

The news that Arthur hadn't killed himself without explanation, that he hadn't deliberately taken her sleeping pills and laid down in their bed to die… Perhaps knowing that had helped.

And Manny, who'd actually been shot at, was the calmest of all. They couldn't go back to the house yet, so he'd booked a hotel, acquired pajamas for all three of them, and ordered hot tea, bacon and pancakes to be sent to their connected suites.

"Sugar for shock and comfort food for comfort," he said, when Aerope wanted to know why they were eating breakfast for dinner.

And while Aerope and Cassie ate, Manny took on a task Cassie hadn't even considered yet, and started calling various concerned parties and conveying the news before they could learn about it via the media. There was a brief moment where he had to hand his phone to Aerope so that she could order Augie not to drive up in the middle of the night, but otherwise he had everything handled.

Cassie steeled herself for a quick video chat with her family, but warned them beforehand that she could only handle a few minutes of discussion. Hecuba managed to drag the time out to twenty minutes, and then Manny said, off-screen, but loudly, "Cassie, I'm sorry, we need to answer a few more questions for the police."

"Sorry, Mom, gotta go," Cassie said, and cut the feed. She smiled gratefully at her boyfriend. "That was a bold-faced lie, Manfred."

"You're welcome, Cassandra." He gestured towards the bathroom. "I ran you a bath."

"Well, if I hadn't already realized I loved you, that'd do it," Cassie said, and tried to get off the bed. Her muscles protested viciously and she froze halfway up. "*Ow.* Why does everything *hurt* so much?"

Manny helped her off the bed. "You kicked through a wall, you badass."

"I have regrets," Cassie said, before honesty compelled her to add, "Not many, though." Staying locked in that archive room another minute, not knowing what Theo was doing to Manny—that would have been even more painful. And she'd known that if she could just make it to a phone, she could get the police on their way.

"I regret making Mom put down the shotgun," Manny said. It didn't seem to be entirely a joke.

"Honestly, how are you being so chill about this? I'm about two seconds from screaming at any given moment."

Manny shrugged. "It's okay. You can be the strong one tomorrow. Tonight, let me take care of you."

"Oh," Cassie said, and stood still. That was it. She was so used to being the smart one, the practical, independent one who could solve other people's problems. But she could trust Manny to do the same thing for *her*. She was stumbling right now, so he'd catch her. It was the easiest thing in the world. All she had to do was let him.

So she let him take her clothes off and ease her into the bath, let him scrub her aching limbs, and gently massage shampoo into her hair, working out the plaster dust that had caught in her curls. He talked as he worked, telling her that she'd done incredibly well in a terrible situation, that she'd probably saved both their lives by talking Theo into the new plan and calling the police. Cassie let him praise her for a while, and when that started to feel self-indulgent she asked him to talk about his nephew and nieces instead. He switched seamlessly into a story about Geni's first soccer game.

Cassie floated on the sound of his voice as much as she did in the water, and felt the tension finally drain out of her.

"Hey," Manny said quietly, sometime later, and she opened her eyes. The water had cooled, and he was supporting her head with his linked hands.

"I fell asleep," she said, astounded, and Manny helped her out of the bath, and gave her painkillers and a glass of water. She managed to pull it together enough to climb into pajamas and brush her own teeth, and then she tumbled into bed and dropped into a deep and dreamless slumber.

She woke at some point in the night, confused and disoriented, and felt strong arms around her waist.

"You're okay," a voice she trusted murmured in her ear.

"I know," Cassie said, and went back to sleep.

***

Around 10 a.m., when it was clear Cassie would sleep as long as he let her, Manny went down to reception, meaning to thank them for the care they'd provided last night.

"Oh, good, Mr. Pelopson," the concierge said. "This way, please."

Manny was led to a storage room, ordinarily reserved for luggage. Instead, there was a table, covered in items. The Weeping Rock gossip network had evidently gone berserk.

The protocol for deaths was flowers and casseroles, and they'd been flooded with both when Arthur had died. Had been murdered, Manny internally amended. It would be a while before he could fully believe that. This time, it seemed that people weren't quite sure what to do, but their instinctive generosity had led them towards making gestures anyway. There *were* flowers and fruit baskets, although no one had got as far as casseroles, or perhaps wasn't sure if they'd be able to freeze them. There was a massive care package of toiletries and some clothes from Aerope's library co-workers, another bag of clothes for Cassie from Steph, who was close enough to the same size, and notes and cards from people who had "heard the news." Jacques had even left an enormous box of bon-bons, in Pie in the Sky's distinctive packaging.

The concierge tactfully withdrew, while Manny tried not to tear up at the thoughtfulness, and then wondered how he'd get everything upstairs. Maybe he could borrow a luggage cart. He went back to the lobby to ask, and was there just in time to see the two women come striding through the door.

One of them looked very similar to Cassie, with the same pink cheeks, dark eyes, and generous proportions of her sister. Her hair was as dark and thick as Cassie's, though she wore it in long, loose curls that flared behind her pink wool coat as she walked determined towards the desk. The other woman was a little younger, with the same exaggerated curves, but she was at least a foot taller. A real Amazon of a woman, she had dark green streaks in her straight black hair, and Manny thought a fair amount of her bulk was probably muscle. She was wearing expensive athleisure wear, and a pair of snow boots that looked brand new.

They were both bearing down on the concierge with identical frowns.

Manny stepped forward. "Laodice and Polyxena?" he said.

"Yes," said the pink one.

"It's Xena," said the tall one.

The women exchanged a look. "Are you Manny?" Laodice said. "Where's Cassie?"

"Yes, and upstairs. Come on." He nodded at the concierge, who appeared grateful for the intervention, and went up the elevator with them, trying not to feel intimidated. This wasn't really how he'd planned to meet Cassie's family. Although maybe it was what he deserved, given everything she'd dealt with at the hands of his.

Cassie was just waking up, bleary-eyed and pink with sleep, but the moment she saw her sisters she jumped out of bed and they all went down in a pile of hugs and tears. Manny backed out of the room and left them to it.

An hour later, Tyron turned up and firmly turned out the Troiadeses, except for Cassie, and sat down with her, Aerope, and Manny in the lounge area.

"There have been a few developments," he said, eyes serious in his lean face. "We were able to corroborate your accounts from the physical evidence. Theo's conscious. He's admitted to killing Chris and Arthur—he could hardly do otherwise, having confessed to both of you—but he claims he was just trying to scare you two."

"That's a lie," Manny said levelly. "He was planning to shoot both of us, and destroy the evidence with a fire."

"We've charged him with attempted murder too," Tyron assured him. "The precinct that was handling the Chris Ipith homicide has reopened that case, and the local coroner is reexamining Arthur's autopsy report with this new information in mind. Even if Theo recants, I think both of those charges will stick." He steepled his fingers. "Now. Speaking of fires. Can any of you spread some light on why Theo's house went up in flames in the early hours of this morning?"

Aerope gasped.

"What the hell?" Manny said.

"It was almost certainly arson," Tyron said. "At the moment our working theory is that it was revenge for what he did to you and Arthur. Who did you tell last night?"

Manny began listing the names, and Tyron's face grew gloomier as he realized the extent of the suspect list. "So it could have been almost anyone in town," he said heavily.

"It wasn't revenge," Cassie said suddenly. "Or...it might have been, but there could be another possibility. He wasn't just worried about being caught for murder, Manny, do you remember? He was upset that you'd been looking into the accounts."

"He offered me money," Manny said, with a start. "A lot of money, and he was cagey about how he'd gotten it."

Tyron's eyes narrowed. "Tell me," he said, and they gave him all the details they remembered.

Tyron took careful notes. "Did he do much of the bookkeeping for the business?"

"Just the cellar door," Manny said. "Could it be drugs? I wouldn't think we do enough exports."

"It could be a few things," Tyron said, his voice neutral. "It's definitely worth looking into. Thanks for your help. If you folks don't mind staying here another night, we'll be done with your place by tomorrow morning."

"Of course, Tyron," Aerope said. "Thank you." She escorted him to the door, and then came back to stand in front of them, looking thoughtful. "Now, have you two worked out your next steps?"

"We haven't really had time, Aerope," Cassie said.

"Then there's no time like the present. If it makes any difference to your planning, I don't think I can go back to that house."

"What?"

"I'm moving out, Manfred. I love you very much, but I don't think we should live together. I'm going to stay in Beverley's spare room for a little while, and then I'm going to get my own place in Weeping Rock. I'm sick of rattling around that big relic, and you'll be better off living close to the business. Not to mention that Cassie will need a place to stay when she's here."

"Um," Manny said. Aerope sounded very definite, but he wasn't sure how she thought she was going to pay for all this. A part-time librarian's salary wouldn't buy a home in Weeping Rock, or even cover rent, unless she planned to sell the manor house. "Mother, were you hoping I could buy you out of the big house? Because I don't really have the equity for that."

"No," Aerope said. "I'm going to use your father's life insurance policy. He increased the coverage early last year, and that reset the clock on the suicide exclusion clause. The insurance company refused to pay out. But now that it's murder, I should be in line for a tidy lump sum. I'm going to use half of it to buy a house, and I'm investing the other half in the carriage house project." She fixed Manny with a steely eye. "No arguments, Manfred. And I *will* be expecting dividends."

Manny felt as if she'd buffeted him around the head with a soft but heavy pillow. "Yes, ma'am," he managed, and Aerope nodded, satisfied.

"Good," she said, and took her coat off the hook. "I'm going to take your sisters to lunch, Cassie. You two should have a chance to talk." And she turned on her heel and left, leaving a stunned silence echoing in the room behind her.

"Oh, man," Cassie said, and started to laugh. "Did your mom just invite me to *move in* with you?"

Manny looked at her. "Would you?"

Cassie's eyes went wide. "I—" she started, and then visibly gathered herself. "You know what, we cheated death last night, so fuck it. Yes. I'll move in with you. Let's jump over all the sensible steps and commit."

"Are you sure?"

Cassie met his eyes. "I'm ready to take the risk if you are."

"Yes," Manny said. He'd never been more certain of anything in his life. "Let's do it. You can go wherever your job takes you, and I'll make a home for you to come back to."

"Oh," Cassie said, in that soft voice that always made his heart swell. "We should probably discuss all the practical matters. But I can't help noticing that we've been left alone for a good hour, and we've got a real bed with no headroom restrictions in that room, so would you mind if we had sex right now and saved the practicalities for another day?"

"I'd love to. Though I might be too sore for anything too athletic."

Cassie took her shirt off and breathed deeply. She was wearing the red silk bra.

"I'll heal later," Manny said, and grabbed her hand, tugging her off the couch. She flowed laughing into his arms, the perfect fit, and he caught his breath, stunned by just how lucky he'd gotten.

He spun her towards their bedroom, the movement turning into an impromptu waltz step, and she laughed again as he turned her under his arm, her free hand flying out as she twirled.

"Admit it," he said, tugging her back into his embrace. "I got you with my first dance."

Cassie smiled up at him. "Nah, that was pure lust. I fell for you when you fed me."

"Copy that," he said, and walked her backwards to the bed, kissing her until they tumbled down together. Getting rid of the rest of their clothes involved a fair amount of wriggling and laughter, not to mention the occasional gasp or sharp exhale as they teased each other.

Manny groped for a condom and slid it on, while Cassie drew her nails lightly down his chest. "Wait, is this our first time doing missionary?" she asked. "Does that attempt where you kept banging your head count?"

"It doesn't," he said firmly, and settled himself between her thighs, teasing the entrance of her pussy with the blunt head of his cock.

"You can do better than that," Cassie told him, and he eased into her, taking his revenge with the slow tease of his stroke.

She clenched tight around him, not yet fully open, and he took his time, moving at the same torturous pace, until she softened and melted, and he could sheathe his entire cock inside her. He was panting with the effort of control, his balls drawing up tight and hard.

Cassie's eyes had gone glassy, her glorious mouth open and soft, and he leaned down and took it, sliding his tongue between her lips. She moaned, and his hips stuttered at the sound.

"I love you," he said urgently, and her focus sharpened.

"I love you too," she said, and shoved at his shoulder. "My turn."

He rolled with her, the tangle of limbs resolving itself with her straddling him. His cock was still buried in her, even deeper now, and she rocked forward, her hips rolling in a movement that made him thrust up in helpless response. He couldn't move very far, pinned down as he was, and Cassie's smile turned wicked as she realized it.

"Give me your hand," she told him, and he willingly obeyed, watching as she brought it to her mouth and curled her tongue around his first two fingers. She slid the hand between their bodies and positioned his fingertips exactly where she wanted them, to either side of her clit.

Manny pressed, and was rewarded with Cassie's gasp. Then she narrowed her eyes, braced herself on her spread knees, and started bouncing on his cock in earnest. Manny gripped the bed with his spare hand and held on for dear life as she drove down onto him, again and again. He could feel the swell and slide of her clit between his fingers, increasingly slippery as her arousal intensified. She let out a choked cry, her face contorted, and froze on top of him, her pussy clenching around his cock in quivering pulses that went on and on.

When she finally collapsed on his chest, panting wildly, he put his arms around her and rolled them again. "My turn," he whispered, and as she cried out, partly in pleasure, partly in disbelief, he fucked her through the lingering tremors of that orgasm and right into the next one, until her pleading pulled him over the edge.

He came so hard he nearly blacked out, and when he revived, he was lying in Cassie's arms, exhausted, and breathless, and full of joy.

And sore. Definitely sore.

"That might not have been too smart," he said, easing out of her and wincing with the motion, as a number of abused muscles, no longer drowned out by endorphins, shouted their displeasure at him.

"Probably not," Cassie said cheerfully. "My thighs are pretty mad at me right now. Worth it, though."

"Definitely worth it," Manny said, and rolled onto his back. There were a number of things he was uncertain about, like whether the carriage house project would work out, or if they could save Tantalus. He still had questions about where Theo had got all that money, or why his house had been burned down. But the woman snuggling into his chest wasn't the source of any of those uncertainties. He stroked her curls, vastly content. "This is it, isn't it?" he asked. "It's you and me from now on."

"Yes," Cassie said, and kissed him soundly. "I can tell. You're my future."

Love, Laodice

If you're interested in learning more about Manny's disastrous first wedding, check out the free prequel novelette, *Penelope Pops the Question* (and then read the first three Olympus Inc. novels, now available on Kindle Unlimited!)

The mystery continues in *Love, Laodice*, the next novel in the Trojan Women arc...

Laodice Troiades has always been in love with love. Working at Olympus Publishing's famous Bridal section, she's been able to indulge her most romantic dreams. Now, with her editor retiring, Laodice is aiming at the big chair, and there's only one person standing in her way: Telfer Terzi; tall, dark, and *extremely annoying*.

Telfer Terzi doesn't have time for romance. Bridal is big business, and he knows he can maximize the bottom line. Laodice is an excellent writer, a notorious fool for love, and an unfortunately gorgeous distraction he doesn't need.

But when the two of them are sent on undercover assignment to a pre-wedding retreat for loving couples, the festivities turn deadly. They'll have to work together to solve the mysteries of murder -- and the heart.

Also by Kate Healey

Olympus Inc. Series:

Penelope Pops the Question (a series prequel and newsletter freebie, available when you sign up at http://thathealeygirl.com!)
The Love Labyrinth (standalone novella)

Arc One: The Olympians (now available on Kindle Unlimited!)
#1 *Persephone in Bloom*
#2 *Aphrodite Unbound*
#3 *Hera Takes Charge*

Arc Two: The Trojan Women
#4 *Ask Cassandra*
#5 *Love, Laodice*
#6 *XO, Xena*

As Karen Healey:

The Movie Magic Series:

"Jingle Spells" (a newsletter freebie, available when you sign up at http:
//thathealeygirl.com)
Bespoke & Bespelled
Savory & Supernatural

The Hidden Histories Series (with Robyn Fleming):

The Empress of Timbra
The Spymaster's Apprentice

Young Adult Works:

Guardian of the Dead
The Shattering
When We Wake
While We Run

About the Author

Kate Healey lives in New Zealand and writes spicy contemporary romance and urban fantasy. Karen Healey, who looks suspiciously similar, lives in New Zealand and writes less spicy fantasy romance, science fiction and young adult fiction. They both drink a lot of coffee.

Sign up for Karen's newsletter at http://thathealeygirl.com . You'll get the first news on new books, weird research rabbitholes, and occasional freebies!

Acknowledgements

As ever, my most fervent thanks go to Robyn Fleming for stalwart editing and Americanization with a Z. My sister Gina Healey did her usual excellent proof-reading scan. They both found *different* spelling errors in a sex scene, and I must cover my head in shame. Appropriately, perhaps, this is a family effort: my brother Scott Healey answered dumb questions and gave smart advice on guns. Writing sprints with Courtney Clark Michaels got me through some recalcitrant scenes. Kristen Smirnov is so good at location scouting it could be her job, except she's already so great at her job.

Erin Kimber generously met with me to explain the details of an archivist's day-to-day *and* sent me some excellent spreadsheets. Her assistance was absolutely crucial in describing Cassie's work, and any errors are mine, either unintentionally, or because I thought it worked better for the story.

My colleagues at *my* day job were sympathetic as I got increasingly frantic about the approaching deadline and generous about buying paperbacks of the Olympus Inc. series. My friends in the Speculative Collective, Lamplighters, Canterbury Romance Writers, Ultimate Bitches and Best Ladies were, as ever, charming, encouraging, and distracting.

I am obviously a big advice column nerd, and I reference a few of my favorites, but my *very* favorite is Captain Awkward, a source of consistent, clear-eyed, and kind advice on all sorts of interpersonal issues.

I was into Greek mythology the way some kids are into dinosaurs, but it wasn't until I studied Classics that I became aware of the astonishing work of the Greek dramatists. I am indebted in particular to Adrienne Lambeth and Robin Bond for introducing me to Aeschylus, Sophocles and Euripides.

The prophetess Cassandra, cursed to know the future but never be believed, appears in Euripides's *The Trojan Women*. She anticipates her death with relish, as it will contribute to the downfall of Agamemnon, the leader of the Greeks who sacked Troy, but the despairing Trojan Women merely think she's mad. In Aeschylus's *Agamemnon*, her prophecy is realized. Agamemnon, full of the hubris of victory, returns home a conquering hero, only to be cut down by his wife Clytemnestra and her lover. He thoroughly deserved it. He'd spent ten years besieging a foreign city to retrieve Helen, his brother's absconding wife (and Clytemnestra's sister), and he'd actually sacrificed his and Clytemnestra's daughter Iphigenia to the goddess Artemis, so that the Greek ships could sail.

Cassandra, enslaved to Agamemnon, and possibly already with children by him, is caught in the crossfire and murdered alongside him. She knows it's going to happen. She's known everything that will happen in the whole horrible saga of the Trojan War, and no one has ever listened to her. (Menelaus, in the meantime, takes Helen home. What a fun marriage that would have been.)

I'm writing in a different time period, in a different genre, and I get to give some people happier endings. When Helen leaves Manny, he lets her go. Augie would never hurt his daughter. Ness might cheat on her husband, but she's probably not going to kill him. And Cassie is not divinely cursed, but merely pretty good at giving advice.

Sometimes, people even listen.

www.ingramcontent.com/pod-product-compliance
Lightning Source LLC
Chambersburg PA
CBHW031251120726
47906CB00003B/695